CRIME IN THE SALON

A fiercely addictive mystery

CATHERINE MOLONEY

Detective Markham Mystery Book 21

Joffe Books, London
www.joffebooks.com

First published in Great Britain in 2024

© Catherine Moloney 2024

This book is a work of fiction. Names, characters, businesses, organizations, places and events are either the product of the author's imagination or are used fictitiously. Any resemblance to actual persons, living or dead, events or locales is entirely coincidental. The spelling used is British English except where fidelity to the author's rendering of accent or dialect supersedes this. The right of Catherine Moloney to be identified as author of this work has been asserted in accordance with the Copyright, Designs and Patents Act 1988.

Cover art by Dee Dee Book Covers

ISBN: 978-1-83526-491-1

For Kelly B

CAST OF CHARACTERS

The Police

DI Gilbert 'Gil' Markham
DI Kate Burton
DS Doyle
DS Carruthers
Ex-DS George Noakes
DCI Sidney
DCI Jack Moriarty, cold-case supervisor
DI Mike Hart, cold-case detective
DI Chris Carstairs
Superintendent Ebury-Clarke
Superintendent Bretherton
Doug 'Dimples' Davidson, pathologist

Olivia Mullen, Markham's partner, teacher at Hope Academy
Muriel Noakes, Noakes's wife
Natalie Noakes, Noakes's daughter

Salons

The Mane Event
Andrew 'Andy' Coxley, proprietor
Ed Collins, Andrew's deputy
Sandra Crowley, stylist
Becca Drew, stylist
Cassie Johnson, beautician/nail-bar technician
Helen Mathews, former stylist sacked by Coxley
Stella Casey, former trainee/apprentice with a crush on Coxley
Philip Casey, Stella's father
Karen Bickerstaff, ex-customer who sued Coxley and lost the case
Evelyn Brady, customer
Mark Brady, Evelyn's son
Jean Gibley, customer
Gordon Rushworth, Jean's brother

Cutting Edge
Des O'Grady, proprietor

Bromgrove folk
Carol Davidson, fundraiser
Sarah Moorcroft, author and wannabe celebrity
Doggie Dickerson, proprietor of Bromgrove Police Boxing Gym
Gavin Conors, reporter with the *Gazette*

Simon McLeish, Fire Investigation Unit
Hoskinson & Garrett, Andrew Coxley's solicitors

Cold-case victims

Ethel Taylor
Jeanette O'Donnell

PROLOGUE

Becca Drew felt her spirits lift as she walked down Greenbank Avenue early on the morning of Saturday 15 April. Normally she resented having to work at weekends — an occupational hazard for hairdressers — but the post-Easter lull meant that it was just her, Sandra Crowley and Ed Collins holding the fort. Oh, and Cassie Johnson would probably show her face at some stage, but the nail bar didn't really count. Plus, she'd be seeing the boss, so there was that to look forward to . . .

Her thoughts turned to Andrew Coxley, proprietor of *The Mane Event*, a small but prosperous little hair salon situated a short way out from Bromgrove town centre on the way to Old Carton.

What *was* it about Andy?

Of course there were the darkly brooding, almost Mediterranean good looks: that gleaming smile against the trim, black beard . . . thick wavy hair, romantic sideburns and languorous sloe-eyed smile that made her shiver deep inside. Granted he was on the short side, but somehow that didn't matter, such was his charisma. Even his accent was exotic . . . caressing, with an indefinable lilt that hinted at some kind of sultry backstory far removed from mundane suburbia.

Becca's partner Phil, of whom she was decidedly bored if truth be told, said 'the whole Greek gigolo get-up' was tragic, but that was just jealousy because there was no way *he* could ever rock Andy's 1970s vintage wardrobe. She sniggered disloyally at the very idea of her Meat Loaf lookalike other half attired in the suede bellbottoms, psychedelic shirts and flared trench coats that fitted Andy like a second skin. Some folk just had it, while others . . .

Despite the flamboyance and theatricality, she would swear that Andy wasn't gay. He played up the ambivalence deliberately . . . to titillate the old dears who constituted a large part of his clientele. It was clever the way he hinted at sexual fluidity (mysteriously decadent) while at the same time managing to suggest that he was drawn to older females . . . Of course, since every woman liked a challenge, this conveyed the message that he was ripe for seduction if he could only meet "The One". Oh it was heady stuff all right, but Andy never dropped a clanger or struck the wrong note, pushing their buttons without them ever realising it was part of his strategy.

She supposed at a level there *was* something almost immoral about it, but the best hairdressers always put on a show. It was all part of creating an *experience* and making women feel special . . . queen for a day . . .

And it *was* mostly women who patronised the salon, though the odd young bloke popped in 'to try something new' (usually marking the acquisition of a new girlfriend). In the main, male visitors tended to be elderly husbands dropping their wives off, rarely emboldened to enjoy a coffee in the waiting area and instead casting looks of profound suspicion around the premises as though they privately regarded the salon as just one up from a bordello and considered 'grooming products' to be the first step on a slippery slope. *Give me a decent barber's any time*, their anguished expressions seemed to say. The occasional brave soul lingered for a chat, but this had sometimes proved traumatic. Poor old Gordon Rushworth from Porlock Drive and that nice bank manager from Medway practically passed out when she told them the cost of a full head of highlights. Ever since then, she fudged prices, remembering to deduct twenty-five percent whenever the issue was broached by easily scandalised visitors. Wouldn't do to give the poor things a coronary . . .

Yes, with the rest of the staff on holiday, it would be more relaxed than usual. Mind you, Ed seemed to have gone sour on Andy recently. She wasn't sure what was at the bottom of it . . . something to do with that woman who left Ed a load of money when she died. Andy hadn't liked that at all . . . She overheard him having a rant at Ed about 'professionalism', so presumably he thought there was something iffy about it. And it was true Ed *could* be pretty smarmy with the older ones. She supposed he wasn't bad looking . . . beefy and blonde, with a way of *leaning in* and getting all confidential . . . whispering to them out of the corner of his mouth like something out of a corny soap opera. Mind you, the technique seemed to work a treat and there was no question it was good for business, but *still* . . .

She got on okay with Ed. But Cassie was a different matter. 'Lash artist' my backside! She looked like Victoria Beckham's twin and smiled just about as often. Catching herself up for being bitchy, she supposed there was no great harm in the woman but couldn't help wondering what on *earth* had possessed Andy to take her on? Most likely it was a favour for someone or other, since he liked to do a good turn where he could. She knew Cassie had kicked up a stink when Andy raised the rent on her beautician's booth, but times were hard and in Becca's opinion she was lucky to have it at all. Des O'Grady from *Cutting Edge* sacked *his* beauty therapist because the business had become so cut-throat, so she wouldn't be surprised if Andy didn't eventually do the same and give Cassie her cards. *No big loss!*

She hoped godawful do-gooder Carol Davidson wouldn't come round trying to cadge freebies for *True Care Bromgrove*. She had a cheek constantly pestering them to put up posters and donate goody bags to the charity for nothing.

Never gave them any custom herself, needless to say. Not that you could do much with such terrible flyaway hair anyway... But she might finally have got the message after Andy gave her the brush-off at Easter. I mean, *imagine* coming in and badgering them to use the salon as a food bank donation point. Too classy for words. Said no-one ever.

Yes, she could definitely do without a dose of Davidson. Of course that other pain in the backside Sarah Moorcroft was coming in to get her roots done, but Ed took care of her these days after she'd got the hump with Andy for not being able to fit her in when she did that thing in Waterstones... what was it... oh yes, *An Evening with Sarah*. I mean, pass the sick bag. It wasn't even as if she was properly famous like Jojo Moyes or Lynda La Plante. Just churned out Mills & Boon type stuff, though of course *she* called them 'historical sagas'. Soft porn more like. Ed was welcome to her!

Business wasn't too bad right now, even if that bitch Helen Mathews *had* done her best to poach clients after she was sacked. It wouldn't surprise her if it wasn't Helen who went running to the *Gazette* with those spiteful stories about Andy, she thought darkly... little drops of poison perfectly calculated to cause maximum damage.

Well, as the boss always maintained, all PR was good PR because it meant people were talking about you. Ed said that made him sound like Donald Trump but so far it seemed to be working.

Becca's pace slowed as she passed the little key park at the top of Quickswood Lane. Andy was a member on account of living in the right postcode, though he had never offered to show any of them round despite Sandra hinting like mad.

She grinned, remembering... It was *so* obvious Sandra had a thing for the boss, always flicking her hair and sticking her bony chest out at him. Plus there was the way her eyes followed him everywhere and she laughed just that bit too loud whenever he was in the vicinity, sending clear signals of hero-worship. Not that the anorexic looking brunette stood a chance with him, Becca thought wryly. He was never snide or unkind, but his indifference was obvious. She could totally see why Sandra fancied Andy, but it just wasn't cool to be so pathetic and needy.

The cherry blossom trees at the gates of the key park frothed and foamed invitingly in the mild sunshine, and Becca suddenly wished she could play hooky instead of reporting for work . . .

But she had to open up.

With a heartfelt sigh, she moved down the road, calling into the little coffee shop for her accustomed skinny latte before heading for the salon.

To her surprise, the front door was unlocked, though no-one was visible through the window that ran the length of the unit.

Inside, everything looked just as usual.

There was the waiting area with its black marble tiles, cream leather sofas, magazine table and reception desk, immaculate and pristine, set off by silk flower arrangements that looked even better than the real thing. A sleek stainless steel coffee machine and water dispenser completed the effect. Nothing, including the cash till, appeared to have been disturbed.

From the doorway, her gaze scanned the interior.

A little flight of steps led up to the mezzanine area with its row of gleaming floor to ceiling mirrors, green glass counters, wall-mounted drying hoods and comfy black leather tub chairs. Towards the back were the sinks, with a beauty counter tucked away in the right-hand corner. Sliding doors in the opposite corner concealed customer toilets. A door behind the sinks led to a separate room for customers who preferred to be shielded from the gaze of passers-by, and next to that was the tiny staff kitchen with adjoining loo. Discreet spotlights throughout were complemented by two crystal ceiling pendants front and back, adding a touch of understated luxury.

Normally Becca would have felt reassured by the mere sight of it all.

But deep down, she sensed something was wrong, the blood beating in her ears so that it almost seemed the whole salon was thrumming with it and a trickle of fear creeping along her spine. Though it was mild outside, she suddenly felt desperately cold.

Taking shallow gasping breaths, she went up to the mezzanine area.

No-one there.

Now to check the toilets and staffroom.

All clear.

Finally, the back room.

As she opened the door, she felt her stomach lurch, the way it used to do when she was a kid riding the big dipper.

Almost as though she knew what she was going to find.

Andrew Coxley sat under a dryer hood, a pair of scissors protruding from the side of his neck. His eyes opaque and unseeing, Becca's boss resembled some ghastly mannequin from a sci-fi movie. Like *I Am Legend* or one of those horror films, she thought, marvelling that one part of her brain was able to make the comparison at such a moment.

Shaking uncontrollably, she stood rooted to the spot, unable to tear her gaze from the most chilling thing of all.

His assailant had put a silicone highlight cap on Coxley's head and viciously pulled strands of hair through it, like some hideous parody of a colour treatment.

As though to send a message . . .

CHAPTER 1: FIRST STEPS

The morning of Sunday April 16 found DI Gilbert ('Gil') Markham sitting on his favourite bench in the old-fashioned, tranquil graveyard of St Chad's Parish Church round the back of Bromgrove Police Station. With a view across to leafy Hollingrove Park and a gentle breeze caressing the back of his neck, it seemed to him that everything spoke of the miracle of new life even as he contemplated the moss-covered monuments and headstones slumbering in the dappled shade of yews and elms.

His was a lean, high-cheekboned, almost gaunt face, topped with thick black hair just beginning to show silver at the temples. The aquiline features customarily wore an expression of thoughtful reserve — almost hauteur — leading to his station nickname of 'Lord Snooty'. But away from CID, lost in contemplation, his keen dark gaze turned inwards as he recalled the discovery of Andrew Coxley's corpse the previous day . . .

'Quite the joker, this one,' the pathologist Doug 'Dimples' Davidson said with a moue of distaste. The bluff, tweedy medic, who looked more like a country vet or farmer than a police surgeon, fastidiously removed the scissors protruding from Andrew Coxley's neck before pronouncing,

'No mystery about cause of death. Penetrating neck trauma which severed the carotid . . . CNS shut down . . . all over very quickly.'

'Time of death?' Markham pressed him, doing his best not to think about Coxley's assailant lunging at him in a blind frenzy of hate.

'Rigor's fully established . . . Judging from that and by the look of him, I'd say sometime between nine and midnight but don't quote me on that. I'll know more once I've had a rummage.'

Had a rummage! The medic's bleak insouciance was distinctly reminiscent of Dr Max DeBryn from *Inspector Morse*. Actually, he wouldn't have been surprised if Dimples wasn't deliberately modelling himself on that old curmudgeon.

'Too early for runners and riders, I suppose?' Davidson asked in another echo of TV's most popular sawbones.

''Fraid so,' the DI replied. 'But I understand the salon's quite a local institution.'

'Yes, I believe my wife's come in here for, er, whatever . . .'

Markham suppressed a smile in the face of Davidson's obvious mystification. But the other recovered his aplomb, resorting to poetry.

'"Th' inferior priestess, at her altar's side, Trembling, begins the sacred rites of pride,"' he quoted with sarcastic emphasis.

'Ah, *The Rape of the Lock*, very apposite.'

Dimples sighed. 'I never *can* catch you out, Inspector. Well, I'll get him moved now.' With a note of anger, he added, 'That get-up on his head . . . downright *nasty*. See you catch this one, Markham.'

'I'll do my best.'

But as the paramedics moved in, Markham felt a pang of self-doubt. What on earth was going on here? A hairdresser murdered in his own salon and posed in such a grotesque fashion . . . what *had* the man done to inspire such malevolence?

Now, as a burst of birdsong recalled him to the present, he said a swift prayer for Andrew Coxley's soul and vowed to make good on his promise to Dimples.

In addition to revisiting the call-out, it was a ritual on such occasions for Markham to take stock and contemplate the merits of his team, reminding himself of the quirks and idiosyncrasies of that tight little unit known (with more than a hint of jealousy) as 'Markham's Gang'.

It comprised his fellow DI Kate Burton plus the two sergeants Doyle and Carruthers.

Not forgetting his oldest friend and ally ex-DS George Noakes.

Noakes.

Markham's naturally austere features softened as he thought of that perennial thorn in the flesh of DCI Sidney ('Slimy Sid' to the troops) and Bromgrove Station's high command.

These days, the powers that be seemed more or less resigned to Markham's former bagman being a fixture around CID, even after collecting his carriage clock. Despite taking up the position of security manager at Rosemount Retirement Home, Noakes still 'had his fingers in every pie', as DS Doyle inelegantly but accurately put it.

But with DCI Sidney's own retirement now on the horizon and Superintendent Ebury-Clarke in the ascendant, it was by no means certain that Noakes's gleeful "infiltration" of his old stamping ground would be allowed to continue. Ebury-Clarke, a virtuoso when it came to bearing grudges, had never forgotten Noakes's heckling when the superintendent addressed Bromgrove's Police Benevolent Fund, none so adroit as Markham's former sergeant when it came to sabotaging the great moments in life:

Ebury-Clarke: 'I am conscious . . .' (*Could've fooled me!*)
Ebury-Clarke: 'That I've been done . . .' (*Too right!*)
Ebury-Clarke: 'A great honour.' (*Is that what you call it!*)

From there, it was all downhill, Ebury-Clarke becoming so unnerved by Noakes's mischievous "noises off" that he crowned his peroration by saying 'he prided himself on being a policeman who had the courage of his previous convictions' (to the unmitigated delight of many in the junior ranks). This line (or was it a Freudian slip?) brought the house down, though not in the way that the superintendent had intended. Certainly, he had never forgiven Noakes. Nor was Mrs Ebury-Clarke, a decidedly rotund lady, likely to forget Noakes's description of her as being 'the only woman who could fill this hall'.

'She's committee mad,' he had groused to Markham when the latter reproached him for his lack of tact.

'Very big on local literacy initiatives, though,' the DI had pointed out.

'Oh aye, the type who wants to publish a book called *Teach Yourself Reading*, the daft bint,' came the blunt rejoinder.

No, there was definitely no love lost on that front and Markham knew he was going to have to box clever to keep Noakes in his unique position as "civilian consultant".

His partner Olivia Mullen, teacher of English at Hope Academy (aka as 'Hopeless') and de facto member of 'the Gang', adored Noakes, being the only one, other than his wife, to call him 'George' and revelling in what, as an ardent ballet fan, she termed his 'faux pas de deux'. On occasion, he had the capacity to extend this into an entire conversation, out-blarneying his opponent. The barbed verbal wit, or one-upmanship, delighted Olivia, since she shared the same subversive instincts, regularly getting on the wrong side of her school's senior management team for her outspokenness. Never had the maxim "Opposites Attract" been more bewilderingly apparent than in the conspiratorial affinity between Markham's former DS and his highly strung, quixotic other half. Never had he seen her more delighted than when regaling his friend with a recent sick note from one of her parents: 'I kept Joe home as I am very tired because I have been under the doctor all this week.' The two of them were regularly in hysterics over the utter ludicrousness of such gems and pronouncements by Ofsted, particularly relishing anything that exposed pretentiousness and pomposity. When Noakes performed verbal atrocities and unleashed insults that made Markham's eyes water, she only laughed the harder.

His friend's Yorkshire make-up was composed of a genial yet unshakeable view of races and characteristics which led him to regard everyone outside that county with a cheerful irreverence that in no way detracted from his essential humanity and that Markham found a refreshing antidote to the achingly PC strictures that poured out of the station's HR department. It appeared to him that Noakes's casual xenophobia was somehow far more honest and authentic than all the nicey-nicey carefully curated pronouncements of a police force which seemed increasingly out of step with the concerns of ordinary people. And if there was one thing that Noakes understood, it was what he called (with a nod to his Methodist Sunday School antecedents), 'ornery sinners'. Still, the Noakesian philosophy was definitely an acquired taste, he thought ruefully, recalling Noakes's infamous retirement speech — de rigueur, or 'de rigueur mortis' as DI Chris Carstairs wittily dubbed it — which had long since passed into legend as a valediction that managed to insult virtually every senior officer in the upper echelons. He suspected that it would be long, very long, before DCI O'Rourke forgot that jovial banter about the Irish Parliament being known as 'the dole' and their PM being called 'tea shop' . . . though in fairness, as Doyle was quick to point out, Noakes was cheerfully insulting about the Scots too, having caused mortal offence to DI McNabb with his denunciation of 'bogpipes' and sly allusions to folk sowing their wild porridge.

Suddenly, out of the corner of his eye, Markham spotted Reverend Duthie's wife slinking round the left-hand side of the church. It was obvious she had seen him but preferred to maintain "custody of the eyes" in case that appallingly uncouth ex-sergeant was with him. Markham grinned at the recollection of Noakes holding forth to the vicar's wife about 'the epistle to the fallopians'. He guessed Noakes just hadn't been able to resist riling one of those he called 'happy-clappy ecumaniacs' or 'holy harridans' — a tribe who, in his books, were definitely fair game.

Making sure Mrs Duthie was out of sight, Markham got up and wandered along the terraces, stopping now and again to read poignant inscriptions and testimonials to the late lamented.

But his mind was still running on Noakes, his best friend and ally, the man whom he found he could not do without but who was utter anathema to his superiors.

Returning to his bench, he looked across at St Chad's cenotaph. In doing so, he mused that his friend's unique patois to some degree derived from his background as an ex-serviceman, with gags, punchlines and a gung-ho indomitability that came straight from the parade ground. It was a unique culture that the likes of Sergeants Doyle and Carruthers regarded with amused tolerance but did not remotely understand and an inheritance that the higher ranks regarded as embarrassing luggage to be discarded on their travels to the top of the greasy pole. Olivia's marked partiality for Noakesy's army jokes and anecdotes no doubt contributed to her reputation for "eccentricity", a trait which DCI Sidney and Mrs Muriel Noakes invariably referred to in terms that suggested they considered Olivia ('your lady friend', as Sidney called her with leery emphasis) ripe for psychiatric intervention.

He smiled as he recalled an army joke that had particularly tickled her fancy (his too). It concerned a weary group of army squaddies trudging around the square and saluting by numbers, when a doom-laden voice, with touching pathos, moaned: 'O death, where is thy sting?' The immediate response from the apoplectic drill-sergeant was, 'Oo said that?' An even wearier voice responded, 'No idea, sarge, but I think it was Shelley.' Next day, on Part-One orders came the announcement: 'Private Shelley to Adjutant's Office. On report. Insubordination. Twenty-one hundred hours.' The more lugubrious Noakes's recital, in a variety of mock-comic accents, the greater his partner's enjoyment.

Olivia and Noakes could not have been further removed from each other by all the normal social rules and expectations, but Markham thought of them as his twin pillars. Let the disciples of Freud and Jung make of it what they would, but when his friend and lover were in alignment, all was right in his world, it was a simple as that . . .

He sighed.

Understandably, Mrs Muriel Noakes didn't see things in quite the same light . . .

Noakes's snobbish, social-climbing wife whom he had first met, almost unbelievably, on the ballroom dancing circuit, had never taken to Olivia. Sitting there in the mild spring sunshine, Markham's thoughts reverted to their sparring about it . . .

'Muriel's so caste-bound, Gil,' Olivia had lamented. 'And no, I don't mean the sticking-your-pinkie-out-from-the-teacup kind of snobbery . . . not Hyacinth Bucket. Just that godawful sliding scale based on class. You know the kind of thing . . . like when she has a fit of the vapours if George says "lounge" instead of "drawing room", or pulls that sour face when he talks about seeing his pal Don down the Legion to swap army stories . . . Whenever we're with her, there's that feeling of net-curtain twitchery. And I just *know* she thinks of me as some kind of ex-hippie who snared you through Mata Hari practices.'

Markham had laughed at this. 'You're a respected English teacher, Liv,' he remonstrated, 'not some kind of degenerate flower child. And anyway, certain of Muriel's tastes are decidedly, er, *populist*. Noakesy says she never misses Simon Cowell on *Britain's Got Talent*.'

His partner giggled. 'God, she'd *kill* him for letting that out.'

'Indeed . . . in the same way that she hides her true crime books under Joanna Trollope and the Aga sagas when she's coming out of the library. It's all about *appearances* and *maintaining standards* . . . perhaps because she hasn't always felt on top of her circumstances . . . I think,' he observed compassionately, 'Muriel's fixation with "commonness" has its roots in her past.' By which he meant the youthful indiscretion prior to her marriage which resulted in the arrival of daughter Natalie . In his opinion *that* was the key to Muriel's obsession with gentility, though Olivia struggled with such a charitable interpretation. 'I suppose George was her safe harbour after things spun out of control,' she conceded reluctantly. 'I kind of get that,' she added with a grimace, 'even if she dies a thousand deaths whenever he says "toilet" instead of "loo" . . . or worse still, "the bog".'

Noakes's discovery that Natalie wasn't his biological daughter nearly derailed his career during the notorious Bluebell investigation, but he had somehow weathered the storm, and it had drawn himself and Markham even closer together. For his part, Noakes knew that Markham was the victim of an abusive stepfather whose malign influence resulted in the premature death of his brother Jonathan from drink and drugs, but very little on the subject had ever passed between them. It was as if they didn't need an exchange of explicit personal confidences to shore up the unusual relationship that was a source of endless bafflement to all in CID.

The fact that Noakes and Olivia had mysteriously and inexplicably "gelled" — Noakes regarding Markham's willowy red-haired partner with the kind of awed reverence appropriate to a knight in Mallory's *Morte d'Arthur* — irritated his wife no end (to say nothing of his beautician daughter, the perma-tanned, buxom Natalie, former doyenne of Bromgrove's nightclubs), but both women for Noakes's sake somehow connived at the pretence that they were the best of friends, which ensured that an uneasy truce prevailed . . . though Olivia was always threatening to break it . . .

'*Cooee!*'

Markham flinched at this interruption of his thoughts, freezing as two middle-aged ladies hallooed to each other before passing under the lychgate into the church. But they were oblivious of him, so he was able to relax, slowly exhaling as he lingered in the ancient churchyard with its reassuring atmosphere of time immemorial. The sun's rays gilded the crumbling monuments and headstones, with clumps of spring flowers softening the overall prospect of granite and marble in a way that soothed his nerves and reminded him of nature's glories. The Easter season was always guaranteed to put Noakes in a bad mood — 'like it's this great bring an' buy sale in honour of the Easter Bunny or some pagan wotsit,' he grumbled, only for DS Carruthers to interject sardonically that of course it was all about 'the great god Thaw', earning himself a portentous frown for the execrable climate change pun and a hasty change of subject by DI Kate Burton.

Kate Burton . . .

Markham's fellow DI had faced a difficult path to success in her chosen profession. An earnest psychology graduate whose parents staunchly opposed her choice of career ('No job for a woman,' was her father's verdict), Burton fought for every square inch of professional renown and was never at ease with CID canteen culture, she and Noakes initially circling each other like two prairie dogs before eventually bonding over their mutual unshakeable devotion to Markham and commitment to the job. The two also shared an indefatigable enthusiasm for true crime documentaries and a keen interest in forensic psychiatry, though Noakes affected profound scepticism whenever Burton had recourse to her beloved *Diagnostic and Statistical Manual of Mental Disorders*. Despite massive differences of character and outlook — Burton being as earnest and right-on as Noakes was slobbish and relentlessly un-PC — they both possessed an almost poetic sensitivity (well-hidden in Noakes's case) that made them sympathetic to their cultured boss's refined temperament. Noakes, in particular, was decidedly proud of having a boss infamous for using 'Big Words' ('keep your Thesaurus handy' went the refrain) and having esoteric interests in 'mouldy old churches', ruins and the like.

Noakes, ever watchful on Olivia's behalf, had early guessed that Burton carried a torch for the guvnor. For his part, Markham felt a strange kind of tenderness for his colleague, having been increasingly drawn to the vulnerability and sensitivity that she only revealed gradually over time and finding that it possessed an unusual power to move him.

Did it mean that he was half in love with her? Certainly Olivia resented their closeness. As did Burton's on-and-off fiancé Professor Nathan Finlayson of Bromgrove University's Psychology department (nicknamed 'Shippers' by Noakes on account of his startling resemblance to the serial killer Harold Shipman) who Markham guessed was inclined to regard their affinity as an obstacle to Kate agreeing to marry him.

Not that Olivia could really claim the moral high ground, given that she had recently been involved (to what degree Markham was never entirely sure) with a colleague from her school. On said colleague — Mat Sullivan, the deputy head — deciding that his orientation was exclusively homosexual, she had come back to Markham. More recently, there had been another hiatus in their relationship due to her struggle to accept the prospect of childlessness (an earlier abortion having left her infertile). When Natalie Noakes became unexpectedly pregnant, Olivia had even nurtured mad schemes of adopting the child, before Natalie's miscarriage rendered all such speculation redundant. Nowadays, she was quietly resigned, rejecting both Markham's proposal of marriage and suggestion that they should adopt. He found he couldn't always read his partner, whose spiky cynicism stemmed from the conviction that life had dealt her an unfair hand, but sensed her suspicion of his fellow DI had by no means abated.

Markham wondered uneasily whether Kate's deferential attitude towards him (she was always punctilious about calling him 'Sir' even though they were now the same rank) played a part in his affection for her. No doubt he was as chauvinistic as the next man (possibly excepting Noakes!), but he knew that there was more to it than that, having become very close to his colleague during recent investigations in Oxford. Noakes would doubtless have dismissed the scenario as 'bleeding Mills & Boon,' but it was damnably complicated for all that . . .

A flurry in the cemetery's dense undergrowth startled Markham. Seeing, however, that it was just a couple of squirrels playing footsie in and out of some brambles to the far right of the cenotaph, he relaxed again as he thought about his two young sergeants.

DS Doyle, proud possessor of a degree in criminology, had been briefly destabilised by the departure of Noakes, his mentor in everything from football (they were both passionate supporters of Bromgrove Rovers) to affairs of the heart. His romantic life had been something of a shambles until recently, when Kelly, a primary school teacher, had entered his life and restored some equilibrium. Markham liked the lanky, auburn-haired youngster (the 'ginger ninja') with his artless enthusiasm and ill-concealed ambition to get to the top. He had no doubt that Doyle would one day make inspector and do a fine job of it. The DS was his own man and had resisted pressure to disassociate himself from Noakes, which made Markham like him even more.

He had initially felt no such liking for Noakes's replacement DS Roger Carruthers ('Roger the Dodger', as Noakes had christened him), not least as Carruthers was the nephew of Superintendent 'Blithering' Bretherton and rumoured to spy for the higher ups. But despite Carruthers's unprepossessing exterior — albino pallor, savage short back and sides haircuts, horn-rimmed specs, Gestapo raincoats and an impression of overall geekiness — he had somehow won over both Burton (they had an interest in psychology and a formidable work ethic) and Doyle (via their mutual love of the Beautiful Game and penchant for wry humour). Most surprising of all was the way Carruthers took to Noakes, clearly respectful of the grizzled veteran's experience and loyalty. Markham had initially wondered whether this was an act, before being compelled to conclude that Carruthers genuinely admired the old warhorse, even to the point of calling him 'sarge' like the rest. The DCI when he got to hear of this hadn't liked it one bit.

DCI Sidney. Markham's line manager . . .

Olivia and Noakes were united in their loathing of Sidney, or Judas Iscariot as Olivia called him. 'Such a *creep*,' was Noakes's uncompromising verdict. 'I can't even feel sorry about him an' his missus splitting up.' For it appeared that the DCI and Mrs Sidney (aka Brunhilde on account of her Valkyrie-like attributes) were experiencing marital difficulties. 'Whass the betting he complains about her being small-minded an' childish then whinges that she's allus going an' hiding his teddy . . . jus' like Hazza said about King Charles.' Mrs Noakes, an ardent royalist, would strongly have disapproved of her other half making such a comparison, but Markham was only too familiar with Sidney's jealous resentment of his Oxbridge credentials and good looks (most particularly a full head of hair). Of late, however, he felt that Sidney had mellowed, and he was grateful to the DCI for backing him in a few tight corners despite his avowed repugnance for 'Markham's fey mystical streak' and preference for 'good solid (i.e. unflashy) legwork'. They would never be natural allies but, as with Muriel Noakes, he increasingly sensed some unacknowledged hinterland in Sidney — some personal insecurity about his background and antecedents — that meant the barriers were always up between them. Perhaps once Sidney retired and the competitive element was removed, there would be a chance to understand his boss fully. Olivia was convinced that Sidney was hellbent on a career in media punditry (like John Stalker), but Markham thought it more likely he would return to the force on a consultancy basis . . . who knows, maybe ending up working cheek by jowl with his old nemesis George Noakes. Now that *would* be worth seeing!

Suddenly, the grin was wiped off Markham's face by the Reverend Simon Duthie's appearance over at the lychgate. He kept very still, feeling he was not up to the forced, over hearty chat in which the clergyman (a late vocation to the priesthood after a career as a bank manager) felt obliged to engage seeing as the station was in his parish. Of course, if Noakes had been there, the DI could have been sure of Duthie giving him a wide berth since the two men had an almost allergic antipathy to each other. Most recently, the vicar had been mightily offended when, after a particularly turgid homily on Moses at St Chad's Police Memorial Service, Noakes complained, 'Preachers these days wanna beat about any bush jus' so long as it ain't burning.' As a commentary on the fairly dire standard of ecclesiastical oratory, Markham was inclined to think his friend had a point, but Duthie had been in high dudgeon about it. Olivia was convulsed by this latest example of what she called *Noakesypropisms*, but relations with Duthie had been pretty much in the deep freeze ever since.

Thank God, the vicar either hadn't spied him or was doing an excellent job of pretending not to have seen him. With it being Sunday, no doubt he was thinking about higher matters, such as his sermon for the nine o'clock service.

Time for Markham to head over to CID.

Yet it was so peaceful in the little cemetery, and his heart rejoiced in the rising sap of spring with its signs of new life and the feeling of hope intrinsic to Eastertide.

But there was a murder to investigate.

Shades of the prison-house begin to close.

He took one last look round the peaceful little cemetery whose ghostly residents seemed to urge him, '*You are not dead yet. Get down to life!*' And in that moment, he imagined the dead hairdresser's plaintive voice joined to theirs. '*Get down to life!*'

* * *

CID felt stuffy and stale after his interlude in the fresh air, but at least the team would be ready and waiting in his corner office with its unrivalled view of the car park. It being tacitly accepted that the trio would be scrambled at short notice when Markham was heading up a murder investigation, he could count on them being free to give their full attention to the salon homicide.

There were few others around the department, but one or two shot Markham appraising glances as he disappeared into his office. As usual, Bromgrove CID's wunderkind was wearing his impeccable three-piece pinstripe and looked as unlike a policeman as it was possible to imagine. With his stellar record, promotion was no doubt his for the asking, but it was rumoured the handsome inspector had no desire to be a desk jockey.

Unaware of this covert scrutiny, it cheered Markham to see that his colleagues looked alert and eager, in notable contrast to the drabness of their surroundings, the DI's office being indistinguishable from CID's other glassed-in cubicles with generic office chairs, metallic filing cabinets, rickety sash windows and generally faded décor.

Kate Burton was a far cry from the dowdy, frumpy sergeant of yore addicted to dreary trouser suits and pudding bowl haircuts. Now she sported a chic geometric bob with a set of blonde highlights to rival Cameron Diaz and wore a softly tailored mint green midi dress. True, she still had schoolmarmish habits — 'perching on chairs with her bum one half on and one half off, like she's getting ready to take dictation' (Carruthers) and ever ready to whip out scary specs that did strange things to intelligent hazel eyes that were normally the size of enormous brown lollipops. But altogether, she was transformed from the sexless neophyte whose main objective appeared to have been to pass unnoticed in the boisterous melting pot of CID. 'Actually she's pretty fit these days,' was the irrepressible Doyle's verdict. Normally Markham would have disapproved of such laddishness, but it was true that Kate had somehow blossomed and come into her own. Now a highly regarded inspector, she demonstrated a new confidence and authority in her dealings with subordinates which, while it provoked the occasional bout of grumbling, became her very well.

Both Doyle and Carruthers — today casually attired in chinos and sweaters — paid careful attention to appearance, unlike Noakes whose chunky physique and fondness for junk food meant that the pug-faced ex-sergeant with his pouchy prize-fighter's features, dreadful dress sense (his cardigans being particularly awful) and wildly waving salt and pepper thatch was hardly a poster boy for modern policing, inducing shudders whenever the 'gold braid mob' clapped eyes on him. Luckily, the two young sergeants distracted bilious superiors from his friend's sartorial deficiencies. Markham still winced whenever he recalled Sidney irritably enquiring of Noakes, 'Why are you always scratching yourself, man?' only to receive the scowling reply, 'Cos nobody else knows where I itch.'

One Noakesian tradition that the team had enthusiastically continued was the provision of eatables on such occasions. Sarcastic commentary from Sidney and others was water off a duck's back to Doyle and Carruthers. Faintly embarrassed by her colleagues' preoccupation with what Noakes called 'commissary', Kate Burton nonetheless saw its value in terms of team bonding and was happy to provide chocolate muffins and cappuccinos from Costa when it was her turn while generally sticking to a granola bar and soy latte for herself. Today it was Carruthers doing the honours, proudly producing a lemon drizzle cake made by his girlfriend Kim. During the wedding boutique murder inquiry, Carruthers had shown himself in a more vulnerable light when he confided that Kim was plus-size and had suffered abuse for being a 'fat girl'. His chivalrous protectiveness had made the others warm to him, with Kim and Doyle's fiancée Kelly now vying to outdo each other in the baking stakes.

Just like family, Markham thought in amusement watching them tuck in, even Burton being tempted by the deliciously moist offering ('Kim uses fromage frais, that's the secret,' Carruthers told them proudly). The DI was pleased to note that Burton appeared more bright-eyed and cheerful than of late. Hopefully that meant her romantic prospects were looking up again. Nathan Finlayson was a decent man — to say nothing of patient — and there was every prospect of him making her happy if she would only give him a chance.

Predictably, Burton was the first to finish her cake and get down to business, briskly stating the identity of their victim before rattling off the pool of suspects.

'Mr Coxley was found by Becca Drew, one of the stylists. It was just her and two other stylists — Ed Collins and Sandra Crowley — due in, along with Cassie Johnson who runs the nail bar . . . The rest of the staff are away on holiday.'

'Narrows it down,' Doyle said with satisfaction.

'Hmm.' Burton frowned. 'I wouldn't be too sure about that. There's a rival hairdresser name of Des O'Grady and some bad blood,' she bit her lip, 'sorry — unfortunate choice of words — with Helen Mathews, a stylist Coxley had sacked . . . he thought she was poaching clients and bitching about him to the *Gazette*.'

Typically, Burton had been swift in extracting background information from Becca Drew.

'In terms of other people he had issues with . . . there's this woman called Carol Davidson from *True Care Bromgrove* who was apparently "always on the cadge" and a local writer, Sarah Moorcroft, who threw a hissy fit because Coxley couldn't fit her in for an appointment when she had some kind of a launch or promo at Waterstone's.' Burton scanned her notes. 'Things weren't hunky dory with the nail-bar woman because he'd jacked up her rent and, reading between the lines, it sounded as though he and Ed Collins weren't getting on too well. Also, there's this girl Stella Casey who was a trainee at the salon and started hanging round the place after her apprenticeship was over, making a bit of a nuisance of herself.'

'*A stalker!*' Carruthers sat up. This sounded promising.

'Well, I'm not sure if you could call her that,' Burton demurred. 'But apparently her father Philip seems to think Coxley had led her on . . . encouraged her . . . Becca also mentioned an ex-customer called Karen Bickerstaff who sued Coxley after a treatment went wrong and damaged her scalp. She lost the case and has been bad-mouthing him ever since.'

'Well done, Kate,' Markham thanked her. 'That's all useful intel . . . It certainly sounds as though Mr Coxley wasn't universally popular.'

'He was very charismatic according to Becca,' Burton replied handing out a head and shoulders shot of the victim. 'I'd say she and Sandra Crowley were fairly smitten.'

'That clobber's a bit dated,' Doyle scoffed.

'Yeah, like something out of *The Sweeney*,' Carruthers agreed, 'though he looks more of a pretty boy than some kind of macho man.' His voice held a question.

'Not homosexual according to Becca,' Burton replied smartly, 'though he liked to keep the customers guessing . . . made him glamorous and mysterious.'

'Ah yes, there's the clientele to consider,' Markham said thoughtfully.

'His regulars were mostly elderly ladies by the sound of it,' Burton said. 'They're really the salon's bread and butter, though there's some young ones come in as well. I've asked Becca to email me a list.'

'What about next of kin?' Markham asked. He was never one to foist condolence visits on subordinates and liked to pay his respects to the bereaved.

'He was an only child,' Burton replied. 'Both parents dead. There's an aunt and a couple of cousins. The FLOs are on it.'

Markham nodded slowly. 'Get them to give me the details, Kate.' Even semi-detached relatives needed to know that Andrew Coxley was not just another statistic and *mattered* to the team.

There was a brief pause, his colleagues aware of the guvnor's intense respect for the dead. Unlike some hard-bitten SIOs, he never tolerated anything that approached an affront to their dignity. Indeed, those who had been on the receiving end of his icy disdain for displaying inappropriate gallows humour never made the same mistake again.

Finally, Doyle broke the silence.

'Who gets to inherit the business?' he asked.

'I'm checking with his solicitors tomorrow,' Burton answered. 'Hoskinson & Garrett in the town centre.'

'What's the plan then?' Carruthers was clearly eager to get cracking.

'Obviously the salon's closed for the time being,' Burton informed them. 'But staff are being re-directed to Mr O'Grady's premises . . . *Cutting Edge*.'

'Kate and I will interview them there tomorrow morning while you two get the incident room set up and make a start with background checks,' Markham instructed. 'We also need as full a picture as possible of Mr Coxley's clientele. Dimples is doing the PM at three tomorrow afternoon.'

The two young men looked at each other. 'Why not attend together,' the DI's tone was wry. 'For moral support,' he added, being well aware of their squeamishness. 'I doubt there will be any surprises, but I want a full report.' He steepled elegant musician's hands with long, thin, tapering fingers. 'You also need to liaise with the SOCOs processing Mr Coxley's flat and find out what his computer shows in terms of social media activity. Whoever killed him didn't take his mobile, so the phone records also need following up.'

'Any chance this could have been random, boss?' Carruthers asked. 'Some nut job?'

'Apparently Mr Coxley always kept the salon locked when he was there by himself . . . he was pretty paranoid about security after a burglary at the newsagent's. Which means he most likely opened the door to his attacker—'

'Because he knew them,' Doyle finished.

'Precisely.' Markham let this sink in. 'I believe he probably met his killer by appointment.'

It was a sobering thought.

'Is sarge coming in on this one?' Doyle enquired disingenuously.

'Is the Pope Catholic?' Markham asked deadpan.

His colleagues grinned.

'I'll swing by Rosemount tomorrow afternoon and see what Noakesy makes of it all. I imagine Natalie and Mrs Noakes will have something to contribute in due course.' Plenty of highly-spiced gossip, no doubt.

He smiled at them. 'Right, get off and enjoy the rest of your day. Tomorrow we have to hit the ground running.'

CHAPTER 2: ALL AT SEA

Monday April 17 looked set to be fine and sunny as Burton and Markham drew up outside *Cutting Edge* on Quickswood Lane. Part of a short terrace of shops and houses on the other side of the street from Andrew Coxley's salon, its dimensions were much the same as the rival establishment, though Markham noticed that the frontage was shabbier with the paintwork peeling in places and worn signage.

'It's just Becca Drew, Sandra Crowley, Ed Collins and Cassie Johnson this morning, sir,' Burton said with her usual punctilious deference (clearly he was never going to break her habit of calling him 'sir'). 'The rest of them will be coming in tomorrow . . . We don't have to worry about staff who were away on holiday, so essentially it's just the key players I went through yesterday — folk who knew Mr Coxley or locked horns with him at some point.'

'Good. What about customers?'

'The others are still working on that, guv, though we've got some names from Becca and hopefully people will fill us in tomorrow . . . The clientele's largely elderly and it doesn't seem like any of his regulars could be in the frame, but you never know.'

'Indeed,' he nodded thoughtfully. 'Anything useful come through from Mr Coxley's flat . . . anything from social media?'

'Doyle's emailed you the SOCO pictures and report. It's just a typical bachelor pad — nice little terrace, décor safe and neutral,' she grimaced, 'not like his dress. By the look of it, he liked a quiet life . . . no red flags, nothing to show he did drugs or anything like that and the neighbours weren't aware of overnight visitors. His social media stuff's all about the salon, nothing personal.'

'Sounds like he guarded his privacy.'

'Well, I suppose in his job he was more or less on stage all the time — projecting an image,' Burton replied. 'It was probably a relief to drop the act when he was at home.'

An astute observation, Markham thought.

'Phone records?' he asked without much hope.

'Still waiting on those, guv . . . But I checked with his solicitors before we came out. After a bit of arm-twisting, the senior partner told me Coxley never made a will, so it looks like his next of kin are set to inherit.'

Markham suppressed a smile at the reference to 'arm-twisting'. Burton must have borrowed one or two techniques from the playbook of infamous George Noakes!

'I spoke with the FLOs last night,' he said. 'The aunt's in a nursing home and his cousins have cast-iron alibis for the time in question.'

'So, not a case of "Follow the Money",' she said regretfully.

'Definitely not,' he confirmed. 'The cousins have power of attorney and apparently want to keep the salon running until they decide what to do with it.'

So the bottom line was, they had nothing to go on.

And the interviews with Andrew Coxley's employees didn't yield anything useful either.

Sandra Crowley was a droopy brunette with long witchy hair and a somewhat dopey manner which gave her the appearance of being half a beat behind everyone else. Becca Drew, on the other hand, a gamine blonde, was clearly sharp as a cartload of monkeys though, like her colleague, she appeared woebegone with red-rimmed eyes. Ed Collins struck Markham as good-looking in the manner of one of those handsome lifeguards from *Baywatch*, giving little away behind a cool, bland exterior.

In terms of alibis, all three were technically unsatisfactory since they were home alone slumped in front of the TV. Of course, given that they were due into work bright and early on Saturday morning, it was understandable if none of them fancied whooping it up on Friday night.

'Andy was a decent boss,' Ed insisted, though neither Markham nor Burton missed the sidelong glance Becca shot him at this. An unspoken message passed between the detectives.

It would definitely pay to probe the relations between Andrew Coxley and Ed Collins.

Cassie Johnson was a scrawny, almost emaciated, woman wearing so much make-up that it practically entered the room before she did. Apparently, she had spent the night with her boyfriend and was feeling fairly hung-over on Saturday morning. 'Andy was a skinflint,' she told them bluntly. 'And yeah, I was angry about him putting my rent up. But not enough to kill him, *no way!*' Petite and bird-like, it was difficult to imagine her plunging scissors into Coxley's neck or lugging his body about, but Dimples Davidson had made it clear that a woman could have done it.

All four employees remained tight-lipped on the issue of personalities and possible disagreements.

'Almost as if they'd made a pact to keep schtum,' Burton lamented afterwards. 'O'Grady too.'

The proprietor of *Cutting Edge* had been even less forthcoming than the others although, being thick-set and brawny, it was easier to imagine him as the attacker. For an alibi, he referred them to the landlord of The Quickswood Arms round the corner.

Once back outside in the sunshine, the two detectives regarded each other in some dismay.

'Let's get back to the station and touch base with the others,' Markham said finally.

'Think I'll drop in on the PM this afternoon, sir,' Burton told him before adding with a thin smile, 'Doyle's always a bit green about the gills when Dimples gets out his Stryker saw.'

'Excellent. Meanwhile I'll see if Noakesy can add anything in terms of background.'

That *had* to be better than spending the rest of the afternoon dodging Sidney.

Burton must have read his mind. 'The DCI's over in Liverpool today, sir . . . conference on digital forensics. Not due back till around four tomorrow '

'Nothing like putting off the evil hour,' he said, the relief clear in his tone.

'And don't forget, sir, he's knee-deep in preparations for the Coronation — that junket down at the Town Hall and the concert in Hollingrove Park. It'll be a while before he gets round to the Coxley case.'

'Thank heaven for King Charles III,' Markham exclaimed. 'Looks like royalty may buy us a reprieve!'

There was a twinkle in Burton's eye as she joked, 'At least with this one they aren't going to be screaming "E.R."!'

He groaned in mock-horror. 'Kate, that sounds worryingly Noakesian.'

'Give sarge my best,' she grinned. 'Looking forward to indiscreet inquiries!'

* * *

Rosemount Retirement Home was a two-storeyed white stucco Georgian building whose classical facade and beautifully landscaped grounds were a source of no small satisfaction to Mrs Muriel Noakes with her penchant for what Olivia called Downton Abbey Toffdom. The layout of knot and rose gardens, along with regimented topiary, created a soothing impression of symmetry and order before the formality gave way to lawns and a lake surrounding a small island with willow oak in the middle. Beyond that, a wildflower meadow blended imperceptibly into a landscape worthy of Constable or Gainsborough.

Since Markham was generally regarded as part of the furniture at Rosemount, the cheery clinical manager waved him through with a smiling welcome. 'Mr Noakes is in the library setting up for a poetry recital tonight,' she told him, since the retirement home regularly played host to a range of local societies.

The Jacobean style panelled room with its deep red walls and drapery, maroon leather wingback chairs, highly polished round tables and thick pile antique carpet was graciously proportioned, with floor to ceiling leaded windows looking out onto the woods and up towards Weston Ridge. Recessed mahogany shelving along one side of the room held row upon row of gold-tooled volumes, while a full-length portrait of George III in his Coronation robes dominated the opposite wall. Markham was amused to note there were fewer paintings of the nymphs-and-shepherds variety dotted about than formerly, these having been replaced by watercolours of British naval heroes due to Noakes's Bulldog Drummond enthusiasm for men who ruled the waves. The DI wasn't entirely sure that Horatio Nelson with eye patch and sleeve pinned up would have been his own choice for the library of a retirement home, but at least it wasn't General Gordon being butchered at Khartoum or Captain Cook facing down cannibals, both of these worthies being much admired by Rosemount's security manager. And most probably Noakes's apple-cheeked young assistant Kevin, who belonged to the Bromgrove Sea Cadets, eagerly endorsed all his line manager's choices.

His friend looked almost respectable, in a brown tweed suit which, despite being rather too warm for the day and straining at the seams, doubtless reflected Muriel's *Home and Garden* aspirations, though she hadn't succeeded in parting Noakes from his beloved George boots (the only footwear an alumnus of 2 Para would countenance) or the regimental tie knotted somewhere under his left ear. Seeing Markham, he beamed with pleasure, ushering the DI towards an armchair. As if by magic, Kevin appeared and after a brief exchange of pleasantries betook himself to rustle up tea and biscuits ('the good ones, mind').

'How goes it, Noakesy?'

'Not too bad. Jus' a case of shifting things round a bit in here an' sorting some chairs.'

'A poetry evening, I understand.'

'Yeah, William Blake.' Noakes scowled. 'You wouldn't think someone like that could write *Jerusalem*, would you?'

'How so?'

'Well, with him being a holy joe an' a dirty old man.' Noakes spoke as if it were self-evident.

'I suppose we've got to make allowances for morally flawed artistic geniuses.'

His friend didn't look as though he supposed they had to do anything of the kind.

'Any road, it couldn't be worse than the bloke we had in last week from the Biblical Archaeology Society . . . some beardy weirdy from the university banging on about ancient manuscripts.' He let out a guffaw. 'Weren't too happy when Kev called them the Dead Chuffed Rolls.'

Markham's lips twitched. It sounded as though Kevin, for all his youth, was a kindred spirit.

'Guess you're here about that hairdresser getting murdered,' Noakes said with elaborate casualness, though he was transparently desperate to be involved ('all the subtlety of a hang-gliding flasher', as Carruthers had memorably observed).

'Did you know him . . . not personally, of course,' Markham added hastily, aware that his friend expected to get change from a fiver when he went for a haircut, 'but perhaps Muriel and Natalie had dealings?' The DI suspected that Mrs Noakes might well have been susceptible to the practised blandishments of a man like Andrew Coxley.

'Dunno about Nat, but I think the missus went in there a few times,' Noakes replied. 'Said it were a bit embarrassing, though, the way some of the old dears competed for his attention . . . kind of fighting over him.' From which it might be deduced that Mrs Noakes did not care to be lumped together with the sort of women who lapped up the attentions of their hair stylist. No, she wouldn't want to patronise an establishment as part of the common herd.

Kevin was back with their refreshments, Noakes dispatching the cheery youngster on various errands before getting stuck in to the tea and shortbread (perk of the job).

'Strange how women had the hots for someone like that,' he said finally, coming up for air. 'Especially with him wearing all that poncey gear, like a disco king.'

'Oh I don't know, Noakesy,' the DI said with a mischievous gleam. 'Vintage wear is in vogue again, what with *Life on Mars* and DCI Gene Hunt.'

'Oh aye . . . that series about the policeman who gets knocked over an' wakes up in the nineteen seventies . . . ends up working for some right bastard straight out of *The Sweeney*. Dead sexist an' homophobic,' Noakes added primly. Pot calling the kettle black, Markham thought with an inner eye roll.

'The very same. But "the Gene Hunt look" went down a storm.'

'Mind you, that hairdresser didn't look like anyone from *The Sweeney*,' Noakes grunted. 'More like Donny Osmond or one of them Bee Gees, if you ask me.' With some compunction he added, 'Not that the poor bloke deserved to end up like that . . . with scissors sticking out of his neck an' a bathing cap thingy on his head.'

Markham didn't ask how his friend knew this, well aware that the other had his own hotline to CID in the shape of DS Doyle.

'I'll check with Mu an' Nat to see what they know about the setup,' Noakes said affably. 'You c'n come over for your dinner an' they'll tell you all about it . . . Thursday suit you?'

'Great, but please don't let Muriel go to too much trouble.' Vain hope!

'Bring your Liv,' Noakes urged. 'I were thinking the other day how she looks like she could do with a square meal.' Which, roughly translated, meant that 'the missus' had made noises about anorexia or an eating disorder.

'I'm sure she'd love to,' Markham lied valiantly, aware with what little relish Olivia would greet the prospect of an evening chez 'Mu'.

There was a brief silence before his erstwhile wingman's thoughts returned to the murder. 'Anyone looking good for it yet?' Noakes asked, shovelling in more shortbread.

Markham outlined the list of suspects. 'The stylists Becca Drew and Sandra Crowley seemed genuinely upset,' he said. 'Ed Collins — Coxley's number two — less so, but he still made the right noises. The beautician Cassie Johnson was upfront about having rowed with Mr Coxley, rather a hard-faced character, but it's a long way from murder.'

'What about O'Grady . . . handbags at ten paces with him an' Coxley?' Noakes demanded in an unconscious imitation of DCI Gene Hunt.

'O'Grady's short, stocky and balding. Definitely not the histrionic type,' the DI replied drily. 'Looks like a real spit and sawdust barber, or a prize-fighter . . . He insisted the place was big enough for the two of them and Coxley was welcome to his "old tabbies".'

'How about the stalker lass an' the rest of 'em?'

'Doyle and Carruthers are chasing up alibis and arranging interviews with all of them for tomorrow morning. O'Grady's letting us use his place again.'

'Probl'y good for business, him being close to the action,' Noakes commented cynically.

'Do you fancy sitting in?' the DI asked, observing the naked longing on his former wingman's face. 'I'd be interested to hear your impressions,' which would no doubt be of the unvarnished and brutally frank variety.

Noakes beamed. 'Thought you'd never ask,' he said. 'Kev can hold the fort for a couple of hours.' Then, a shade anxiously, 'What about Slimy Sid?'

'It'll be fine,' Markham said with more conviction than he felt. 'You leave the DCI to me.'

There followed a pleasant interlude, with Noakes enquiring cordially after Dimples Davidson. The pathologist didn't have the requisite 'bed-pan manner', in his opinion, but the two men had acquired a grudging respect for each other over the years.

Gradually, Markham made his way round to the delicate subject of Natalie's health, feeling he could safely introduce the subject now that her name had been mentioned between them.

'Well, it knocked the stuffing out of her for a while an' she had a bit of a depression, but Rick really stepped up,' Noakes confided, referring to Rick Jordan, her fiancé and proprietor of a fitness empire whose hardboiled mother hadn't exactly welcomed Natalie into the family. 'The lad's stuck by her through it all.' His piggy eyes were sad though, Markham noticed. Thinking of everything that could have been. His first grandchild. Of course he was no doubt tip-toeing round Muriel for whom this was all equally traumatic though in a different way, reviving memories of that turbulent chapter in her own life when it looked as though the world was falling around her ears.

'Just two more years and then Natalie will have her degree,' Markham said swiftly, moving on to a happier subject. The Noakeses had been inordinately proud when their 'late developer' offspring — a beautician and 'holistic practitioner' — retook her A levels before signing up to do a part-time degree in History at Bromgrove University where she was now in her third year. 'Yeah, jus' think of that.' Noakes sighed happily, 'She'll have letters after her name . . . like your Liv!' And Muriel would doubtless be insufferable on the strength of it. 'God, talk about *Educating Rita*, we have to deal with *Educating Natalie!*' Olivia had lamented even though no-one could fail to be touched by Noakes's delight in his daughter's achievement.

'Funny thing, this with your hairdresser an' the oldies,' Noakes said gnomically as they wandered out to the forecourt where Markham had parked.

'How so?'

'Well, I ran into Chris Carstairs in The Grapes the other day an' he said Jack Moriarty's looking at a couple of unsolveds from ten years back.'

'*Really?*' Markham had a lot of time for DCI Moriarty who ran the station's cold case unit.

'Couple of old biddies who lived somewhere off Quickswood Lane . . . yeah, thass right, one were Montclair Drive an' the other Canterbury Close. Each of 'em smothered with a cushion or pillow or summat but no sign of a break-in or burglary or owt like that . . . dead peaceful an' quiet, a bit like Shipman.' Noakes had always been vastly interested in Doctor Death's murderous career.

'So they knew their killer then?'

'More'n likely, yeah . . . Jus' seems a weird coincidence with it being in the same area an' Coxley having that OAP fan club.'

Markham couldn't help laughing at the reference to the 'fan club', though he felt a sudden chill on hearing this, as of someone walking over his grave. It was not long since the high street murder investigation had raised the spectre of a homicidal gerontophile, and he had no desire to revisit such territory any time soon.

'An' there's more . . . Apparently the two women got their hair done by Coxley,' Noakes announced while eyeing Markham shrewdly. ''Course, I know you don' like coincidences, guv.'

The DI certainly didn't. And this all felt oddly incestuous, especially the fact of the victims being former customers of their dead hairdresser.

Calmly, he replied, 'I'll check in with DCI Moriarty, Noakesy. As you say, it's an odd coincidence, but we need to cover all the bases.'

'Him an' DI Hart don' reckon there's much gonna turn up after all this time, but you never know.'

Markham unlocked his car and looked back at the elegant mansion behind them.

'I reckon you've landed on your feet here, Noakesy,' he said. 'A gentler pace of life.'

'Happen so . . . but I ain't ready for the old invalid chair an' cocoaholic haze jus' yet, guv.'

More like a rum-and-coke, the DI thought wryly. Britannia waives the rules as far as Noakesy's concerned, he reflected as he headed down the drive.

But there was considerable affection in his glance as he drove away. As Olivia often said, if cycling from the pub to Evensong past cricketers on the village green was no longer what it was, there were nevertheless still certain enduring signs of what it meant to be *Made in England*, one of which being George Noakes. As he headed away from Rosemount back to the station, Markham strove to remind himself of this essential truth.

* * *

That evening at The Sweepstakes, a complex of ultra-modern apartments off Bromgrove Avenue where Markham had his flat, Olivia was waiting for him with Chinese takeaway (from her current favourite, *The Lotus Garden*) and a new hairstyle.

'*Wow, Liv,*' Markham said, contemplating her new side-parted pageboy with a bizarre mixture of pride and nostalgia. 'Where have the pre-Raphaelite tresses gone?'

'Way too Burne-Jones, my love,' was the prompt reply. 'I felt it was time for something more hard-edged and Anna Wintour.'

'Suits you,' he said. And it was true, though he wasn't sure how he felt about the somewhat severe, almost androgynous new look. The Joan of Arc style brought out Olivia's fine-edged, almost medieval, bone structure as never before, however, and he was impressed by the overall effect.

'Of course, Noakesy will be outraged.'

'Not to mention Her Nibs,' Olivia retorted. 'She'll probably decide I'm "gender fluid" or a Tatu follower and thus even more unworthy of the honour of being your partner.'

He chuckled at the allusion to the lesbian pop duo.

'Where did you get it done?'

'Mobile hairdresser who does someone at school,' she said, smiling broadly.

As the timing seemed propitious, Markham quickly broke the news of their invite to the Noakeses for Thursday but was relieved that his partner took it quite well.

'Oh well,' she sighed, 'I suppose I'll get through it somehow.' With the aid of gallons of Pinot Noir.

'How's Natalie doing?' she asked kindly.

'Noakesy says okay, but it's got to have left emotional scars.'

The whole topic of Natalie's pregnancy being freighted with difficult memories, he sought to distract Olivia with an account of his visit to Rosemount.

'A poetry evening, eh . . . Wasn't it Milton who said, "Some books are to be chewed and digested"?' she laughed. 'Though I guess in George's case, they're probably ulcer-inducing.' Spearing a won ton, she giggled endearingly. 'He loved it when I told him Milton had a hernia . . . fell about when I said that's probably why people talk about his "epic strain" . . . Honestly, Gil, it's priceless. I'll never forget Hope's Open Evening last year . . . George announced he'd always liked Keats's *Belle Dame Sans Merci* and then went on about how all the Romantics were high on "deadly lampshade". I don't know how Doc Abernathy managed to keep a straight face, even when George started on about his favourite Tennyson poem being *The Lettuce Eaters* . . . It was too much for Mat, he had to leave the room before he died laughing.'

Despite a sharp pang at the mention of Mat Sullivan, Markham played along. 'Better not get Noakesy started on John Donne then,' he cautioned. 'Wasn't he alternately a convert and pervert at regular intervals?'

Olivia smiled delightedly. 'Think I'm safe there, Gil . . . They didn't do The Metaphysicals on George's school syllabus. Apparently most of it was modern stuff about cup-finals and the queen's birthdays.'

'Thank God for small mercies,' Markham chuckled. 'The cynicism of his outlook is bound to curdle the enthusiasm of the most dedicated poetry-lover.' Given his friend's anti-Scots prejudice, what he might make of Robert Burns did not bear thinking about.

'She smiled reminiscently. 'It was a real conversation-stopper when Abernathy said, "I'm sure your peers have all gone to higher things" and George told him, '"You mean jails." You should have seen the Doc's face! But I think he really *rates* George, not like the rest of that po-faced lot . . . enjoys all his mis-quotations and taking the mickey . . . Actually, I reckon he secretly wishes *he'd* had the guts to kick over the traces and be a bit more of a rebel.'

'Hmm . . . career suicide for a deputy head, my love.'

'Probably,' she gurgled. 'D'you know what George said to my friend Linda, that PGCE student I was mentoring last term . . . "Don't talk too quickly at assembly, luv, or most likely they'll all get up and start dancing." She was pretty scandalised, but at least I managed to stop her repeating it to the head — don't think it would have gone down well with our Dear Leader!'

Markham had no doubt of it, nor of the fact that such *bons mots* would inevitably somehow have found their way to DCI Sidney and the station's top brass.

'Damage limitation, Liv,' he said wryly. 'Well done.'

'Seriously though,' she went on gently, 'how are you doing with this hairdresser murder?'

'We're all systems go tomorrow,' he said. 'Witness statements and alibis and all the rest of it.' Then, as she regarded him quizzically, 'Only we're really none the wiser. Pretty much all at sea.' Almost as an afterthought, he told her about the parallel cold case inquiry.

'Spooky,' she said thoughtfully. 'D'you reckon there's a connection?'

'I don't see how,' he replied, 'but it's uncanny nonetheless.'

Rousing himself to show an interest in his partner's day, moving the chow mein round his plate, he said, 'What did *you* get up to, sweetheart?'

'Oh, just a mental health awareness forum,' came the laconic reply.

'What's one of those then?'

'You really don't want to know, Gil.' Then, with a sudden grin, 'The last time we were in The Grapes, George said students are all "bleeding snowflakes".'

'Sounds a familiar refrain.'

'He said back in the day nobody gave a stuff about mental health. Him and his mates just got given Cascara tablets . . . fed them to the school nurse's dog . . . poor bugger ended up passing himself away.'

Markham couldn't help laughing despite himself.

'You know what he's like once he gets started with all that Dotheboys Hall malarkey!'

'Well, he says kids these days are all so wet you could wring them out — the victim culture and all that — and no-one's prepared to tell it as it is. I mean, all that twaddle about "micro-aggressions" . . . You can't even say someone's fat any more. Apparently the correct terminology is "Chronic Appetite Dysregulation"! George thinks it's bloody ridiculous.'

'I'm sure you managed to reassure him that at least *one* teacher was on his side!'

'Oh yeah.' The shiny new bob swung with the vehemence of her enthusiasm. 'Actually, I suppose today could've been worse . . . At least there were *some* laughs.'

'Indeed?'

'Yep . . . One of the speakers told us this anecdote from Rabbi Lionel Blue . . . There was this time when a student burst into his office ranting that he was going to commit suicide and screaming, '"What are you going to do about it?" In his memoirs, the Rabbi says, "For the next half an hour or so, we practised jumping off the sofa."'

Markham found his voice after nearly choking on a prawn cracker. 'I'm not sure that kind of, er, *robust* approach will find much favour with Hope's senior management team . . . *Just saying.*'

'Don't I know it.' Olivia's face was alight with mischief. But it's *such fun* when someone goes off-message. They say the pen is mightier than the word, right?' she demanded, head on one side. 'Well, I reckon the Biro Platoon is my best chance of cocking a snook at Slimy Sid and your creepy bosses.'

'Good luck with that, Liv.'

'I've saved something special for the *Bromgrove Police Newsletter*.'

Oh, God. He might have known. 'How's that, Liv?'

'It's George's favourite traffic-cop story.'

No, oh no!

'You know . . . the one about the policeman who cautions the female motorist, "Madam, you don't have to say anything, but whatever you say will be taken down and may be given in evidence," and *she* says, "Please don't hit me with your truncheon, officer."!'

Hell, that should go down a bomb when it came to the Federation conference on *The Place of Humour in Modern Policing*.

'Sorry, Gil.' Only she didn't appear remotely contrite. 'It's just too good to leave out.'

'*Hmm*.' He liked to see her looking bright and bushy-tailed, so was loath to puncture the merriment.

But she sensed his anxiety.

'This case has got under your skin,' she observed softly.

His lips twisted in a resigned smile.

'It just doesn't add up,' he sighed. 'No rhyme nor reason, but there's something malicious and hateful at the back of it . . . and now some ancient history that feels as if it might be connected . . . only I don't see how . . .'

In other words, the kind of case that gave him the professional heebie-jeebies.

She met his gaze levelly. 'You'll crack it Gil, of course you will.'

He wished he felt so sure.

'I'll be seeing Noakesy tomorrow . . . for scabrous commentary amongst other things,' he added wryly.

She grinned.

'Wish I could be there.'

'Yes, well, I could do with a few penetrating insights before Sidney inflicts a press conference on us . . . Hopefully Kate'll be on top of that.'

He missed the way her face tightened at the mention of Kate Burton, but all she said was, 'Oh, I'm sure she'll be on top of all the bollocks-speak.' *Not half!*

After an awkward silence, Olivia forced a laugh. 'You'll be okay with the "Press Gang"'

'Not if Gavin Conors has anything to do with it, I won't,' he replied gloomily, referring to the *Gazette*'s lead gossip columnist and Noakes's sworn enemy with whom the former DS had on one occasion come to blows. 'He'll be looking for some kind of personal angle.'

'"Putting a nose on a piece," I believe they call it,' she smiled. 'Like that headline in the *Yorkshire Evening Post* after the sinking of the *Titanic*.'

He looked at her quizzically. 'What headline was that?'

'"West Riding Lad Feared Drowned."'

Markham burst out laughing and his gloom momentarily lifted.

'Right, what's tonight's bill of fare on the box?' he enquired.

'Kirsty and Phil with *Love It or List It*.'

Oh well, he'd take what he could get.

'You're on,' he said.

Outside, the spring shadows deepened. Even as they watched the anodyne property improvement gurus, Markham's mind never stopped niggling at the all-consuming question.

Who killed Andrew Coxley and why?

CHAPTER 3: WASH AND GO

The following morning, Markham and Noakes arrived at *Cutting Edge* before the rest of the team.

'The place could do with a lick of paint,' Noakes said, his eyes narrowed against the sunshine as he surveyed the premises. 'Bit tatty compared with Donny Osmond's gaff over the way.'

'*Noakes*.' The DI's voice held a warning. It was always risky once Noakes got started on nicknames.

'Okay, okay . . . But you gotta admit Coxley's got the edge — *geddit!* — when it comes to kerb appeal.'

Ignoring the execrable pun, Markham said evenly, 'His salon certainly looks the more prosperous outfit, but it's possible Mr O'Grady doesn't care about window-dressing provided the punters keep coming.'

As the brawny, bullet-headed proprietor ushered them in, Noakes gave him a quick once-over. Well, the bloke was no oil painting, he thought to himself. Put him in mind of Charles Bronson or some other prison psycho . . . all he needed was the beard. Self-consciously, he rumpled his own salt and pepper thatch the wrong way, heightening his resemblance to a startled porcupine. No, he wouldn't fancy letting Mister Muscle anywhere near him with a pair of scissors . . . too much like an offensive weapon . . .

A harried-looking young receptionist appeared to have her hands full fielding enquiries from two shrill-voiced elderly women, while a man of similar vintage — stooped and thin with thick NHS spectacles and pencil moustache — hovered uselessly in the background.

'Sorry gents,' O'Grady muttered, drawing Markham and Noakes through to a distinctly frowsy back office, 'some of Coxley's oldies descended on me once they heard about the murder.'

'S'pose they'll all be flocking to you now John Travolta's copped it,' Noakes said beadily.

'My colleague's little joke,' Markham cut in, squelching his friend with a look. 'On account of Mr Coxley's unique . . . nineteen seventies look.'

'Oh right, I'm with you,' though O'Grady regarded Noakes uneasily. He scratched his chin. 'You're probably right about his regulars coming here while things are up in the air,' he continued. 'What with me being practically smack next door to Coxley, it makes sense . . . At that age, familiarity's everything, right? Plus, they don't want the hassle of finding someone new in town or Old Carton.'

Markham gestured encouragingly towards the front of house. 'You mentioned Mr Coxley's, *regulars*,' he prompted. 'Perhaps you could fill us in?'

O'Grady was clearly pleased to be consulted, his tone turning confidential.

'The spindly bloke with the specs and sprout coloured jumper who looks like an asthmatic stork . . . that's Gordon Rushworth . . . retired teacher from Medway High.' He rolled his eyes. 'Difficult to imagine the likes of *him* keeping order in the classroom . . . *way* too prissy. Mind you, back then it probably wasn't all about crowd control the way it is now.'

Markham was amused to note that Noakes looked as though he had found an unlikely soulmate in the politically incorrect hairdresser.

'What about the Maggie Thatcher lookalike?' his friend demanded.

O'Grady's pugilist features broke into a grin.

'Rushworth's sister, Jean Gibley . . . She's a widow . . . lives with him and keeps house.' His tone was indulgent. 'No harm in either of 'em. Devoted to each other . . . he squired her to Coxley's every week come rain or shine.' A grim chuckle. 'Even stuck it out and waited around for her, though it nearly killed him . . . dead embarrassed about being seen in a "Poofs Parlour" if you ask me.' Markham winced, thankful that Kate Burton wasn't there to hear this, but Noakes looked as though he strongly approved of such full-fat sentiments.

'And the other lady?' the DI prompted.

'Evelyn Brady.'

Markham sensed a certain constraint in the hairdresser's voice.

'Whatever you tell us will remain confidential, Mr O'Grady.'

Except insofar as it helps us nail a killer.

'She's a widow too . . . Staff here call her the "Witch lady",' the hairdresser replied. 'A bit sharp and hatchet-faced, so Coxley was welcome to her.' Professional respect came reluctantly to the fore. 'But fair play to the guy, he worked wonders considering the raw materials . . . Plus, he was always kind to her, even though she's a tricky old biddy, went on about her having fabulous bone structure, that kind of thing . . . made it sound sincere, not smarmy.'

The hairdresser hesitated, Markham sensing there was more to come. His eyes flashed a warning to Noakes. *Wait!*

'Her son Mark didn't like it, though,' O'Grady volunteered.

'How so?' The DI's voice was mild, almost relaxed.

'Got it into his head that she and Coxley were too cosy . . . thought she might've given him money?'

Noakes couldn't restrain himself. 'An' *did* she?'

'You'd need to ask Mark about that.' O'Grady looked uncomfortable. On Markham fixing him with a level stare, he conceded, 'Okay, yeah, word on the grapevine was, she'd bunged the odd nice thing Coxley's way . . . presents, if you like . . .'

'*Presents?*' Noakes wanted specifics. 'As in *cash?*'

O'Grady looked cagey, making Markham wonder if Coxley's rival had himself ever accepted gifts from customers.

'Dunno . . . Like I say, it was just gossip . . . stuff about gifts . . . the odd antique, that kind of thing . . . but who knows . . .'

The DI made a mental note to check the inventory for Andrew Coxley's terraced property.

'Are you saying that Mr Brady thought his mother was being exploited?' he asked.

O'Grady shuffled his feet, clearly wary of saying too much. 'You'd have to check with him,' he mumbled once again.

Markham began to wonder about the dynamics of this strange environment that he was attempting to navigate. The DI himself got his hair cut at *The Pony Club* in Medway and never thought much about it (other than getting out as quickly as possible). Devoid of vanity about his handsome looks, he took "personal grooming" for granted, but could see that female customers in particular might well regard their hairstylist in the light of a therapist — someone to whom they could safely confide their private secrets, their hopes and fears . . . Suddenly he wondered if Olivia had ever gone down that route. It was an uncomfortable thought.

He needed to learn more about Andrew Coxley's approach to customer relations, but from what he had seen of them it appeared unlikely that Gordon Rushworth and Jean Gibley would be in any hurry to divulge juicy titbits. The sister, in particular, looked as though she required careful handling. And Rushworth had the buttoned-up air of a desiccated clergyman, so it seemed unlikely there was much to be gleaned from that quarter. Hopefully the team would learn more about Coxley's business practices from the morning's other interviewees, but for the time being it would be counter-productive trying to pump OAPs, not least as Evelyn Brady had the dazed look of someone in shock.

He wondered why O'Grady had chosen to tell them about Mark Brady's suspicions. Could it be that the hairdresser wanted to steer them away from himself? Or had the rumours about Coxley made him genuinely uneasy, so that he felt compelled to tell the police?

'No need for me to get in the way of your work here, Mr O'Grady,' the DI said blandly without giving any hint of his thought processes. 'One of my officers can take preliminary statements from Mr Coxley's regulars as to their whereabouts on Friday night, but we'll leave the interviews till tomorrow . . . That will give them a chance to recover after hearing such distressing news.' It wouldn't do for Mark Brady to accuse the police of bullying his vulnerable widowed parent, Markham thought grimly, so best if they did mother and son together. He'd take Doyle with him for the morrow's visits, since the gangling fresh-faced young detective generally made a favourable impression on such occasions, not least as he appealed to older women's maternal instincts.

O'Grady didn't attempt to hide his relief.

'I'll get someone to give the ladies a wash and set,' he said. 'Gordon can come back for Jean when she's done.' Clearly the idea of Rushworth cluttering up his salon didn't appeal.

With that, he left the two men alone.

Noakes smirked. 'Don' reckon there'll be any surprises with the crumblies' alibis for Friday night . . . most likely Horlicks an' *Newsnight*.'

Markham sighed. 'It's a wonder to me, Noakesy, how you ever managed to swing that job at Rosemount given your galloping ageism.'

His friend grinned unrepentantly. 'Must've been my winning personality an' glittering CV.'

'Well for God's sake don't let anyone hear you talking like that.'

The other held up his meaty paws propitiatingly. 'Kid gloves, guv,' he said, causing Markham to smile at the sheer incongruity of the phrase.

'Watcha reckon to that about Coxley fleecing Ma Brady?' Noakes asked.

'Hmmm it's not clear we're looking at undue influence or grooming or anything of the kind . . . more a case of Mrs Brady being fond of him and wanting to show her appreciation.'

'Mister Scissorhands looked dead shifty when you asked about exploitation, though,' Noakes observed thoughtfully. 'Wouldn't be surprised if he didn't have a little side hustle of his own,' he added philosophically.

'It's a complication all right.' And one they could well do without.

'The Giblet woman looked a right tartar.'

'It's *Gibley*, Noakes.'

'Whatever . . . She's one of them born with a silver sock in their gob, that's for sure.'

'More than likely,' the DI said imperturbably.

The other frowned. 'Pretty weird, though . . .'

'What is?'

'Lover boy's regulars coming to get their hair done when he's jus' been found stabbed to death.'

'Not really,' Markham demurred. 'It could be their usual day . . . or they're aware that Mr O'Grady will have his ear to the ground and want to find out what he knows. Plus, you have to factor in shock . . . everyone reacts differently to something like this.'

'The Gibley one looks like she's got a black belt in bossing folk around. Didn't O'Grady say she keeps house for the brother? Well, God help him. It'll be martial arts at the Aga . . . one chop and you're crippled for life.'

Markham's voice was dry. 'Well, whatever service Mr O'Grady is offering — be it some post-trauma counselling with the wash and set or a cup of tea and a kindly word — let's hope it softens them up for a visit tomorrow.'

'Taking Doyle along, are you?' It was a rhetorical question, since Noakes knew as well as Markham that the youngster had a way of getting round oldsters.

Suddenly O'Grady was back, ushering Burton, Doyle and Carruthers before him as though anxious to get them out of sight as quickly as possible. He opened a back door, disclosing a small courtyard with table and chairs. 'With the weather being so nice, reckon you might like to interview folk out there,' he said awkwardly. In other words, well away from his customers.

'An excellent suggestion, Mr O'Grady,' Markham said politely. 'It looks quite the suntrap.'

'Shame about the rubbish bins, though,' Noakes said with pursed lips before the hairdresser was barely out of earshot.

Doyle and Carruthers grinned. While Burton went into a huddle with Markham about the interview schedule, the other three engaged in a spirited discussion about the merits of the new signing at Bromgrove Rovers.

They had just been supplied with tea and stale custard creams by the receptionist when she returned, escorting an attractive blonde with a good figure whose undeniable good looks were marred by her petulant and sulky expression.

This turned out to be Sarah Moorcroft, the local celebrity (in her own mind, at any rate) who had objected to Andrew Coxley's refusal to fit her in for an appointment at the last minute. 'I felt so *let down*,' she said plaintively in a husky contralto, gesturing theatrically with her designer sunglasses. 'I mean, I was *counting on him* for some moral support.'

'And a power blow-dry,' Carruthers put in quietly. Most likely she expected it on the house too, he thought sardonically.

The woman shot him a venomous look. 'He insisted he couldn't cancel some old dears . . . But I'm sure they wouldn't have minded me queue-jumping seeing as I'm by way of being a *local figure*. Of course,' with a spiteful inflection, 'I don't tip or *take care of him* the way they do.'

'What do you mean by "take care of him"?' Burton asked quickly.

'You can put your own interpretation on it,' was the reply. 'Let's just say everyone knew Andy had *very* expensive tastes . . . definitely high maintenance . . . And then he had all the old dears *fawning* over him.'

'God, that one's *trouble*,' Doyle burst out after the truculent divorcee, having told them that she was 'enjoying a quiet evening at home' on Friday night (yet another unsatisfactory alibi), departed with a toss of the thick glossy plait that suggested she was pretty high maintenance herself.

'But at least she confirmed that there were rumours about how Coxley funded his lifestyle,' Markham pointed out.

'His flat's nothing special,' Burton mused. 'But it's in a pricey postcode and he took some luxury holidays — Pyramids and the Nile this year, and the Greek Islands last summer . . . He drove a BMW and had subscriptions to all kinds of sporting events plus membership at *Quads*.'

Carruthers whistled at the mention of Bromgrove's premier health club. 'That won't have come cheap.'

'Any sign that he was involved with an expensive partner?' Markham asked.

Burton shook her head. 'By the look of things, he pretty much enjoyed the bachelor lifestyle.'

'What about phone records?'

'They've come through, but nothing jumps out,' Burton sighed. 'Same with his PC.'

Carruthers was anxious to inject some optimism. 'We're going through his contacts, boss. Alibi-wise, almost all of them were out pubbing and clubbing — plenty of witnesses — so at least we can cross them off and look for a local connection.'

'Someone he rubbed up the wrong way,' Doyle chipped in eagerly. 'Someone connected to the salon.'

Burton's mind was still running on the issue of sidelines.

'If he got given pricey gifts, he could easily have sold stuff on,' she said, 'built up a nice little nest-egg for himself . . . There's a hundred K in his Halifax account and he's got wardrobes full of retro gear.'

'We're getting everything checked out,' Carruthers reassured Markham. 'Looks like he spent a small fortune on clobber — collector's items most like.'

Noakes's expression suggested this confirmed his worst fears about male hairdressers, but he plainly struggled to reconcile the dead man's wardrobe with his reputation as some kind of suburban Rasputin who hypnotised elderly women into subsidising his lifestyle. At last he couldn't contain himself.

'Whass Coxley's secret then?' he demanded. 'Was he some kind of stud muffin on the sly?'

Doyle and Carruthers exchanged delighted glances. *Stud muffin! OMG, just clock Burton's face! She looks like she's swallowed a wasp!*

Before Noakes could get stuck in to the subject of Andrew Coxley's sexual endowment, Markham smoothly interposed, 'It's unlikely anyone's going to give us any information on that point, Noakesy.'

'And we can hardly go round asking *pensioners* about it,' Burton expostulated. 'The DCI would have us working Traffic if something like that got out.'

Noakes looked disappointed. Suppressing a smile, Markham said, 'It's more likely to be some kind of psychological thralldom than anything X-rated.' He turned to Burton. 'Would that be your take on it, Kate?'

She nodded vigorously. 'Definitely, sir,' before adding shyly, 'you can get, well, sort of emotionally *dependent* on your hairdresser... With everything these days being about image, it's quite a big deal.' Seeing that Noakes looked as though she was spouting Swahili, she explained, 'Not necessarily for *blokes*, sarge, but women spend a lot of time and money... A new look can make all the difference if you're looking to get some confidence.' This was obviously her own experience and Markham found himself touched by the admission. 'Well, looking at you I'd say it's a worthwhile investment, Kate,' he said gallantly, causing the colour to creep into her cheeks.

She ain't over the guvnor, Noakes thought crossly. Not by a mile!

Aware of the piggy eyes boring into her, Burton said hastily, 'There's nothing so far to suggest that Mr Coxley was some sort of Lovejoy character or doing anything fraudulent . . . nothing that anyone could pin on him at any rate . . . just the usual Ebay stuff, nothing sinister.'

There was a glum silence before Markham said, 'There could be a possible connection to a cold case.' He nodded to Noakes. 'Tell them what you told me.'

The others listened attentively as Noakes repeated what he had learned via DI Carstairs.

'I'm having a breakfast meeting with DCI Moriarty and DI Hart tomorrow morning,' Markham resumed. 'I'll take you along for that, Noakes . . . should oil the wheels seeing as they were your intake.'

'Yeah, only I wanted to pound the streets an' nick scrotes while them two mainlined on paperwork . . . Thass why I never made Inspector.'

Along with an ocean-going ability to antagonise his superiors, Markham thought, careful not to meet his colleagues' eyes.

'There may be nothing in it, but those murders took place in the same locale and involved elderly victims who got their hair done by Mr Coxley,' he resumed. 'That being so, I think they're worth revisiting.' The DI gestured towards the premises behind them. 'Afterwards, Doyle, you and I will touch base with Mr Coxley's regulars—'

'Batting those baby blues,' Carruthers said sotto voce as Doyle surreptitiously gave him the finger.

'In the meantime, Kate, I want you and Carruthers to liaise with the criminal profiling team,' Markham instructed, careful not to specify any particular psychologist in light of her troubled relationship with Professor Nathan Finlayson. 'See if you can pinpoint some useful markers, factoring in whatever I get from the cold case people.'

Carruthers looked distinctly perky on hearing this. Po-faced Burton was good to work with when it came to the psychiatric stuff.

'Right, who are we waiting for now, Kate?' Markham asked.

'Carol Davidson, the charity fundraiser.'

Doyle pulled a face. God, the do-gooder. That should be a barrel of laughs.

'And after that?'

Burton consulted her notebook. 'Well, I'm still trying to track down Karen Bickerstaff... She's the woman who lost a negligence claim against Mr Coxley. But Helen Mathews and Philip Casey are due in ... the sacked stylist and—'

'The bloke who thought Coxley was giving his daughter one,' Doyle burst out delightedly. Then registering Burton's thunderous expression and Noakes's smirk, he amended hastily, 'I mean, the fella who got the idea there was something iffy going on cos his daughter went all lovestruck and stalkerish.'

'Let's try and avoid any prejudgment shall we, Sergeant,' Markham said mildly. He didn't reprove the vulgarity, since Doyle's sheepish expression was evidence enough that he knew he had overstepped the mark.

'What's going to happen to *The Mane Event*, guv?' Carruthers asked by way of diversionary tactic as Doyle shot him a grateful glance. 'Who's going to take it over?'

'I believe Mr Coxley's cousins plan to keep the current team in place until any decisions are made ... Presumably Ed Collins will step up, seeing as he's been there the longest.'

'That reminds me,' Burton said. 'Becca Drew let drop that Coxley and Collins fell out over some client who left Collins a legacy in her will.'

'Interesting,' Markham said thoughtfully. 'So presumably what's sauce for the goose *wasn't* sauce for the gander in this instance.'

'I followed up with Collins,' Burton continued. 'He was upfront about it — didn't seem particularly embarrassed. Apparently he'd been good to the old lady ... used to drive her home so she didn't have to take a taxi, that kind of thing.'

'How much did he get?' Noakes asked.

'Five K, which obviously seemed like riches to Becca.'

'An' Coxley didn't want David Hasselhoff muscling in on the action in case all the old biddies switched loyalties?'

Noakes leered. 'Y'know, on account of him being a blonde with biceps.'

Burton looked somewhat vinegary at this. 'Mr Coxley was the proprietor,' she pointed out. 'He might have felt that what was acceptable in his own case *wasn't* acceptable for his staff.'

'Employer's prerogative?' Markham suggested.

'Exactly, sir,' his fellow DI said. 'Though obviously there could have been mixed motives. The thing is, there doesn't seem to have been anything murky about Collins getting that money, though his colleagues may have resented it, especially the women.'

She broke off suddenly as the receptionist reappeared. 'Ms Davidson for you,' the girl said, whisking off before Noakes had a chance to ask for more tea and biscuits.

Carol Davidson had lots of dandelion-fine blonde hair secured with an Alice band (somehow, perhaps due to the nature of the case, Markham found himself paying close attention to coiffures) and the slightly affected, braying tones of a dedicated upper-class committeewoman. Broad shouldered and well built, with the look of someone who lifted weights on a regular basis, her sturdy physique was somewhat at odds with her thin predatory face, fussy pussy-bow blouse and dirndl skirt. She lost no time in alluding to her 'police contacts', with the veiled threat that she could make trouble for Markham's team should she choose.

The DI found her as uncongenial as Sarah Moorcroft, however he reminded himself that an unattractive personality did not constitute criminality. And while her resentment at Coxley's disinclination to be dragooned into various charitable schemes was clear, she had a stronger alibi than the rest of his suspects having hosted her elderly neighbour for 'kitchen sups' on the night in question. Markham shot Noakes a quizzical look on hearing this — confirmation that at least one 'crumbly' appeared to have eschewed Horlicks and *Newsnight!*

The interview with Helen Mathews, equally, led nowhere. Short and bottle blonde, with tip-tilted features and a cheery open expression, she freely admitted to taking some of Coxley's customers.

'Is that why he gave you the push?' Noakes wanted to know.

'I did mobile clients as well as renting a chair in the salon,' she told them. Seeing Noakes's bemusement, she explained. 'Hairdressers are kind of like independent contractors — strictly speaking, we're not employees cos we pay the salon owner to use the facilities — and there's nothing to stop us taking on other work . . . Well, anyway, he got it into his head that I was poaching customers.'

'Were you?' Noakes again.

She rolled her eyes. 'Not *poaching*,' she insisted. 'Some of the older ones asked if I could do them at home . . . got to the point where they were tired of schlepping out to the salon — too much faff at their age — and I didn't have a problem with it.'

'How about the younger ones?' Carruthers asked.

Her expression turned flinty and a certain set of the jaw that suggested this wasn't a woman to mess with. 'Look, I never touted for trade,' she told them. 'Didn't need to. But if someone asked could I do home visits, then that was a different matter. No law against it.'

'What about slagging off Coxley to the press?' Doyle asked.

'Never happened. That was just Andy being paranoid.' She shrugged her shoulders. 'He needed someone to blame and *voilà*, there I was . . . Plus, I didn't drool over him like some of the other girls, so he saw me as fair game . . . There were a few snide pieces about him in the *Gazette*, but that was thanks to the mysterious gigolo thing he had going . . . sure, it made really good copy, but I had nothing to do with it.'

After she had gone, Burton said, 'I've emailed you the relevant bits from the *Gazette*, boss. It stayed just the right side of libel. Stuff about Coxley's "geriatric harem" and his allure for "ladies of a certain age". Malicious froth really.'

'Wouldn't that be good for business?' Doyle objected. 'I mean, the press making him sound like Liberace would get all the old biddies flocking to the salon.'

'Yeah, but it's tacky,' Carruthers pointed out, 'and he might've minded that.'

'To say nothing of reinforcing the misgivings of people like Mark Brady,' Markham added.

There was a pause while they digested this.

The DI finally broke the silence. 'Where are we up to with Mr Coxley's younger clientele?' he asked.

'We're still going through them, boss,' Carruthers said, 'but so far it looks like they're in the clear — making an early start on the weekend . . . out in restaurants or down the pub, which means they're alibied.'

'Pity the salon lot didn't do the same,' Doyle grumbled. 'Then we could've ruled them out.'

'It was a school day for them,' Carruthers reminded him. 'Wouldn't do for them to rock up with a hangover.'

'Yeah,' Noakes agreed. 'One false move with them scissors an' it could get proper nasty.'

There was a pregnant pause as an image of Andrew Coxley stabbed through the neck flashed through their minds.

This reverie was interrupted by the return of the receptionist with their final interviewees.

Ten minutes later and Noakes was in full spate.

'Jus' think,' he burst out, 'thass the crème de la wotsit of Medway High.' He ratcheted his voice up a full octave in a passable imitation of Catherine Tate's *Am I Bovvered* routine. '"*What even is this! I'm not gonna lie, Andy was, like, well fit . . . He, like, enjoyed a bit of banter . . . It was so random . . . totally sick.*"'

Doyle and Carruthers sniggered. As far as the old warhorse was concerned, Stella Casey might as well have been speaking Esperanto.

Markham smiled. 'That's teenagers for you, Noakesy.'

His friend's complexion had turned puce. 'Bleeding verbal vandals.'

'No way did Coxley give her the come on,' Doyle said forcefully. '*No way*. That'd be totally, well, tragic.'

'Yeah,' Carruthers concurred. 'And besides, it doesn't fit with that camp *Boogie Nights* vibe he had going.'

Recalling the pimply seventeen-year old, with her thin, pointed features, straggly carroty hair and gum-chewing inarticulacy, the DI was inclined to agree. Stella Casey's father, however, had fairly simmered with outrage . . .

Tall and thick-set, face weather-beaten from his job as a construction worker, Philip Casey possessed a shock of grey hair that seemed to sprout in all directions at once and was nearly as alarming as Noakes's.

'He incinerated stuff.'

Incinerated! A malapropism worthy of Noakes!

'What did he *insinuate*, Mr Casey?' The schoolmarm in Kate Burton meant that she simply couldn't let that pass.

'That he was interested in . . . well, messing about . . . He was trying it on, like. The guy was a perv.' When it came to verbal incoherence, clearly the apple didn't fall far from the tree.

'Is that correct, Stella?' Markham asked the teenager.

'Andy said it was nice having me around and we should go for a drink some time . . . to, like, celebrate me getting my Level 2.' She shot an aggrieved glance at her father. 'Nothing funny, he thought I was dope . . . Okay, so I hung out at the salon. Is that, like, an actual crime?'

It sounded innocuous enough, but maybe Stella was the kind of girl a father worried about. Markham knew that Noakes had been through similar worries with Natalie who acquired something of a reputation in her night-clubbing phase. Stella's vulpine streetwise manner certainly suggested she would require watching. But it was a stretch to imagine her attacking Andrew Coxley. Her father, on the other hand, was a different proposition.

'Can you account for your movements on Friday night?' Burton asked calmly.

'Stel was on a sleepover at her mate Shirley's,' Casey told them with a glower. 'Me and the missus had our tea in front of the telly like we always do.'

No doubt Shirley's story would chime with Stella's, but of course she could be covering for her friend. And as for Philip Casey, well a wife's alibi was worse than useless . . .

Now Markham took stock.

'So, no-one exactly stands out at the moment,' he said, raking a hand through the thick dark hair that curled over his collar in elegant dishevelment that seemed the height of unfairness to Noakes. 'Miz Stridently Annoying and the Local Philanthropist may have set our teeth on edge, but neither seems a strong contender for murder.'

'Helen Mathews had more of a motive,' Doyle suggested. 'Getting sacked and accused of stuff she didn't do must've really rankled.'

'My money's on Casey and the screwy daughter,' Noakes grunted. 'She's *gotta* be on the spectrum.'

'They call it "neurodiverse" these days,' Burton corrected him primly.

'She's probably a bit cray-cray all right,' Doyle put in, 'but hard to imagine her sticking it to Coxley.'

Burton looked as though she thought this remark was in decidedly bad taste.

'*Cray-cray*,' Markham said wryly. 'Presumably that's a term of art, Sergeant. But in the circumstances I trust you'll find a suitable euphemism when you do a briefing note for the DCI.'

He allowed this to sink in and then said, 'Right, back to the station.' And at some point a meeting with Sidney. 'I'll drop you off en route, Noakesy, before Rosemount sends out a search party.'

'No worries, guv,' his friend said cheerfully. Then, 'You sure you don' need me to help with Sidney?'

'That won't be necessary,' Markham replied faintly as his colleagues exchanged knowing glances, thinking that if there was one thing guaranteed to get things off on the wrong foot, it was the attendance of Sidney's bête noire. Things were tricky enough without *that!*

* * *

Burton gallantly offered to join Markham for his grilling by the DCI, but he declined the offer with a dry, 'I'm keeping you in reserve for later, Kate . . . when Sidney starts peppering about our lack of progress. That's when you can blind him with data.'

This elicited a thin smile from his colleague. Both psychology graduates, she somehow gelled with Sidney in a manner that Markham had never quite managed. Certainly, she had a remarkable gift for handling the top brass with an adroitness that remarkably never tipped into servility.

Sidney's conference must have gone well, because he was in a relatively sunny mood when Markham was ushered into his office by the dragon PA who could never help peering suspiciously over the DI's shoulder as though to reassure herself that his appalling sidekick was nowhere about.

Even more rabidly monarchist than Muriel Noakes, the impending Coronation and elevation of his all-time favourite royal The Countess of Wessex to become Duchess of Edinburgh had the DCI rubbing his hands with glee. Markham was amused to note that the Hall of Fame, as the photomontage in Sidney's office was irreverently dubbed by the lower ranks, now featured new pictures of HRH at various civic shindigs, with the DCI's bald bonce prominent in the background as though he was intent on photobombing her. It was notable, however, that there were no longer any photographs of Sidney together with Brunhilde on display, though his 'paperless' mahogany desk held framed pictures of his three boys, pride of place going to Jake's passing out at Sandhurst. Despite their mutual antipathy, this army connection had provided some common ground between the DCI and Noakes, the latter conceding that Sidney's eldest boy was a 'top lad'. (Not that Sidney particularly relished the ex-sergeant's habit of jovially saluting Jake's picture with such jovial pleasantries as *'Barrack shun!'* or *'Stand by your beds!'*.)

Sidney's executive buzz cut was unchanged, but he was back to growing the sinister little goatee that he no doubt fancied gave him a philosophical air. Definitely not a success, Markham thought compassionately. More Bin Laden than Johnny Depp.

He fancied that the DCI's manner was less antagonistic than of yore, perhaps due to the fact that they had both suffered "relationship issues", though while Markham and Olivia were now back together it was rumoured that there was little prospect of any reconciliation for the Sidneys. Indeed, if canteen gossip was to be credited, Brunhilde had taken up with a local businessman and was reinventing herself with a vengeance. Less WI and more Cougar, as Carruthers was wont to put it. Whatever the truth of the DCI's personal life, he was definitely more mellow, and Markham proceeded to take full advantage, slipping in the odd patriotic pean which always went down well (although rather despising himself in the process).

Sidney listened attentively as Markham brought him up to date.

When it came to prime suspects for murder, the DCI invariably preferred that suspicion should fall on just about anyone other than respectable members of the community — ideally the mythical "bushy haired stranger" or, failing that, some mentally disordered dropout. So Markham was careful to stress that all options were on the table, including the possibility of a random attack. 'I know you'll be wanting good old-fashioned policework on this, sir,' he said. With a spasm of self-disgust, he laid it on with a trowel, 'No danger of my getting carried away with "hunches" or anything of the kind.'

Sidney's honk affected the DI's nerves as badly as ever, but at least the DCI's expression was now almost benign and he received the news of a possible link to two cold cases with something close to rapture. Cynically, Markham could not help reflecting that a hat trick would be an auspicious start to Sidney's post-retirement career. But he supposed it was fair enough that his boss should be looking for future fame and glory, if only to compensate for failure on the domestic front.

'Be sure to keep me posted, Markham.'

'Absolutely, sir.' God, any more of the Uriah-Heaping and he wouldn't be able to look at himself in the mirror.

Just as well Olivia and Noakes weren't there to witness his abasement.

Noakes.

With Sidney in such a good mood, he should seal the deal.

He got to his feet but turned at the door. 'I hope you don't mind if I consult with George Noakes on this one, sir,' he said almost as a throwaway 'Local knowledge and so forth. Nothing official, *naturally*.'

A brief spasm of something like pain crossed the other's face.

Anything but that, it seemed to say.

Markham forced a laugh. 'We'll keep him on a tight rein, never fear sir.' And with that he salaamed himself out of the Presence before his boss had a chance to reply.

Mission accomplished!

Now it was time for what Doyle called their 'Wash and Go' case to pick up steam.

CHAPTER 4: RIPPLES FROM THE PAST

As he sat in his office at eight o'clock on Wednesday morning waiting for the cold case detectives and Noakes to arrive, Markham reviewed developments so far.

Despite the positive spin he put on things for Sidney, what they had didn't amount to much. The DCI hadn't said anything about organising a press conference, but Markham was in no doubt the evil hour was fast approaching when he would be wheeled out to reassure an anxious public that the police were making progress.

Olivia had been informative on the subject of hair salons when they discussed the case over supper the previous evening. He found that he was coming to like the clean unfussy lines of her geometric bob, despite the odd pang of regret for her previous romantic style.

'There was something so *liberating* about getting it all hacked off, Gil,' she told him. 'Like I was embarking on a new chapter or something.'

He had been startled to learn that mobile hairdresser Helen Mathews was responsible for the new look. 'I heard Helen was going freelance and liked what she did for one of the TAs,' Olivia explained. 'She was able to fit me in straight after school . . . salon prices, but I reckoned it was worth it.'

'Without a doubt,' he murmured gallantly.

Olivia was equally taken aback to learn of her new stylist's connection to Andrew Coxley and the rupture that had led to her being sacked and going solo. 'She was very discreet . . . never said a word about it.'

'What did you make of her?'

'Very good at her job, can cut hair with either hand . . . No nonsense . . . calls a spade a spade.' She grinned. 'But I quite like that.'

'Not the homicidal type then?'

Olivia laughed at that. '*Hardly!* Very down-to-earth and unneurotic. Not at all nosy . . . so you don't feel you have to share every last personal detail.'

So it appeared that Helen Mathews was both circumspect and tactful. Which made it less likely that she was the one who had fed tittle tattle to the *Gazette*.

'It was really interesting what she said about the way they used to do people's hair . . . all those rigid hairstyles, with the backcombing and rock-hard sets held in place by heavy lacquer . . . or chignons which were so stiff, it meant women had to sleep Japanese style with their heads on blocks . . . It was the Dark Ages, really. Stylists even mixed their own shampoo in buckets. And back in the day, when just about everyone wanted to go blonde, they used so much ammonia that they could have cleared the sinuses of whole streets.'

He chuckled. 'So things have evolved?'

'Oh, it's a whole different ball game . . . much more scientific. There are "hair colourists" and all kinds of different specialists . . . incredibly technical.' She smiled. 'Helen's first boss sounded a real character. Apparently, he got sacked from his first salon for being rude to a customer.'

'How so?'

'Well, when he had finished and put his scissors and comb down, she told him she didn't like her hair. He just looked her in the eye and said, "*I* don't like it either but it's the best I can do with what you have" . . . Reminded me of that scene from *Educating Rita* when this woman who looks like the back end of a bus rocks up and asks for a Princess Diana makeover.'

'Ah, I imagine there's a real art to managing people's expectations.'

'*Definitely*. Helen told me another story about a sleb in the fifties who told a top stylist that she wanted a whole new look and fancied going grey-white. He gave it a go and cracked on for about eight and a half hours while she worked her way through a packet of digestive biscuits. At the end of it, she complained, "I've been here all day and I'm still not grey-white". He was so fed up that he said, "Madam, when you see the bill you will be"!'

Now, as he sat there, Markham decided that Andrew Coxley had been a past master at massaging his clients' egos.

It still hadn't stopped him from turning up dead stabbed through the neck.

So who was in the running for their prime suspect?

He ticked off the names on his fingers:

Becca Drew and Sandra Crowley, two female stylists who most likely both had a crush on their boss despite the camp vibes he gave out.

Ed Collins, the senior stylist whom it appeared Coxley kept on a tight leash.

Cassie Johnson, bolshie manicurist.

Des O'Grady, the bulldog like rival who looked like a wrestler and had none of Coxley's practised charm or *soigné charisma*.

Sarah Moorcroft, a self-obsessed prima donna who resented not getting the red-carpet treatment.

Carol Davidson, professional cadger and tiresome fund-raiser whom Coxley hadn't wanted to help.

Philip Casey, over-protective father, and his "cray-cray" daughter Stella who took vacuity to new heights.

Mark Brady, who suspected Coxley of targeting his elderly mother Evelyn for financial gain.

Then there was Jean Gibley and a clutch of older women who had a proprietorial attitude towards Coxley and competed amongst themselves for his attention. It didn't appear that the likes of Gordon Rushworth or other elderly passers-through had any significant issues with the dead man — other than tongue-tied horror at his prices and their dread of such overwhelmingly female territory — but they couldn't be ruled out.

Also in the mix was Helen Mathews, the sacked employee who was distinctly less dewy-eyed about Coxley than his other female colleagues and who may or may not have been responsible for some bad PR in the *Gazette*. Olivia judged her to be sound, but he knew all too well that appearances could be deceptive.

And finally, Karen Bickerstaff, the unsuccessful litigant who was proving elusive.

Even though it looked as if Coxley's personal contacts and younger clientele were largely in the clear, along with those of his employees who had been away on holiday, there were still too many possibles for Markham's peace of mind . . .

These musings were interrupted by the arrival of Noakes who was irritably jangling his visitor's lanyard. 'I *hate* these things,' he said. 'Whass wrong with a name badge instead of a bleeding necklace?'

Markham smiled ruefully. 'Just try not to get it tangled up in your tie, Noakesy,' he advised. 'Definitely *not* a good look.' Not that anything could really redeem the horribly mismatched combo of crumpled mustard jacket, purple shirt and bright green cords.

His friend grunted, plonking himself down on the other side of the desk and setting the little silver balls of Markham's cradle desk pendulum in motion, this executive gadget being his invariable recourse when in a bad mood. Like one of those fidget toys Olivia used with students who had ADHD, the DI thought in amusement as he rang down for tea and biscuits, nothing being so well calculated to mollify the other as the prospect of refreshments.

By the time their colleagues appeared Noakes had satisfied the inner man and was eager to hear about the two cold cases.

DCI Jack Moriarty was a puckish, merry-eyed officer whose cheerful demeanour belied the grim nature of the investigations that were his professional diet. DI Mike Hart — a good-natured, softly-spoken, well-respected detective (and football fanatic) — had an equally easy manner. After an exchange of pleasantries with their old friend Noakes, both men listened carefully to Markham's summing up of the salon murder, exchanging a long look as he concluded, 'There seemed to be some sort of unusual dynamic between Andrew Coxley and his elderly customers . . . When I heard you were looking at two deaths of OAPs close to Quickswood Lane, I wondered about a possible connection.' Clutching at straws, he thought dourly.

Moriarty nodded at Hart who said. 'Ethel Taylor lived in Montclair Drive . . . just had her ninetieth birthday when she was found smothered with a cushion in her living room. This was December 2011. Then in February 2012 there was another one . . . Jeanette O'Donnell, sixty-seven, round the corner in Canterbury Close. Exactly the same M.O. No forced entry, so they must have let the killer in . . . both of them widows . . . well-off . . . no enemies that anyone knew of. Nothing taken, so didn't look like robbery was the motive . . . Totally inexplicable and the original SIO Phil Clark got nowhere.... died last year, so we haven't been able to go through it with him.'

Noakes leaned in eagerly. 'But he reckoned it was the same guy?'

Moriarty nodded slowly. 'With the two women being friends and living round the corner from each other, Phil figured it had to be. But forensics drew a blank. Didn't look like the perp was in the system and there was nothing from the local mental health agencies, so he wasn't on their radar either.'

He. Markham noticed how the other three assumed the killer had to be male, but statistically it was a reasonable deduction.

'What about the victims?' he asked. 'Anything that stood out background-wise?'

'Ethel lost her teenaged son Preston when he was fourteen,' Hart said in his gentle, deliberate manner. 'She was thirty-nine when he died and there weren't any other kids.'

'How'd it happen?' Noakes asked.

'Accident on a school trip,' Hart replied. 'Nobody to blame. Lost his footing when they were hiking in the Cairngorms. The lad had type 2 diabetes so he most probably felt dizzy and lost his balance. That's what the inquest decided at any rate. Nothing sinister and the school had done all the risk assessments and everything by the book . . . just a freak tragedy.'

Moriarty's eyes were sad. 'He was a brilliant student and sportsman apparently. Ethel and Jack — that's the husband — never talked about it.'

'And the other lady . . . Jeanette?' Markham pressed.

'Retired university lecturer,' Hart told them. 'Quite the scholar with a strong publication record . . . an authority on Henry VI . . . you know, the one who founded Eton.'

The founding of Eton cut no ice with Noakes.

'Thass the bloke who went doolally,' he said disdainfully. 'Ended up in the Tower cos he weren't up to the job.'

Markham hid a smile at this typically trenchant verdict.

Hart blinked. 'Well, they think he most likely had schizophrenia or something like that,' he continued. 'Anyway, Jeanette was a bit of a star in the academic world . . . gave talks to various local societies and volunteered with *Meals on Wheels*. A really nice woman. The husband Frank was quite a bit older than her . . . history lecturer at Leeds uni, died in 2000.'

Markham digested this.

'Andrew Coxley opened *The Mane Event* in 2009,' he said thoughtfully. 'And you say both women were customers. . .'

'That's right,' Moriarty confirmed. 'Ethel got her hair done there every few weeks. With Jeanette it was more . . . sporadic.'

Noakes snorted at this, envisaging the hirsute results of skipping the salon.

'Any issues with Coxley?' the DI asked.

'Nope,' Moriarty sighed. 'Apparently they were pretty loyal to the salon . . . He didn't do mobile, though, and eventually they wanted home appointments. There was another place opened up a couple of doors down and the bloke from there said he could do it.'

Noakes's eyes gleamed. 'Des O'Grady?'

'Yes, I think that was the one . . . I remember it was an Irish surname.'

Another one in the mix, Markham thought wearily, but there was no obvious reason for Coxley's rival to target two inoffensive elderly women. And customers of his at that . . . unless he was some kind of deranged sociopath, and so far they had uncovered nothing to support such a theory.

'What's your game plan then?' he asked Moriarty bluntly.

'Reinterview everyone,' the DCI retorted promptly. 'That is, everyone who's still around. Given the victims' ages, some of the original witnesses are pushing up daisies.'

'We'll try and drum up some publicity,' Hart added. 'But after all this time, it's going to be difficult.'

God, talk about getting the short straw, Noakes thought sympathetically. With the case being about wrinklies and, well, *unsexy*, he couldn't imagine the *Gazette* or any of the tabloids would be interested.

Moriarty's eyes crinkled, as though he read the other's mind.

'We'll give it our best shot,' he announced firmly. 'There may have been someone back then who knew something but was afraid to speak out . . . We're ten years on, so things are different.'

I wouldn't count on it, mate, Noakes's expression said more clearly than words.

After making arrangements for information sharing, the cold case duo departed.

'You need to get back to Rosemount, Noakesy,' Markham told his friend. 'Otherwise I'll be fielding complaints about your . . . extracurricular commitments.' Though he suspected their security manager's police credentials were a definite plus as far as Rosemount's directors were concerned.

'I've trained Kev up so he c'n handle everything,' Noakes said complacently. 'You wouldn't believe how that lad's come on.'

Hmm, Markham thought. No doubt young Kevin was already an expert in outmanoeuvring the bosses, but presumably there were limits to the prodigy's ingenuity.

'You'll let me know how it goes with Mrs Giblet an' the Brady Bunch,' Noakes wheedled as he heaved himself up, wrestling his paunch into the snug-fitting cords as Markham tactfully averted his gaze. 'An' don' forget it's dinner at ours tomorrow.'

'Looking forward to it,' the DI said a shade too heartily. 'I'll update you on developments then. In the meantime I need to make sure the team's up to speed on these cold cases.'

For all the good it would do, he thought morosely, firing up his PC.

His former DS grunted acknowledgment. Then, tugging irritably at his visitor's lanyard as if it was an affront to his dignity, he headed downstairs for an exchange of friendly insults with the desk sergeant.

* * *

In the event, 'Mrs Giblet' proved pretty much impervious to Doyle's boyish charms, while Gordon Rushworth wore an air of wary rectitude throughout the interview.

Brother and sister lived in a solidly unpretentious 1940s four bedroom detached house at 4 Porlock Drive, a short distance from Quickswood Lane and Andrew Coxley's salon. The furniture and décor, in accents of eau de nil and beige, had a strong feel of Old People's Home and looked as though they hadn't been renovated since the year dot. The front room into which they were ushered was particularly characterless, with a musty closed-up odour and only olive-green curtains and burgundy antimacassars to relieve the drabness. It had all the amenities — large flat-screen television, hi-fi system and fitted bookcases — but they did nothing to lift the atmosphere. The world was kept safely at bay with vertical blinds hung between the heavy drapes, and altogether the impression was that of a hermetically sealed bastion on its guard against intruders. The front garden sported no flowers and was laid to lawn with a block paved driveway.

As Noakes had predicted, their routine for Friday night consisted of supper followed by television, after which Jean retired to her own bedroom and Gordon to his study.

Safe on her own territory, stately in a knitted twinset, Jean thawed sufficiently to say that Andrew Coxley was 'a delightful young man with the most beautiful manners and frankly she didn't trust anyone else to do her hair ... couldn't imagine how they would get along without him.'

Rushworth, equally old-fashioned in a tweed suit with elbow patches, was less effusive but readily concurred. If you looked past the flamboyance and the prices, Coxley was a real perfectionist, he told them in his reedy voice, and very easy to talk to.

'You get what you pay for,' his sister snapped, clearly reluctant for the detectives to imagine that cost was an issue, though Markham had a sense of stifling smallness about the pair — not just the ambiance of the property but something suggestive of narrow horizons and prickly self-preoccupation ... emotional as well as material stinginess.

Doyle felt it too. '*Phew!*' he said once they were back out in the fresh air, 'those two are *depressing*.' Quickly, he added, 'I'm not being ageist, boss ... It just felt like they were waxworks or something ... only really came to life when they were talking about Coxley.'

'I know what you mean, Sergeant.' Markham had been intrigued by the transformation that had stolen over Jean Gibley's features when she talked about Andrew Coxley, the hawk-like lineaments softening to a remarkable degree. Rushworth's expression had been indulgent as he listened to her raptures, the schoolmasterish fustiness replaced by something far more natural and likeable.

'Their house felt like a *museum*,' Doyle said with a shudder as they got back into Markham's car, 'but I guess they can't help how they are,' he added magnanimously. 'She looked a bit *glazed* though, boss . . . like she wasn't all there.'

'Could be the side-effects of antidepressants or sleeping pills,' the DI replied. 'Or of course delayed shock.'

'Yeah, it's obvious they considered Coxley to be the best thing since sliced bread . . . Looks like the bloke had everyone eating out of his hand.'

Not quite *everyone*, Markham thought as they headed for the Brady residence a few roads away in Rockbourne Close.

The Bradys' three bedroom detached bungalow was altogether a more inviting proposition than the property they had just left. Bright and airy, with sleek contemporary fittings and a wraparound garden bursting with colour, it felt like they had been transported to a different universe.

Markham had deliberately timed their visit to coincide with Evelyn Brady's shift at *Age Concern* in Bromgrove town centre, calculating that her son, who worked from home, would be alone at the property and thus more likely to speak freely.

After serving the detectives coffee in his comfortable home office (there had been no offer of refreshments at their first port of call), Mark Brady lost no time in setting out his stall. Stocky and silver-haired, with his florid countenance and booming voice he seemed almost too big for the room. But Markham recognised the type and, unlike Doyle who shrank into his tobacco leather armchair, showed no signs of being overpowered.

'I didn't trust Coxley, Inspector,' Brady insisted. 'Mother had her head turned by him and it just wasn't healthy.'

'Do you have any evidence to support that conclusion, Mr Brady?' the DI enquired with a pleasant smile.

'*Not as such* . . . But there was stuff she bought at antique fairs . . . One minute it was in the house and the next it was gone . . .'

'Did you ask her about it?'

'She brushed me off . . . talked about presents for people's birthdays . . . I didn't like to make a fuss. I mean, she can do what she likes with her own money. But I saw the way she behaved around that smooth-talking gigolo,' he added with surprising vehemence, 'and I just *knew* it wasn't kosher.'

Recalling Des O'Grady's reference to gossip on the salon grapevine, Doyle chimed in, 'How about her mates, did any of them ever talk about her giving Coxley stuff?'

'I caught the tail end of an argument between mother and Jean Gibley,' was the surprising retort. 'Jean came over for coffee and I heard her say something about how maybe it wasn't a good idea to make presents like that in case people got the wrong idea and mother ended up making a fool of herself . . . It was obvious who they were talking about.'

The two detectives exchanged a knowing look. Clearly Brady had been earwigging.

Interesting, though, Markham thought, that Mrs Gibley had omitted to tell them she suspected Coxley of milking her friend. In fact, Jean had made a point of stressing the hairdresser's uprightness, bestowing a fishy stare on Doyle when he asked if she had ever observed any 'unprofessional behaviour'. But maybe she felt that the hairdresser was innocent in this business with Evelyn Brady . . . that he reluctantly accepted gifts from the woman because she put him on the spot and he couldn't very well refuse without hurting an elderly customer's feelings. Alternatively, if her own head was turned by Coxley, she could simply have been jealous that her friend was stealing a march on her and gaining ground in his affections. Having seen inside 4 Porlock Drive, the DI was inclined to think Jean Gibley had a parsimonious streak that inhibited her from going so far as to loosen the purse strings. Paying top dollar for a high-end hairdo (and assiduous flattery) was one thing, but giving Coxley expensive gifts quite another.

Brady leaned forward in the padded swivel chair, arms firmly planted on his thighs and face thrust towards theirs.

'Look, Inspector, I run a successful financial planning business. I don't need my mother's money. But I'm damned if she was going to leave it to some oily lothario on the make . . . She was vulnerable after dad died and Coxley played on it.'

'Where were you and your mother on Friday night?' Markham asked quietly.

'I cooked dinner for the two of us — beef bourguignon, if you're interested — and then we played Scrabble for a bit.' Awkwardly, he added, 'I split up with a girlfriend last month . . . giving that side of things a rest.'

'Nice for your mum to have a bit of company,' Doyle (an inveterate home bird) said with such transparent sincerity that the businessman looked mollified.

'That's right,' he said gruffly. 'I was feeling my way round to talking about Coxley,' he said, 'but the time wasn't right and I didn't want to spoil things.'

Outside, Doyle said, 'He seemed on the level, guv.'

'Unlike Jean Gibley,' Markham said dryly.

'Yeah . . . she closed me down when I asked her about inappropriate behaviour. And her brother had a right face on him . . . You'd have thought I made an indecent suggestion or something.'

At that moment the DI's mobile rang.

'Bit of an incident going down at Des O'Grady's,' Carruthers told him without preamble.

'Right,' the DI said, 'we're on our way.'

* * *

By the time they got there, however, the excitement was over.

Des O'Grady's receptionist appeared flustered.

'Des doesn't come in on Wednesdays,' she told them. 'It's early closing and usually quiet. I was checking the appointments book when there was this commotion outside . . . I looked out to see what all the shouting was about . . . I recognised Sandra and Becca but not the other woman. Then they started pushing and shoving and it looked like getting nasty. I was afraid one of them would end up crashing through the front window. Freaked me out, so I called 999,' she finished lamely.

'In view of the connection to Coxley, we got the call-out, guv,' Carruthers said crisply. 'Burton's got them in the back room. Turns out Sandra and Becca were in the bistro three doors down when they spotted the Bickerstaff woman. Apparently they tore into her about Coxley. *Was she satisfied now he was dead? Did it feel good?* That kind of thing. They practically accused her of killing him.'

'I'd better see them then,' Markham said calmly.

Ushered into the small office at the rear of the premises, he found the three women sitting in sullen silence while Kate Burton fixed them with her frostiest gimlet stare.

Sandra Crowley was the first to speak.

'I reckon we had too much rosé in *Coast*,' she mumbled.

'And when we saw her . . . well, we just lost it,' Becca finished.

Karen Bickerstaff was very attractive with striking green eyes, a head of shiny, long dark hair and an air of glowing good health. If Andrew Coxley's ministrations had traumatised her scalp, there was certainly no sign of any lasting damage. Expensively dressed in a powder pink trouser suit, she exuded confidence despite the circumstances. Whereas the other two appeared cowed, she was now in full command of herself.

'This isn't an episode of *Judge Judy*, so I'm not going to ask who put their hands on whom first,' Markham said with a steely inflection in his tone. 'Presumably you started brawling because emotions are currently running high.' His voice dripped with sarcasm in a manner that had the two hairstylists squirming, though the other woman maintained her sang-froid. 'I also take it that no-one wishes to press charges for assault,' the DI continued.

Silence.

Markham turned to Carruthers. 'That being the case, kindly see Ms Crowley and Ms Drew off the premises before I interview Ms Bickerstaff.'

The two stylists left with the DS who was back within minutes, anxious not to miss anything.

'I apologise for what happened, Inspector.'

Karen Bickerstaff didn't sound particularly contrite.

Markham said nothing but regarded her coolly.

'They virtually implied I had blood on my hands.'

'And did you?'

'*No*,' she rapped. 'I lost my case against Andy when I took him to small claims but,' with a slightly strained laugh, 'them's the breaks, as they say . . . It wasn't worth killing for?'

Something in the way she said 'Andy' brought Burton's head up.

'Were you ever involved with Mr Coxley?' she asked silkily. '*Intimately*?'

'We had a fling years ago,' the other replied with an attempt at nonchalance. 'Ships that pass in the night, nothing heavy . . . I only looked him up after the bank posted me back here.'

'Were you aiming to take up where you had left off?'

From the tightening of Karen Bickerstaff's face, it was obvious Burton had hit the jackpot.

So Coxley had turned her down, Markham thought. In which case, suing him through the small claims court smacked of revenge.

'Tell us about your negligence claim,' was all he said, however.

She shrugged. 'He didn't supervise the colour technician properly . . . I fancied going blonde . . . She used the wrong strength peroxide — more than twelve per cent — and mixed it with bleach. I told her it was burning me, but she took no notice and even stuck me under a dryer to speed things up . . . that's a big no-no but I didn't realise it back then.' A bitter laugh. 'I know better now.'

'Who was the technician?'

'Oh, she didn't last long. Andy got rid of her sharpish, but not before she had ruined my hair.'

'And yet you didn't win your case?'

'No.' Her mouth was a thin line. 'The famous Coxley charm swung it . . . At any rate, they decided he'd told the dozy bitch to use six percent and when he came over to check she said that's what she'd done, so he had no reason to think she was frying my scalp. Plus, when she stuck me under a dryer in the back room he believed she was taking me through for a deep conditioning treatment . . . by the time he cottoned on, it was too late.' A harsh laugh. 'All the staff backed him up . . . those love-sick ninnies . . . *everyone*.' She suddenly seemed aware that her voice and colour had risen. 'Galling,' she said more quietly. 'But like I said, not worth killing for.'

'No alibi for Coxley's murder,' Doyle said afterwards. 'Netflix and chilli ain't worth diddly squat.'

'And don't forget, she's a woman scorned,' Carruthers pointed out. 'Despite all the ice maiden shtick, she's obviously got quite a temper on her . . . Looked to me like she works out . . . got the muscle to move Coxley's body without breaking sweat.'

'Let's get back to base,' Markham instructed. 'I have a feeling the DCI will want some kind of media briefing, so better get on it. Plus, I need to bring you up to speed on our cold cases.'

He noticed Carruthers give a guilty start at the word 'media'. For some time now there had been rumblings in CID about tip-offs to the *Gazette* and other leaks. Having gradually warmed to the latest recruit, he hated to think this might be their weak link.

The situation would need watching. If Carruthers was in any way morally suspect, it risked compromising all of them.

And with a possible triple murderer on his patch, Markham was taking no chances.

CHAPTER 5: OEDIPAL RIDDLE

As he had anticipated, Markham was saddled with a press briefing on Thursday morning.

Gavin Conors, reptile-in-chief at the *Gazette* whose animosity towards Noakes was the stuff of legend (the two notoriously once came to fisticuffs), had already done a piece spiced with the usual innuendo. The stuff about Coxley's 'popularity with ladies of a certain age' and 'confirmed bachelorhood' stayed just the right side of being defamatory, however, so there was nothing to throw Sidney into a conniption.

Watching as the local press trooped into the briefing room, Markham was struck by the porcine Conors's increasing resemblance to Eamonn Holmes, though without any of that TV personality's genial charm. Dress-wise, with his somewhat spivvy blue suit, psychedelic tie and built-up shoes, he looked more mobster than respectable press correspondent. In fact, in the event of a sartorial run-off with Noakes, the reporter would definitely come off second best.

Conors was particularly adept at confected outrage and this occasion was no different.

Given that a local entrepreneur had been murdered *on his own premises*, what were the police doing to protect the local community, he wanted to know.

Kate Burton was ready for him, reeling off details of increased foot patrols and crime prevention initiatives to the accompaniment of approving nods from Sidney.

But Conors wasn't squelched for long. As Doyle said, he was like India rubber when it came to bouncing back from put-downs.

Could the police say if this was the work of someone waging a *vendetta* against successful businesspeople (a self-satisfied smirk at the PC term) . . . or, oozing fake concern, was Andrew Coxley's *personal life* the reason why he had been targeted?

Again, Burton stepped up to the plate. Inscrutably, she answered that at this stage they had found nothing to suggest either of those motives were behind the murder.

So essentially the police had *nothing*, the journalist's hatchet-faced peroxide blonde henchwoman said in an accusatory tone.

Not at all, Burton replied blandly. In fact, they were following up various lines of enquiry after helpful tip-offs from members of the public.

This was a stretch, Markham thought, but it undoubtedly covered what they had learned about Coxley's customer relations and the reasons certain people had for hating him.

Was it true that the police were looking at a connection with other unsolved murders, a mousy looking woman asked.

Damn and triple damn, Markham thought as he watched the DCI's face turn a shade of magenta (or what Noakes liked to call 'ultraviolent') while his eyes narrowed to slits. How the hell had that piece of information got out? His eyes wandered to Carruthers, but the sergeant's poker face betrayed nothing.

Of course they weren't in a position to comment on other investigations, Burton said after an infinitesimal pause. It was standard practice for different teams to share data with a view to identifying common denominators, but this was *precautionary* and designed to *narrow* the pool of potential suspects rather than linking multiple murders to a specific individual. (She was careful not to say 'serial killer'.)

At this calm rejoinder, the DCI's angry colour subsided.

Before Conors or his sidekick could get their second wind, Burton said that nothing was being ruled out including the possibility of a mentally disturbed assailant, which is why the police were liaising with local agencies. Then she segued smoothly into her well-worn "scientific shtick", throwing out statistics about "customer crimes" and "customer-facing workers" — generally bludgeoning the assorted journalists with statistics and psychological jargon until they practically screamed for mercy. Watching their stampede for the exit, Markham complimented his colleague, 'Well done, Kate, that was pretty seamless.'

Pudgy press officer Barry Lynch (a notorious Handy Andy now safely corralled in matrimony) also telegraphed his approval with a thumbs-up before scuttling off, while Sidney likewise bestowed a gracious smile before leaving them to it.

After dispatching Doyle and Carruthers to finish their background checks and exhaustive trawl of databases (with particular attention to social care hubs), the DI murmured to Burton, 'We've got a leak, Kate.'

His colleague's face was unreadable, and he wondered if she shared his misgivings about Carruthers.

'I'd like you to see if you can find out who it is and then have a word in their shell-like . . . they're looking at a disciplinary if it should come out.'

'Got it, sir.'

He had no doubt that she did. With her sedate, discreet manner, she would have made an excellent spy. But if their mole was Carruthers, he was a cool hand and Burton would need to tread carefully, not least given that the DS was 'Blithering' Bretherton's nephew. Hopefully they could stop this in its tracks before Sidney weighed in. As things stood, it was unlikely that the DCI suspected any of Markham's team, but with Gavin Conors in the mix there was always the possibility that things might get out of hand. Right now, a potentially explosive inside "exclusive" about CID corruption was the last thing he needed.

* * *

That afternoon found Markham and Noakes lounging in Doggie Dickerson's 'premium locker room' at the Bromgrove Police Boxing Gym. When it came to the gym's 'VIP facilities', this merely meant a changing area, badly grouted showers and sauna marginally less mildewed and insalubrious than the rest of the premises. Somehow, Environmental Health had never managed to catch up with the proprietor, thanks not least to Markham's partisanship, another black mark as far as his superiors were concerned.

DCI Sidney and the higher echelons intensely disapproved of the dingy outfit in Marsh Lane, not least because of its popularity with CID detectives and the local criminal fraternity alike, both sides happily slogging it out in the ring before reverting to their normal roles of cat and mouse on the streets of Bromgrove.

Today, the proprietor took them by surprise, his head now shaved with what looked like a squirrel's tail bisecting his bald pate.

'*Jesus, mate.*' Noakes preserved an awed silence before resuming. 'Never thought you'd go Huron or Mohawk or whatever . . . Looks like you're auditioning for *Last of the Mohicans* or summat.'

Markham disliked profanity but shared his friend's utter bemusement. The last time they had seen him, Doggie was doing his usual impersonation of Long John Silver crossed with a Napoleonic re-enactor — funereal frockcoat, skew-whiff horsehair wig, eye patch, yellow tombstone gnashers, the whole nine yards. But today, in addition to the mullet and suede leather get-up, he sported a set of pearly whites that wouldn't have disgraced a Hollywood star and had dispensed with his signature eye patch, unveiling the false eye that heightened his disconcerting resemblance to Blofeld or some other James Bond baddie. The extraordinary physiognomic transformation was enough to make one giddy, all that remained of the old Doggie being an overmastering scent of nicotine, Johnnie Walker and mothballs.

Aware that Doggie regarded him expectantly, Markham found his voice.

'Quite a makeover, Dogs . . . very, er, *striking*.'

And brave too for a man of his age.

Doggie beamed, highly gratified that his 'fav'rite 'spector' approved.

'I thought it might be too much, Mr Markham. But Evie's Clare said to go for it. So I did. Got my teeth fixed an' all.'

Evie (Evelyn) was now Doggie's 'romantic partner', having put him back together when he was left on the ropes and reeling after the defection of his previous girlfriend Marlene (of bingo hall fame). Her daughter Clare had clearly decided to take the old devil in hand.

'I was kind of in a rut, Mr Markham . . . needed a new image to bring in the punters, see.'

Doggie turned to Noakes, sensing that half his audience remained to be convinced. 'You gotta ring the changes, Mr Noakes . . . else folk think you're past it.'

'No danger of that in your case, mate . . . Them veneers are quite something.' Which was one way of putting it. 'Plus, you look like you're ready to throw a tomahawk if anyone cuts up rough.'

The other cackled, his distinctive phlegmy laugh more suggestive of a tubercular sufferer than a tomahawk-wielding frontiersman. Well pleased with the compliment, he sketched a few feints and lunges, tapping his bulbous nose between moves with the finesse of an old pro.

'Those were the days eh, Mr Noakes,' he said at the conclusion of this comically balletic divertissement, 'when the likes of us showed them officer-cadets a thing or two.'

Markham had never cared to enquire too closely into Doggie's time in the forces (where he had apparently acquired his infamous moniker), but his wingman certainly regarded the gym's proprietor as a brother in arms, delighting in a world view that was, if anything, even more reactionary and un-PC than his own.

'Who sorted your bonce?' Noakes wanted to know.

'*Ben Hair* in the shopping centre . . . special rates cos Clare knows the main man.' Doggie put a hand to his head with the shy self-consciousness of one who couldn't quite believe his own daring. 'He said tufts are big now . . . sends a message, see . . . *Don't Mess With Me.*'

'And does Evie, er, like the new look?' Markham was genuinely intrigued to hear the answer.

'Well, she's not 'xactly used to it yet, but Clare'll talk her round . . . Zac says if I want, he can dye it blue for more of an impact.'

Noakes's mouth fell open. *OMG. Forget Last of the Mohicans and noble savages. This sounded more like ancient Britons.* Visions of druids and demon kings danced before his eyes.

The DI found his voice. 'Well, you're certainly on trend, Dogs.'

The other preened for a moment before recalling his obligations as host.

'I heard from Mr Carstairs about that hairdresser who copped it,' he said turning serious.

Like Markham and Noakes, DI Chris Carstairs enjoyed chewing the cud with Doggie, secure in the knowledge that everything stayed within the walls of the gym. Remarkably, given the old villain's reputation for ducking and diving, he was surprisingly close-mouthed when it came to police secrets and had never betrayed their confidence.

'Did you ever come across him on your travels, Dogs?' Markham enquired.

'Nah . . . saw him once or twice . . . bit of a ponce, if you ask me. Mind you, I heard he was handy with his fists . . . knew how to take care of himself.'

'Oh?'

'Yeah . . . got into a ruckus with that big Irish bruiser who has the place a few doors down . . . gave him a terrific thumping.'

Noakes's button eyes narrowed. 'D'you know what the fight was about?'

'Paddy probl'y made some joke about poofters an' the other fella got the hump.'

Markham was used to Doggie's blithe disregard for social nostrums, but hearing this made the DI glad he had never inflicted him on Kate Burton. The man was one of a kind, but like Noakes definitely an "acquired taste".

'Clare's friendly with one of the girls from the barber's.' (The word 'salon' was unlikely ever to pass Doggie's lips.) 'Sandra something . . . Any road, *she* told Clare the poncey one had a cut lip afterwards but was dead cool about it.' Another alarmingly wheezy chuckle. 'Said he'd tripped over a hairpin.'

'Did Clare or Evie ever use him?' the DI asked.

'Nah . . . Costs an arm an' a leg to go there . . . You're just paying for frills an' fuss . . . "Yes Modom" an' all that jazz. My two can't be doing with all that mwah-mwah air-kissing an' stuff,' Doggie added approvingly, showing a surprising mastery of the hairdresser's lexicon. 'According to this Sandra, the place was full of Karens.'

'*Karens?* Afraid I don't quite follow you, Dogs,' Markham told him.

'He means snotty middle-class women who like sounding off an' bossing folk around,' Noakes translated. 'Up their own backsides, right Dogs?'

'Couldn't have put it better meself, Mr Noakes,' the other confirmed with a satisfied leer. 'By all accounts their boss knew how to handle 'em but the others got well browned off. Of course,' with an air of pious recollection that made Markham want to laugh aloud, 'you shouldn't speak ill of the dead, but he sounded a right greaser.'

The DI was thoughtful. 'Did you ever hear anything about the, er, patrons giving him money or presents?' (For the life of him, he couldn't use the millennial slang.)

Doggie's shaggy eyebrows shot up. 'Nothing like that,' he said. 'But he looked a flash git, so no surprise if he was up to some type of scam.'

The DI suppressed a smile. Takes one to know one, he thought. And Doggie Dickerson was no slouch when it came to dodges.

'P'raps some bloke didn't like him making up to the missus,' Doggie suggested helpfully. 'Got jealous, like.' With his head on one side, he added philosophically, 'Mr Carstairs says it always comes down to sex or money.'

Or perhaps in this case both, Markham thought grimly.

After their frowsy friend had sloped off to his office (and a libation courtesy of the bottle of whisky in the top drawer of his filing cabinet), the two men got changed, Noakes shooting somewhat resentful glances at Markham's athletic physique as he poured himself into billowing aertex shorts and top.

'The missus is pulling out all the stops for our tea,' he said gruffly, 'so reckon I need a decent workout.'

'I'm the man for that,' Markham retorted.

'It were dead tactful how you got us out of having a bite with Dogs,' Noakes said admiringly.

'Well, the last time we adjourned to his flat, I discovered what Napoleon meant when he said that an army marched on its stomach,' Markham observed wryly. 'I also learned why it was that in very rough seas old sea-dogs used to sing "Heave away me hearties"!'

Noakes was delighted. 'I'll have to remember that one for Kev,' he guffawed. 'With him being a sea cadet an' all.'

The DI regarded his porky opponent affectionately. 'Thought you'd appreciate it,' he said. 'Right, let's get out there. Time for us to see what you're made of!'

* * *

George had been right about his wife pulling out all the stops, Olivia reflected that evening as she and Markham sat over their post-prandial coffee at the Noakeses, prawn cocktail having been followed by Beef Wellington and all the trimmings with walnut and coffee gateau for 'afters' (Noakes received a basilisk glare from their hostess for this vulgarity).

Sartorially also, it looked like Muriel had made a special effort, resplendent in a sticky out taffeta cocktail dress that

Olivia privately thought was ridiculous for a casual supper with friends.

But of course, she fumed, the lady of the house was unlikely to look on any encounter with Gilbert Markham as run of the mill, such was her enthusiasm for Noakes's handsome boss whose old-world courtesy and grave attentiveness never failed to charm her.

Always gushes like an oil well whenever he's in the vicinity, whereas she thinks *I'm* nowhere near good enough for him and a neurotic clever clogs into the bargain . . .

At least Muriel had eased up on the fake concern about her and Markham's 'bumpy period' and stopped dropping those snide little digs about the importance of *making an effort* and the *honour of being a police spouse*. She'd even managed a complimentary remark about Olivia's new hairstyle, though being Muriel it was barbed. 'So dramatic and . . . *courageous* . . . reminds me of Princess Charlene of Monaco's new look,' said the devoted royal-watcher (patting her own corrugated coiffure complacently).

Oh God, ran Olivia's internal monologue, wasn't Charlene the one who went doolally and had some sort of butch transformation? She was pretty sure the last time she'd flicked through *Hello!* magazine, there was this double-page spread on the Monégasque princess's 'debilitating battle with mental frailty' and 'androgynous chic'. Either way, she was pretty sure that spacey Charlene wasn't someone she aspired to resemble.

At least she'd been ready when Muriel started dropping hints about being too thin and the danger of 'going under' (through want of self-discipline was the subtext).

'I've always been scrawny,' she riposted cheerfully. 'Not one of those anorexic types secretly doing star jumps in the loo or running on the spot every chance they get.'

Muriel hadn't expected such a frank response and, frowning at this reference to toilets at the dinner table, swiftly changed tack.

She was more comfortable when they got on to the subject of hairdressers, her face losing its pouting double-chinned look of disapproval as she discussed Andrew Coxley.

'Wonderful manners,' she said in an echo of Jean Gibley. 'And such an *original* way of dressing.' A sentimental little sigh. 'Put me in mind of dear Perry Como.'

Poor, poor man, Olivia thought fighting back hysterical laughter. That carefully cultivated image, only to be compared with Mister Housewives' Choice. Coxley must be turning in his grave!

'I gather he was very popular,' Markham ventured.

'Well,' Muriel's prunes and prisms expression was back, 'there were always the *needy* types looking for attention . . . *possessive* about their hairdresser . . . inclined to *monopolise* him. That's when it got a *teensy bit* embarrassing.' She patted her stiff lacquered bouffant complacently. 'These days I go to *Jules* in Old Carton.' An arch twinkle at Markham, 'I must be a sucker for tall, dark and handsome . . . and he's such a *genius* with hair . . . instinctively *knows* what one wants.'

To look like Margaret Thatcher, Olivia thought darkly as she listened to Muriel whitter on over the coffee and biscotti (Fortnum's, *naturally*). Then, catching sight of Noakes's proud glow, she reproached herself for bitchiness. Like Gil said, no-one knew the truth of what went on in other people's relationships (thank God they didn't know the half of what went on in *hers*), and Muriel's desperate attempts to impress everyone with her plummy-voiced social sophistication was the product of low self-esteem and a lack of confidence. Her smarminess around Gil was *beyond* irritating, but she was the sun, moon and stars to George and *that* was what mattered . . .

By the time she tuned back in to the conversation, Muriel was on to the subject of King Charles's impending Coronation, trilling excitedly about the WI's plans to mark the occasion while Markham listened with his customary impenetrable courtesy. Olivia's sympathies were republican if anything, but she knew better than to interject with caustic asides about inherited privilege, anarchist sans-culottes being regarded by their hostess as totally beyond the pale.

She had never thought the day would come when she would actually be *glad* to see Natalie Noakes, but the prodigal daughter's arrival was a welcome diversion from Muriel drooling over the royals.

Appraising Natalie with a critical eye, it appeared she had rebounded from the 'setback' (her mother's word) of miscarriage. The hookerish attire and Polyfilla make-up that had characterised her reign as doyenne of Bromgrove's nightclubs had been replaced by a more demure look (the redoubtable mother-in-law elect no doubt had something to do with it), but she still had the brassy, defiant air (and embonpoint) with which she was wont to bulldoze through life.

Natalie's smile didn't reach her eyes as she greeted Markham's partner. She could never rid herself of the suspicion that Olivia Mullen looked down her nose at anyone without a massive IQ — always excepting her dad who she couldn't get enough of for some reason.

It was cringe the way her mum tarted herself up whenever Markham was around, but she had to admit the inspector *was* pretty fit for an older guy . . . He never made you feel stupid, like he had this big brain or something. *And* he was interested in *ordinary* things like her and Rick's plans for expanding the business and how she was doing at uni . . . whereas Olivia just sat there with a secretive, sneaky, superior expression that made Natalie want to punch her in the face.

But for all that, Ms High and Mighty Mullen wasn't so perfect herself. For a moment, Natalie wondered if childlessness was behind Olivia's split with Markham, having never quite bought the story of her hooking up with Matthew Sullivan. I mean, who'd seriously *look* at that drippy beanpole if they had the likes of Markham waiting at home. She needed to get her head screwed on straight.

As she tucked into coffee and a ginormous wedge of walnut and coffee cake (nothing wrong with her appetite, Olivia thought sourly), Natalie basked in Markham's attention, highly gratified by his request for her take on Andrew Coxley.

'That place just wasn't *me*,' she confided. Then, with a wary glance at Muriel, 'To be honest, there was something a bit creepy about him and the gerries . . . the way he kind of oiled up to them . . . played them off so they were all looking daggers at each other . . . it felt uncomfortable.'

'That's just what *I* said, darling,' her mother gushed. 'Though of course there was never anything *inappropriate*.'

Olivia suppressed a smile. God forbid any joint Muriel patronised should turn out to be a gigolo's hunting ground.

Natalie noticed and shot her an unfriendly look.

''Course not,' she said. 'But I figured maybe he had "mommy issues" or something like that.' (She didn't watch *Descent of a Serial Killer* on CBS Reality for nothing.) 'That other bloke . . . wossname . . . Ed Collins . . . well, *he* said Andy didn't have a great childhood . . . was really close to his mum but his dad was a bully. She got cancer and died when he was sixteen.'

'That's most interesting, Natalie,' Markham said thoughtfully. 'So you reckon he was drawn to older women as mother substitutes.'

She cast a swift glance at Olivia, but this time there was a triumphant gleam in her eye.

'Yeah, the Oedipus Complex innit.'

Olivia just couldn't help herself.

'*Oedipus-Schmedipus, just so long as he loves his mother!*'

'Very droll, Liv,' Markham said suavely as Noakes sniggered before subsiding at a glacial stare from his wife. 'But if Natalie is correct, it's potentially a new light on Mr Coxley.'

'Don't forget, he's the *victim*,' his partner said sweetly. 'Surely it's the *killer's* mindset you have to probe . . . Perhaps *they're* the one with hang-ups about older women.'

Natalie's enthusiasm for true crime documentaries won out over her dislike of Olivia. 'Yeah, like the Stockwell Strangler,' she said with a relish that made her mother frown.

Muriel wasn't at all sure she cared to revisit such distasteful topics. It had been bad enough during the high street murders when everyone was full of Shipman, Kenneth Erskine and other degenerates, but they really weren't suitable for discussion over her Queen's Blend coffee and biscotti with Richard Clayderman on the stereo crooning *All the love in the world won't take me away from you.*

'For a moment back there I was afraid you were going to break into Tom Lehrer,' Markham said afterwards as they walked home arm in arm.

She giggled before carolling,

'There once lived a man named Oedipus Rex
You may have heard about his odd complex
His name appears in Freud's index
'Cause he loved his mother.'

'Behave yourself,' he admonished as a startled pedestrian crossed to the other side of the road.

'Shame you never got to telling them about the cold case "gerries",' Olivia continued. 'Then Natalie really *would* have been in clover.'

'Noakesy's expression said, "Please don't go there",' he laughed. 'Muriel can only cope with so much shop talk over the Royal Doulton.'

'Especially when it's about middle-aged women with *crushettes*,' she said in a mischievous allusion to Muriel Noakes's susceptibility to smooth-tongued charmers.

'Natalie looked well,' he said neutrally.

Olivia snorted. 'That Peter Pan collar was a bit much . . . I thought there was a bit of tension between her and Mommie Dearest, but that's hardly surprising. . . She probably reckons that deep down a part of Muriel's almost *relieved* there's no sprog to be explained away or any awkwardness like that,' she added with a bitter twist to her mouth. 'Onwards and upwards with the degree course, big fat wedding and fitness empire.' She flushed awkwardly before adding, 'I'm not explaining it very well, but you can tell Muriel wants everything glossy and picture perfect . . . career, marriage, kids. Everything in the right order. No messiness . . .'

'I'm sure both of them bear scars,' Markham said gently, squeezing her hand. 'And Muriel's desperate for Natalie to make something of herself. Maybe avoid some of her own mistakes? After all those years worrying that Natalie might be on the wrong path — flunking her A levels and hanging out with losers — perhaps it's not surprising that she's obsessed with everything being perfect. Particularly as there's the new mother-in-law still to be won over.'

Smiling at him gratefully, with a supreme effort, Olivia pushed the subject from her. 'Is that stuff about mother complexes really going to help you find out who killed Andrew Coxley and the other two?' she asked.

'Somehow it feels significant,' he replied, 'though as yet I don't see *how*.'

They continued walking in companionable silence.

Suddenly he remembered.

'Mr Coxley's funeral is tomorrow, eleven o'clock at St Mary Magdalene.'

Olivia was startled. 'So soon?' she exclaimed. 'I mean, it's not even been a week.'

'The Coroner's released the body . . . Presumably Mr Coxley's family has influence, given the absence of red tape.' He shrugged. 'Ours not to reason why.'

'I'd like to come with you for moral support, Gil, but it's a full timetable for me tomorrow morning.'

'Thanks, sweetheart. But Noakesy and the team will be there . . . The woodland burial out at Old Carton is private, but there's some sort of bunfight laid on at a local café — Coast, I think it's called — so we'll probably drop in on that.'

'If George has anything to do with it you will,' Olivia chuckled. 'The woodland bit sounds quirky,' she added. 'Coxley must have been some sort of eco-nut on the sly. Didn't look like one, mind you.'

'*Eco-nut* . . . you're worse than Noakes,' he sighed. 'No doubt *he'll* have plenty to say on the subject . . . but hopefully not within earshot of the grieving relatives.'

'Oh I nearly forgot,' she said.

'What?'

'While you were getting your guided tour of Muriel's Coronation glassware, Natalie mentioned something about Bromgrove TV having planned to do a documentary on *The Mane Event* but then they got cold feet and it never came off.'

'Interesting,' he murmured. 'Thanks Liv, that looks like being another avenue of enquiry for us.'

'My pleasure.'

They were nearly home. All in all, Markham thought, it had been a good evening.

Tomorrow Andrew Coxley would be laid to rest.

And then he would redouble his efforts to find an elusive killer.

CHAPTER 6: RENDEZVOUS WITH DEATH

'Who's the patron saint of hairdressers then?'

Markham smiled at his friend's enquiry.

'Appropriately enough, I believe it's Mary Magdalene, Noakesy . . . Artists normally depict her with abundant flowing hair, don't they.'

'Is she the same one who gate-crashes a party an' slobbers all over Jesus so everyone's dead embarrassed an' don' know where to look?'

'Well, she's popularly identified with the woman who kisses his feet, anoints them with ointment and then dries them with her hair. And yes, it's a safe bet that caused a certain amount of awkwardness,' Markham replied gravely.

'An' Jesus tells the guy who's giving the party that she's got much better manners than *him* cos *he* never let Jesus have a wash an' brush up.' Noakes, predictably, liked the idea of some snotty Pharisee getting his comeuppance.

'No-one's quite sure who Mary Magdalene was,' Markham said thoughtfully. 'She could have been a prostitute or the woman with seven demons whom Jesus exorcised—'

'At any rate, she sticks by him,' Noakes said with satisfaction. 'Never scarpers when the bad stuff happens . . . I guess thass why she gets to see him first . . . y'know, when she thinks he's the gardener an' then tries to grab hold of him once she's twigged what's going on.' A censorious note crept in as he added, 'Mind you, with her being the hysterical type an' having demons an' things, stands to reason his mates think she's making it up.'

'And there was I thinking you might be a fan,' Markham teased. It occurred to him that Noakes, for all his assumption of male rationality, was himself very much a creature of instinct and quite unconsciously capable of magnificent impulses.

'What about barbers?'

'Sorry?'

'There's gotta be a different saint for barbers, right?' Markham might have known Noakes wouldn't be happy to have a woman take top honours.

'I'll have to get back to you on that, Noakesy,' he laughed.

The church of St Mary Magdalen in Old Carton blended traditional and modern architecture to dramatic effect, with its neo-Gothic tower and spire attached to a low concrete extension faced in granite which replaced the remains of a nineteenth-century building that had been destroyed by fire. Markham generally preferred older places of worship but had liked the strikingly modern interior on a previous visit and was curious to see what his friend would make of it.

Despite the single storey extension being constructed entirely of concrete, the overall effect was not oppressive, thanks to abstract designs in coloured leaded glass that filled the tall slender windows and space between the roof and walls, a skilful contrast of warm and cool colours varying the light and producing an almost prismatic magic-lantern effect. The altar was a single beautifully carved piece of granite on a white marble plinth towards the centre of the sanctuary, surrounded by double rows of pine pews on three sides (almost like a theatre in the round, Olivia had observed when she first saw it). Long triangular roof lights enhanced the impression of luminous airiness, offsetting the austere grey limestone flooring, granite fittings and wooden stations of the cross in a manner that felt daringly innovative while somehow liturgically appropriate. Notwithstanding all the exposed brickwork and the three-sided box beams on freestanding tapered concrete columns, the overall effect struck Markham as sensuous, though he wasn't too sure about the copious statuary depicting various holy figures. By far his favourite feature was a vast tapestry on the wall behind the altar which depicted Mary Magdalen, Titian hair tumbling about her shoulders, soaring upwards from a granite rock into some mysterious light-filled fourth dimension where wheeling, fiery Seraphim waited to serenade her with silver trumpets and strange creatures like burning coals or streaks of lightening capered joyfully at her approach. With admiring eyes he took in how the rocky desert landscape echoed the church's brutalist architecture while the vision of Paradise seemed to absorb the rainbow brilliance of its stained glass. Truly a strong uncompromising statement of religious conviction.

Noakes, being a traditionalist in such matters, was unimpressed by the Corbusier architecture but liked the kaleidoscopic coloured glass (if not the abstract symbolism) and the tapestry. 'You kinda get the feeling that she don' have to worry any more cos there's gonna be a slap up party,' he mused, in a comical nod to the Magdalene's antecedents as Good-Time Girl.

Markham chuckled. 'Well, doesn't the Bible say something about entering into the joy of the Lord?'

'Yeah, if you've been a good an' faithful servant,' his friend intoned. Looking around, he said, 'Strange kind of church . . . What's the connection with John Travolta then?'

'Apparently *Mr Coxley's* parents were parishioners. They donated that bronze sculpture in the porch . . . the one of St Michael defeating the dragon.'

Noakes's mouth turned down at the corners. 'Didn't do Sonny Jim much good in the end, though, did it? I mean, sounds like they were decent enough types . . . an' then their lad ends up with a pair of scissors through the neck.'

'Who knows what's in store for Mr Coxley,' Markham said quietly. 'Maybe all those seventies costumes of his meant that he felt himself to be a misfit and his soul somehow out-at-elbows . . . *lacking* or inadequate . . . And it's only now after death that he understands what true freedom means.'

Noakes looked dubious.

'A bit like our friend back there,' Markham added mischievously, with a nod towards the tapestry. 'I mean, the demon queen wasn't exactly saint material to start with.'

'Yeah, but she got her act together in the end,' the other objected. 'Went off to the desert an' fasted an' all sorts . . . proper *holy* . . .' Whereas Coxley, his tone implied, was not exactly worthy to pass through the Pearly Gates.

Markham's lips twitched. 'Well, the Good Book assures us that death is swallowed up in victory, Noakesy, so we must just trust to Mr Coxley becoming his best self once all the hindrances and perplexities are taken away . . . "through a glass darkly" and all that,' he added encouragingly.

Falling back on his Methodism that discouraged fanciful speculations on eternity, Noakes muttered. 'Oh aye, reckon he'll get there in the end . . . with his parents being church folk.' He spoke as though heaven was for ticket holders only and Coxley would have to negotiate some celestial enclosure, Markham thought, suppressing his merriment.

Whatever his private feelings about the dead man, Noakes had certainly made an effort with his appearance, attired in a sober lounge suit and plain white shirt that seemed to fit pretty well, though a pigeon-toed walk suggested he wasn't entirely comfortable with the pair of squeaky black oxfords that had replaced his beloved George boots. His hair, however, waved wildly on top of his head in agitated tufts that gave him an air of having been plugged into the mains and receiving an electric shock.

Now he was surveying the church's interior with pursed lips.

'D'you reckon there'll be much of a crowd for the lad's funeral?' he asked, gesturing around at the cavernous interior.

'Hard to imagine there'll be enough of 'em to pack the place out.'

'There's nearly half an hour till "curtain up",' Markham observed lightly. He looked towards the porch. 'And if I'm not mistaken, the undertakers have arrived.'

As they watched, a couple of portly middle-aged men bustled in and in no time at all had arranged the catafalque with black pall and tall candlesticks at each corner. A young woman joined them, carefully placing pedestal arrangements of arum lilies on either side of the candlesticks.

'Let's hope they don' plonk a massive photo of him on top of the coffin,' Noakes muttered. 'With that whole disco look, it'd be like taking the mickey . . . I mean, you want it to be *dignified* . . . like he's ready for heaven—'

'As opposed to getting down with the kids,' Markham finished drily.

'*Just saying!*'

They went and sat down towards the back, Noakes looking suspiciously round at all the statues as though he shared Markham's estimate of their artistic merit. The DI meanwhile contemplated the giant tapestry, wondering at its hold upon his emotions.

Noakes respected the guvnor's meditative silence, completing his survey of the various painted saints and ending up at the tapestry. He fancied its subject had a look of Olivia in the days when she had long hair — at least as far as the colouring and swan neck went, since this Mary Magdalene appeared extremely well fed compared to Markham's partner. 'Anorexic, you mark my words,' had been Muriel's dire verdict after they had seen the couple off the previous night, causing him some anxious moments as he questioned whether all was truly well with his friends. It *seemed* to him that they had weathered their domestic storms, but then with Markham it was difficult to penetrate the personal reserve that enveloped the DI like an invisible forcefield. *Keep Out!* and *Do Not Enter!* signs were all over the shop and, with an instinctive delicacy which belied his uncouth exterior, Noakes hesitated to pry. They had never been much for woo-woo oversharing and he sensed Markham liked it that way. If truth be told, so did he. Somehow they understood each other deep down where it mattered, without soppy navel-gazing . . .

The arrival of Burton, Doyle and Carruthers interrupted Noakes's reverie. Markham's fellow DI had collected their orders of service, her stern gaze daring Noakes to make any wisecracks about the matinee idol headshot that decorated the front cover.

Markham noticed that the two sergeants shared a conspiratorial grin at the sight of his wingman in best bib and tucker while Burton looked apprehensively at the Rieger organ which, unusually, was located at the front of the church to the left of the altar. After his team had cringed their way through Noakes's lusty bellowing on a previous occasion, Markham had admonished them gently, 'There's an old proverb which claims that, "He who sings prays twice",' only for Carruthers to retort deadpan, 'Yeah, but those around he who sings badly pray *three times*.' At least there was no danger of the DCI being scandalised on this occasion, since he was out of Bromgrove on another senior management away day.

For Markham, funerals always passed in something of a blur, with mourners fading into an amorphous conglomerate where no-one really stood out.

And so it was on this occasion, though he located all the key players as the congregation arrived in dribs and drabs. The two side aisles were left empty, but the body of the church filled up pretty quickly and constituted a respectable showing.

Andrew Coxley's elderly customers were notable for being discreetly and appropriately turned out, with Gordon Rushworth ramrod straight and positively regimental ('only army catering corps, though,' sniffed Noakes after scrutinising Rushworth's tie) escorting his sister and a clutch of women, all of them elegantly attired in dark twinsets accessorised with closed court shoes, pearls and neat pillboxes or fedoras. Jean Gilbey and Evelyn Brady, who had gone a step further with netted veils as though to signal their pre-eminence, wore identical expressions of disapproval at the sight of local author Sarah Moorcroft sashaying down the nave with short hemline, stiletto heels and towering plumed millinery more appropriate to a day at the races than a funeral. The charity fundraiser Carol Davidson, heavily made-up, also wore a show-off outfit of tight black dress and jacket with bizarre gold frogging and epaulettes that made it look like she was attending a military review. Her hat was only marginally less distracting than Moorcroft's, being a velvet fascinator with large bow and two feathers. 'Attention seekers,' someone hissed as the well-grouted fundraiser sailed past.

Disapproval turned to outrage as Sandra Crowley, Becca Drew and Cassie Johnson joined the congregation, click-clacking noisily in their high shoes. Sandra's leopard print dress along with Becca's cleavage and Cassie's oompa-loompa make-up attracted hostile glares from virtually every quarter, while an acrid tang of cheap perfume mingled queasily with the scent of the floral arrangements. The young women appeared oblivious but Ed Collins, impeccably well-groomed and almost distinguished looking, cast apologetic glances towards the OAPs as he ushered his colleagues to seats near the front. Neither Mark Brady nor Helen Mathews put in an appearance, but this was understandable given their history with the deceased, though Markham was surprised the businessman didn't wish to support his mother. He was taken aback to spy Philip Casey together with daughter Stella, though the man had the air of a prison warder and was presumably there to make sure his offspring didn't disgrace herself. His sergeants' eyes were out on stalks as they took in her ensemble of tight-fitting black suede dress which came several inches above her knees and was teamed with ripped fishnets, jangling heavy metal chains and clumpy black Doc Martens that made it look, as Carruthers muttered, as though she was off for a spot of S&M. Certainly it had the effect of making Coxley's female employees appear positively upmarket by comparison.

Des O'Grady arrived looking like a nightclub bouncer, but at least his staff were, for the most part, conservatively apparelled in neat black suits and jackets. There was also a smattering of very smartly dressed out-of-towners — presumably friends of the deceased — who cast supercilious glances at the riff-raff and old folk alike, though they appeared to like the church's modernist architecture. 'Bleeding pseuds,' Noakes muttered to Markham as he observed the way they drank in the stained-glass symbolism. He would have said more but for Kate Burton's reproachful nudge in the ribs as the organist launched into *Sheep May Safely Graze* heralding the arrival of the funeral cortege. Andrew Coxley's wicker coffin, adorned with a single tasteful spray of garden flowers, was followed by a small contingent of family along with a surprisingly youthful vicar who looked more like a ruddy-cheeked stockman than clerical incumbent. Mercifully for Noakes's composure, there was no framed photograph as a focal point.

The service itself was solidly conventional with the usual hymns and no surprises. Given that Coxley had died as the result of a violent physical assault and that the congregation was almost certainly light on believers, the vicar did well. Markham found it poignant when the young clergyman asserted earnestly: 'The premature ending of our brother's life is painful indeed but, as with our Saviour's three days in the tomb, this is a very short period to be set off against eternity. We must remember that *Up There*, time is measured differently. Therefore, Andrew is bidden to look forward to the new Life, not back to the wasted and fallen years. Those mistakes he might wish to have put straight can yet be redeemed through the power of the Resurrection.' In that instant, the DI wondered what *was* the fateful mistake that had led to someone plunging scissors into Coxley's neck and malevolently adorning him with that silicone cap . . . a mistake the dead hairdresser never had time to put straight. He shivered involuntarily as though struck by a sudden chill, but only Burton appeared to notice, shooting him a sympathetic glance that suggested she shared his disquietude.

In no time at all, it seemed, the service was at an end, with all the words said that were necessary to set Andrew Coxley's soul at peace and the coffin exiting to *The Lord's My Shepherd*. Unselfconsciously, Noakes roared out the lyrics with a gusto that caused several heads to turn and his longsuffering friends to wish themselves invisible.

Watching the genteel stampede for the exit, Markham noticed the way Jean Gibley twisted her gloved hands and bit her lip, unobtrusively steadied by her brother who, along with a couple of white-moustachioed red-faced retired army major types, shepherded the group of elderly women out of the church. There was something unreal about Mrs Gibley's demeanour, but the DI guessed this was down to a prescription of tranquilisers or other medication. As for bird-like Evelyn Brady, she turned from side to side nodding graciously at people as if she was at a wedding ... almost like the mother of the bride, despite her red-rimmed eyes and dark clothes. But of course, shock often resulted in strange behaviour and this was bound to be particularly true with women at their time of life. He noticed Ed Collins pause to say something comforting to them and reflected that the man showed genuine grace, even if he *did* have a reputation for having an eye to the main chance and sweet-talking elderly clients. Sandra and Becca likewise found time for a kind word, though Cassie Johnson promptly detached herself from the group, her brittle expression denoting a determination to dodge the codgers at all costs. Sarah Moorcroft and Carol Davidson likewise managed not to see them, manoeuvring themselves next to the more fashionable attendees with a ruthlessness that suggested years of practice. Des O'Grady and his staff left with Philip and Stella Casey, O'Grady's bear-like presence a clear reassurance to the distracted parent. Stella looked mutinous, but Markham thought there was no danger of her making any sort of scene — provided they could keep her from getting sloshed at the wake.

Markham's team held back from the rush to join the Christian Carnivora, lingering in the church until the crowd milling outside should have subsided. He noticed with amusement, however, that Noakes appeared distinctly restless. No doubt he figured that his status as an external consultant amounted to a Licence to Scoff, and that the DCI's pointed strictures against 'treating wakes like All You Can Eat buffets' and 'behaving like gannets' could be safely ignored by civilian personnel. 'S'all about not disgracing the uniform innit,' his wingman had confided in Kate Burton. 'I'm not in CID, so reckon that gives me a free pass.'

Now Noakes said, 'What's with the woodland burial caper?'

'It's out next to Old Carton reservoir,' Burton told them.

'Was he a tree hugger then?'

Burton flinched but forced a smile. 'One of the cousins said he was quite interested in green issues — you know, reducing the carbon footprint, that kind of thing . . .'

She faltered in the face of Noakes's satirical expression.

'I wouldn't fancy being dug up by a squirrel jus' for some carbon wotsit bollocks.'

'That doesn't happen sarge, and keep your voice down,' she hissed as a couple of passing stragglers gave them a funny look.

'That vicar struck the right note,' Carruthers said hastily. 'No awful jokes about hairdressers or bad hair days.'

"Cept for his story about that wedding when the bride nipped out halfway through so Coxley could give her a haircut,' Doyle reminded them.

'I thought that only happened to nuns,' Noakes put in. 'Y'know, when they marry Christ an' get their heads shaved to show they're dead serious about it.'

'It's the latest fad, sarge,' the young sergeant explained patiently. 'They're mad about it on TikTok . . . Girls get the chop halfway through the day for a new vibe . . . during the wedding breakfast or halfway through the reception.'

'Not in church then.' Noakes was relieved.

Burton clearly felt that the conversation was becoming increasingly surreal. 'The vicar was being complimentary about Mr Coxley,' she said repressively. 'Trying to say something nice about him being talented and in demand . . . to comfort the relatives.'

'Indeed,' Markham said easily. 'Right, time for us to repair to *Coast* and mingle. You three go ahead and I'll drive Kate.'

After the trio had departed, he smiled at his fellow DI. 'I think we can trust them to keep their eyes and ears open while hoovering up the quiche and vol au vents.'

As they emerged into the church forecourt, Burton's thoughts ran in a different channel.

'Poor Andrew Coxley fancied he was "The Next Big Thing",' she said sadly. 'Never guessed he was headed for some waterlogged hole in the middle of Old Carton Woods.'

Markham gave her a searching look.

'Isn't that so with all of us, Kate,' he said before murmuring softly, '*We paused before a House that seemed A Swelling of the Ground — The Roof was scarcely visible — The Cornice — in the Ground.*'

'Sorry, guv.' She squared her shoulders. 'I'm being morbid.'

'No,' the DI said gently. 'Your compassion does you credit.' He paused. 'It's frightening to think what a slight hold we have on everything and how quickly it can all be whipped away . . . even more disturbing to imagine death stalking us unawares. But at least we can do something to make sure all the balance of injustice and failure and defeat will be set right in the here and now as well as the hereafter.' With a disarming wink, he added, '*Here Endeth the Lesson.*'

Burton gave a shaky laugh. 'Right, guv,' she said.

'Good. Now let's get to *Coast* before Noakesy demolishes everything in sight!'

* * *

Markham hadn't expected they would glean much at the wake, but later when the team compared notes back at base, some interesting nuggets emerged.

'Coxley's rellies didn't skimp on owt,' was Noakes's approving verdict. 'It were a good spread . . . Looked like they were happy to shell out.'

Doyle grinned. 'Not like some of the others then,' he said. 'I overheard Becca Drew bitching about Jean Gibley being a right old skinflint . . . According to Becca, when this friend of hers left *The Mane Event* to have a baby, everyone gave her vouchers or something for the baby, but Gibley's present was a ball of wool—'

'*A ball of wool!*' Carruthers exclaimed. 'How come?'

'Well, here's the best bit . . . It wasn't even a *new* ball of wool . . . She said she'd unravelled one of her brother's old jumpers so there'd be enough to knit the baby a matinee jacket . . . too mean to spend any money, see . . . The poor girl was gobsmacked cos she'd looked after Gibley ever since she came to the salon. Becca said old Gordon was mortified.'

Noakes guffawed. 'Hard on a penny then.'

'Too right. Evelyn Brady as well by the sound of it,' Doyle confirmed.

'Which makes it the more remarkable if she gave Mr Coxley presents,' Markham said thoughtfully.

'There were a bit of a ding dong between O'Grady an' David Hasselhoff,' Noakes said.

'Ed Collins,' Burton corrected automatically.

'Yeah, him . . . the Blonde Bombshell,' Noakes confirmed. 'Well, I jus' heard the tail end, but it didn't sound very friendly . . . O'Grady told Collins he needn't get any ideas an' then "Any time, any place!" like he were challenging him to fight or summat.'

Ed Collins and O'Grady, Markham mused. Well, well, well.

'Becca thinks Helen Mathews was definitely the one who fed stuff about Coxley to the *Gazette*,' Doyle said. 'I heard her saying that Mathews couldn't stand him.'

Noticing Carruthers's imperceptible start at this mention of the press, the DI wondered again if he could be the newspaper's mole and resolved to share his misgivings more explicitly with Kate Burton so she could mark the sergeant's card. DI Carstairs had once laughingly twitted Markham with being CID's "sea-green incorruptible", but he knew himself to be vulnerable when it came to protecting his team and had come to value Carruthers as one of the gang. Please God Burton would be able to nip any nefariousness in the bud before it burgeoned into something that he couldn't ignore.

Noakes appeared struck by something.

'Weird, innit,' he began before lapsing into a brown study.

'What is?' Doyle prompted.

'Well, other times we've gone to a wake, some poor sod usually turns up dead.'

'I apologise for our not being knee-deep in corpses,' Markham said drily. But it occurred to him that Noakes was correct. With *this* case, the deaths weren't coming thick and fast. All they had was Coxley. Unless you counted the two cold case murders . . .

Unabashed, Noakes offered a further titbit from his eavesdropping in *Coast*.

'That washed out lass with the straggly hair . . . Sally or Sophie—'

'Sandra Crowley?' Burton interjected.

'Yeah her . . . got well stuck into the vino . . . Anyway, she were chippy with one of the girls from the other salon . . . said Coxley an' the rest of 'em would have been on the telly cos *Bromgrove TV* had some documentary in the pipeline, only Big Mick put the mockers on it.'

'Hmmm, Mr O'Grady again,' Markham replied as Burton frowned at the pejorative. 'Sounds like we need to pay a visit to the television people.' He was amused to notice how Doyle and Carruthers perked up at that. Nothing like the prospect of showbiz stardust to get them champing at the bit. Burton, of course, wasn't remotely interested in "slebs" or anything of the kind, though something about the set of Noakes's jaw suggested he had no intention of being left out.

'Everyone appeared to behave pretty well at the wake,' Markham concluded. 'No outbursts or catfights or anything like that,' he said in an ironic tone.

'Giblet an' Brady got a bit weepy,' Noakes said. 'But her brother an' some double-barrelled geezer — retired from the Territorials — took care of it.' You could always trust the military to come to the rescue, his tone said clearer than words.

'Mrs Do-Gooder and the writer woman got a bit loud and obnoxious,' Doyle put in. 'Think they were disappointed *Hello!* wasn't covering it.'

'The way Davidson piled up her plate was something else,' Carruthers said with a fastidious shudder. 'You'd think she'd never had a square meal in her life.'

'Yeah, but the woman's a professional cadger,' Doyle reminded them. Idly, he wondered if she was any connection of Dimples Davidson. If so, he couldn't remember her name having ever come up in conversation.

'Philip and Stella Casey disappeared fairly early on,' Carruthers went on. 'Don't know how he managed it, but Ed Collins somehow got them out of there without the kid kicking off.'

'Probl'y bribed 'em,' Noakes concluded cynically.

'*The Mane Event* will be re-opening soon,' Burton said. 'So Collins could have offered her the chance of some work, provided she behaved herself.'

'Okay, so where do we go from here?' Doyle asked.

'Don' forget I c'n help out,' Noakes said with his most winning expression. 'I'm free Saturday.'

Of course you are! Burton thought, resigned to the inevitable.

'You and I will pay a visit to *Bromgrove TV* tomorrow, Noakesy,' Markham said, trying not to smile at the disgruntled expressions of his two sergeants. He turned to Burton. 'In the meantime, see what else you can find on Des O'Grady and Ed Collins. So far they're the ones putting their heads above the parapet.' His fellow DI, unlike her colleagues, looked relieved to be spared a visit to TV Land.

'Any point sniffing round the *Gazette*?' Carruthers asked. 'Find out who was feeding them stories about Coxley?'

'Excellent idea.' Ironically, if the DS was that paper's mole, he was most likely the best person to ferret out any skulduggery by their suspects. 'And you can chase up the cold case team as well, in case they've got any developments for us.'

The DI did his best to sound optimistic, but in reality he was despondent at the lack of progress. Though he supposed he should at least take comfort from the fact that officially they just had one body.

He could only hope that nobody else was headed for a rendezvous with Death.

CHAPTER 7: ANCIENT HISTORY

Later that evening as they enjoyed another *Lotus Garden* takeaway, Markham *did* in fact have some progress to report to Olivia.

'We've come across a school connection,' he told her over their chicken chow mein.

She was instantly riveted. 'Not Hope, surely?'

'No. Holy Martyrs Secondary in Old Carton.' He didn't miss his partner's look of disappointment, but was privately relieved that it wasn't Olivia's school.

'So how does it fit in to your hairdressing investigation then?'

'You remember those cold cases I told you about?'

She nodded, laying down her chopsticks the better to concentrate.

'Ethel Taylor and Jeanette O'Donnell,' Markham recapped, 'aged ninety and sixty-seven respectively. Lived round the corner from each other. The original investigators ruled out burglary but couldn't establish a motive.'

'Yes, I'm with you now, Gil . . . They both went to Andrew Coxley's salon, right?'

'Yes . . . Ethel was quite religious about it whereas Jeanette was more hit and miss.'

'I think you said they were widows . . . and Jeanette was a successful academic?'

'Well remembered, Liv.'

She glowed. 'Didn't they end up deserting Coxley's salon for the other hairdresser?'

'Right again. That was after Des O'Grady from *Cutting Edge* said he could do their hair at home.'

'Sounds like Coxley missed a trick there,' she mused.

'It probably wasn't that big a deal . . . just two elderly ladies . . . he had plenty of other customers on the books.'

She nibbled a prawn cracker. 'Okay, but where does Holy Martyrs come into it?'

'Ethel Taylor's son Preston was a pupil there and died on a school trip—' Markham began.

'But that was an accident, wasn't it . . . some kind of hypoglycaemic episode on an outward-bound expedition . . . nothing sinister?'

'Uh-huh . . . But there'd been *another* tragedy the previous year involving the same school.'

'What kind of tragedy?'

He smiled at her impatience. 'It happened on a field trip to Colomendy. A seventeen-year-old boy called Gerry Beck disappeared during the night. After an extensive search, they found his body in an abandoned well a couple of miles away from the residential activity centre. It was fenced off with warning signs saying *Danger*, but somehow he ended up at the bottom of the shaft in six feet of water.'

'That's the kind of thing kids do,' she said thoughtfully. 'Go exploring where they shouldn't.'

'The inquest brought in a verdict of accidental death.' Markham frowned. 'In the circumstances, that was pretty much the only option since there were no signs of a struggle . . . The PM indicated that Gerry went in head first, knocked himself out and drowned in a matter of seconds.'

'Was he drunk . . . or on drugs?' Olivia asked.

'They found a six pack of Strongbow along with packets of crisps and biscuits, so it looked like he'd planned a midnight picnic or something of the sort.'

She was puzzled. 'On his own?'

'There's the rub,' Markham said slowly. 'Apparently Gerry was the type who'd take the lead in any fun that might be going down . . . but the staff couldn't see him wandering off like that by himself.'

'So a solo escapade was out of character?'

'Very much so. But the other kids swore blind they hadn't been with him and there was no sign of foul play. As things stood, it looked as if he must have had some sort of brainstorm out of the blue.'

'Something about this second accident is bothering you,' Olivia prompted softly.

'Well, I don't like coincidences.' He raked back the luxuriant coal-black hair which was DCI Sidney's pet peeve. 'But it's not just that . . .'

Sensing Markham's need to formulate his thoughts, she reined in her impatience, pouring them both another generous glass of Châteauneuf-du-Pape.

'Half our suspects for the Coxley murder have some sort of connection to Holy Martyrs,' he said finally.

She was startled. 'How come?'

'The OAPs — Evelyn Brady, Jean Gibley and her brother Gordon Rushworth — went there.'

'Blimey,' she digested this information. 'Was this at the same time as Preston and Gerry?'

'Yes, but they were in different year groups and didn't have all that much to do with each other, though they went on the outward-bound expedition up the Cairngorms. When it came to the Colomendy trip, all three were alibied by their roommates . . . it was mainly two-bed dorms and the kids were up half the night with excitement.'

'Why didn't Gerry's roommate notice he'd sneaked out?'

'The sixteen- to eighteen-year-olds got their own bedroom. It was the younger ones who shared. That's how Gerry was able to slip away without anyone noticing.'

'Wasn't there a teacher on duty doing checks?'

Markham grimaced. 'Back then schools weren't so hot on health and safety. It was one of the things the coroner highlighted.'

'Okay . . . So who else has a link to Holy Martyrs?'

'Pretty much everyone and their dog,' he sighed. 'Or at least that's what Doyle and Carruthers have found out.'

'Go on . . . Can't you see I'm on tenterhooks.'

He laughed, admiring the starry eyes and flushed cheeks. Her skin had the translucent pallor that went with red hair and showed every surge of feeling in the ebb and flow of the blood.

'It turns out that Sandra Crowley's mother Margaret was a teacher there. She was disciplined after Preston made a complaint and Ethel kicked off about it.'

'What sort of complaint?' Olivia asked curiously.

'Oh, something about her being sarcastic and undermining his confidence—'

'Makes a refreshing change from "misgendering" and "micro-aggression",' she interjected sardonically.

'We haven't got to the bottom of it yet . . . according to Doyle, the school isn't exactly falling over itself to assist.'

'Now there's a surprise!'

'Anyway, Margaret Crowley ended up under a cloud and left teaching when she was just forty. There were problems with alcohol and a long, sad decline before she died at sixty. The whole family was up in arms over her being forced out of her job and blamed her premature death on the business with Preston.'

Olivia leaned forward eagerly, sensing there was more.

'Becca Drew and Sandra Crowley are cousins,' he told her.

'So, the family background meant she and Sandra both had a reason to hate Ethel?'

Markham's brows knitted, 'Yes, but not Jeanette O'Donnell, beyond the fact that she and Ethel were friends.'

'Did Jeanette go to Holy Martyrs?'

'Yes, she was the form above Preston.' Markham gave another sigh of frustration. 'But she wasn't on the Colomendy trip and had no history with Gerry Beck . . . It's just the coincidence of her being at the same school as two boys who died in unexplained circumstances that troubles me . . . somehow it feels hinky.'

'*Don't let "copper's hunch" lead you astray, Markham,*' Olivia honked in an uncanny impersonation of DCI Sidney, squinnying at him balefully. '*Remember, there's no room for mavericks in CID.*'

'Hilarious.' He took a hefty swig of red wine. 'Unfortunately, any links between Ethel Taylor and the Coxley suspects are pretty tenuous, and there's nothing to link anyone to the O'Donnell murder other than my gut instinct that the school comes into it somewhere.'

'Hmm.' Olivia felt an urge to jolly him along. 'Let's look at the positives, Gil . . . You've got these two elderly women who lived round the corner from each other and were both murdered . . . Then there's the fact that they both got their hair done by Andrew Coxley and had a connection to Holy Martyrs where two boys — one of them Ethel Taylor's son — died in mysterious circumstances . . . Plus, some of those boys' contemporaries from school are knocking round Bromgrove today, including Coxley's regulars.'

He was touched by her transparent effort to raise his flagging morale.

'Who else has links to Holy Martyrs?' Olivia pressed.

'Mark Brady — son of Evelyn, one of Coxley's customers — is a Governor . . . Ed Collins and Stella Casey both went there . . . but they've got no connection to Ethel or Jeanette—'

'And anyway, those deaths happened years before their time.'

'That's right.' He thought hard. 'Carruthers did some digging and found out that Sarah Moorcroft ruffled feathers at the school—'

'The writer woman?'

'The very same... Carruthers tapped someone at Gallery Press which publishes her bodice rippers. They said she originally submitted a proposal for something much darker... a psychological thriller about this school where a murderous teacher is bumping off her students—'

Olivia boggled. '"Her"?'

'Apparently the preliminary draft specified a female serial killer.'

'I take it this idea never got off the ground?'

Markham smiled grimly. 'Gallery got cold feet after various people somehow got wind of the project and,' air quoting, '"made an almighty stink".'

She caught his ironic tone. 'Did the objectors include Ethel Taylor and Jeanette O'Donnell by any chance?'

'Correct... This was twenty years ago when Moorcroft was just getting started, full of ambition and big ideas.'

'Couldn't her publishers have ridden it out?' Olivia asked. 'I mean, what about that disclaimer they stick at the front of books... as in, *Any resemblance to actual persons, living or dead, events or places is purely coincidental*? Surely that would have taken care of it.'

'Good point, Liv, but I guess they must just have been super-cautious for some reason. Moorcroft's an alumnus of Holy Martyrs and apparently tried to make capital out of what happened to Preston Taylor and Gerry Beck.'

'Did that mean there were rumours their deaths *weren't* accidental?'

'I presume so. Anyway, just for good measure she also wove the Margaret Crowley affair into her storyline.'

Olivia stared at him. 'Do you reckon she figured Crowley was somehow involved in murder?'

Markham raised his eyes heavenwards. 'Who can tell what goes on in that woman's head,' he exclaimed. 'Margaret

Crowley wasn't on either of the school trips, but I imagine Moorcroft drew on the poor soul's story when she was inventing motives for her serial killer.'

'Dramatic licence presumably,' Olivia said scornfully.

'Precisely. But whatever Moorcroft was up to, the dissenters spiked her guns and that manuscript never saw the light of day.'

'Was there anything about it in the local press?'

'No, and Carruthers says there's no copy of her draft proposal . . . omertà all round.'

Olivia pursed her lips consideringly. 'Understandable, seeing as it was potentially defamatory.'

She began to clear away the debris of their meal.

'There's chocolate profiteroles for pudding if you're up for it.'

'Always,' he grinned, secretly relieved that despite Muriel's prognostications, his partner didn't appear to be succumbing to anorexia any time soon.

Once they were settled with dessert and strong coffee, she returned to the engrossing subject of his investigation.

'So where does all this stuff about Holy Martyrs leave you?'

'I honestly just don't know, Liv . . . All I've got is this sixth sense and—'

'We know where Slimy Sid would tell you to stick that!'

Her tart riposte raised a reluctant chuckle.

'Carruthers also turned up some intel about Carol Davidson, our indefatigable fundraiser,' Markham continued.

'Don't tell me she's another one from Holy Martyrs.'

'An alumnus of *your* place, I believe. But there was some story about her wanting to do a fundraiser in Preston Taylor's name — one of those school safety campaigns — only Ethel turned her down flat . . . It's an interesting nugget but, again, there's nothing to show that Davidson ever crossed paths with Jeanette O'Donnell.' He stretched and yawned wearily. 'At the moment, there *seem* to be all these points of intersection between the cold cases and our Coxley investigation . . . but from another angle, one could say they're all dead ends.' He grimaced. 'Excuse the pun.'

'Where did Andrew Coxley go to school?' Olivia asked suddenly.

'Medway High.'

He had to laugh at the way her face fell. 'Sorry, my little amateur sleuth, there's no connection with Holy Martyrs.'

'What about the other hairdresser bloke?'

'Des O'Grady was at Calder Vale Secondary,' he grinned. 'Foiled again!' Before she could ask, he added, 'Cassie Johnson — the nails woman — and Karen Bickerstaff who sued Coxley both moved to Bromgrove from London, so nothing doing there.'

She flopped back in her chair, conceding defeat. 'I see what you mean about dead ends, Gil. But the whole Holy Martyrs thing is weird all the same.'

'Yeah . . . but the cold cases have to go on the back burner for now. I'm taking Noakesy over to *Bromgrove TV* tomorrow,' he said before telling her about the aborted reality TV documentary and the conversation Noakes earwigged in which Sandra Crowley claimed that Des O'Grady had screwed Andrew Coxley over.

'Professional jealousy?'

'Looks like it . . . And I wouldn't be surprised if O'Grady hasn't already pitched himself as the perfect replacement.'

'I thought you said he was plug-ugly — not photogenic at all,' she commented with her usual hyperbole.

Markham smiled. 'O'Grady's not a beautiful specimen, certainly. But with his outfit being practically next door to Coxley, he can milk the murder for all he's worth . . . reflected notoriety, so to speak.'

'*Yuk.*'

'Well, that's the cynical world we inhabit, Liv. Good reality TV fodder.'

She grinned. 'At least George will enjoy a tour of the studios. And it's bound to impress She Who Must Be Obeyed!'

He let that pass. 'In the meantime, I have to hope the team can unearth something else to help us.' So far nothing untoward had come to light about Des O'Grady and Ed Collins, nor had Carruthers succeeded in uncovering the *Gazette*'s informant. He wondered whether to tell her his fears about Carruthers's trustworthiness but decided against it.

'I've got a hairdressing story for you,' she said as they washed up together.

'Go on then.'

'Well, an anecdote about Vidal Sassoon at any rate,' she explained. 'He was devoted to his mother, and when she broke her leg, he arranged for her to have the operation in a private hospital run by nuns.'

He waited for the punchline, a smile playing about his lips.

'With it being a convent hospital, there were crucifixes over all the beds. Vidal asked if she was offended by it and his mum replied, "Not at all. He was a nice Jewish boy."'

'Noakesy'll appreciate that,' he laughed.

'Right.' She folded the tea towel and winked at him. 'What'll it be, TV or bed?' she asked in a come-hither tone.

There was only one answer to that.

* * *

Mark Harris, Commissioning Editor at Bromgrove TV, could almost have been Slimy Sid's twin, with his bullet-headed number 2 buzz cut and equally strident tone. This was not the first time he had crossed paths with Markham and Noakes — Peter Wimsey and Bunter, as they'd been christened by his reporters — and he was privately intrigued by their "bromance". So much so, that he had contemplated a feature on their unorthodox partnership. 'Forget it,' his boss counselled. 'Markham's not interested in being a celebrity copper. Hell, from what I've heard, he's not even interested in promotion . . . Apart from Fatty Arbuckle and that teacher he shacked up with, nobody gets close to him. I've heard rumours about a tough childhood, but he never lets his guard down . . . anyone tries to get personal, he just cuts them off at the knees.' Harris had laughed at 'Fatty Arbuckle' before concluding reluctantly that there was no point trying to woo CID's wunderkind. A pity really, since Markham was decidedly eye-catching. The last time he had called on them (during the wedding boutique investigation), his PA had insisted the inspector was a dead ringer for Gabriel Byrne.

Now, looking at the handsome, slightly haggard detective with the unnervingly steady gaze, Harris had no doubt that, for all his immaculate exterior, Markham wouldn't hesitate to fight dirty should that be necessary. Certainly there was no point trying to finesse him.

'What do you need to know, Inspector?' he asked.

'As you will be aware, we're investigating the murder of a local hairdresser, Andrew Coxley who owned *The Mane Event*.'

Harris grunted noncommittally.

'We understand you were thinking of doing a reality show about Mr Coxley's salon but the programme got pulled for some reason,' Markham continued in his blandest voice.

Harris shrugged. 'Happens all the time, Inspector. Fads come and go . . . And it had been done before with *Herbert's*.'

'*Eh?*' Noakes was no great fan of the shaven-headed executive who invariably looked at him like he was some specimen in a lab. And the TV buildings were nothing special — about as exciting as B&Q. You'd imagine it would be all swanky leather armchairs with chrome legs, but Harris's office wasn't much smarter than the guvnor's. Still, you never knew. There was always the chance he might see Holly Willoughby and thus get bragging rights with the missus and Nat.

'Herbert Howe was a celebrity hairdresser from Liverpool,' Markham told his friend.

'Died in 2016 . . . ran salons in the city since 1962,' Harris took over. 'A Liberace lookalike — dyed blonde hair, perma-tanned, taut skin and Botox . . . eventually moved to the Bling Bling building . . . kind of like the Harrods of hairdressing with these copper projecting pods . . . very striking and glamorous . . . The series *Shampoo* on Channel 5 was filmed there.'

'Musta passed me by,' Noakes sniffed with the air of one who was distinctly underwhelmed.

'Herbert owned lots of businesses,' Harris continued undeterred, 'but it was the hairdressing that made him famous. Had this totally outsize personality and when he was young people said he looked like Michael Flatley from Riverdance. Typical Liverpudlian . . . talked about his clients wanting their hair "dead 'igh, dead wide an' a lorra lacqueur!"'

Noakes finally cracked a grin, with a Yorkshireman's condescension for Scousers and their works. 'Sounds a character,' he conceded.

'Oh yes . . . Wore every colour of the rainbow and lived in a pink cottage. His mum worked as his receptionist for thirty-two years and he had this incredible rapport with older women who *flocked* to him.'

'Gay?' Noakes asked with the virtuous air of one who eschewed prurience.

'He was engaged at one point,' Harris replied. 'No-one was ever really sure . . . he most probably played up to that image for the mystery and glamour.'

Noakes's expression suggested that the mystery and glamour were lost on him, but he contented himself with looking sceptical.

It occurred to Markham that there were some uncanny similarities between Herbert Howe and Andrew Coxley. But one had died famous and respected while the other was murdered in his own shop . . .

'Coxley was kind of a Poundshop Herbert,' the commissioning editor said bluntly. 'We weren't sure about the formula.'

'So Des O'Grady had nothing to do with your decision?' Markham asked smoothly.

The other looked wary.

'We met at some charity bash . . . kind of bonded over a dreadful comedian who was doing the entertainment—'

'No turn unstoned,' Noakes quipped jovially.

Harris cleared his throat nervously. 'Well, we got talking and when I found out he was a hairdresser I said something about maybe doing a fly-on-the-wall programme . . . Anyway, he just marked my card and said I might want to think twice about using Coxley . . .'

'Why?' Noakes demanded.

'We'd had a fair amount to drink, so I can't remember exactly what he said,' was the evasive reply. 'It was something about Coxley being a wheeler dealer type . . . I got the idea there were skeletons in his closet, something like that.'

'O'Grady wasn't specific about these "skeletons" then?' Markham pressed.

'Sex an' drugs an' rock an' roll?' Noakes suggested helpfully.

'God no, it was just casual back-and-forth.'

Somehow the DI thought that the commissioning editor's eyes told a different story.

'You see, one or two people were under the impression that Mr O'Grady deliberately sabotaged the project,' he said.

'Did you an' O'Grady ever meet up again?' Noakes's eyes were pebble hard. 'Cos mebbe he fancied his own chances on the telly?'

'No,' Harris rapped.

Markham didn't believe him, but suddenly his mobile trilled.

'Excuse me, I have to take this,' he said.

At the conclusion of the call, his expression was unreadable.

'We may need to speak again,' the DI told Harris quietly, terminating the meeting.

Noakes restrained himself till they were out in the carpark.

'There's been another, hasn't there?' he burst out.

'Evelyn Brady's been found dead,' Markham replied. 'Dimples is over there now.'

'An' it ain't natural causes?' Noakes almost pleaded.

'No.'

Just that one syllable.

The salon killer had struck again.

CHAPTER 8: TILTING AT WINDMILLS

When they got to the Bradys' bungalow, the beautiful wraparound garden was teeming with police and forensic personnel. Recalling the secateurs he had spotted on their previous visit, Markham felt a moment of piercing sadness as he took in the riot of snapdragons, gardenias and peonies that their victim would never tend again.

Noakes's thoughts ran in a parallel groove. 'Nice gaff,' he murmured taking it all in.

Kate Burton appeared in the porch and, once they were suited up, led them through to the living room where Dimples Davidson crouched over Evelyn Brady's corpse which lay face upwards next to the glazed door.

'She was strangled,' he said straightening up. 'You can see the bruising and petechiae quite clearly.'

The woman's nimbus of blue-white hair curling softly around her sharp features looked as immaculate as if it had been freshly washed and set. But that was where normality ended, the silk scarf knotted tightly round her neck in a garotte and bulging red-veined eyes pointing all too clearly to her violent end.

'Can you give us time of death, Doug?' Markham asked quietly.

Unusually for him, the pathologist did not hum and haw. 'Judging by body temperature and rigor, sometime between eight and midnight,' he said. Then, 'She was roughed up pretty thoroughly . . . wouldn't have stood a chance, a small-boned elderly woman like that.'

Markham looked round the airy room which was neutrally but tastefully decorated in muted shades of taupe and soft yellow. He figured the modernist fittings, flat-screen TV on a sleek pine console and vintage leather three-piece suite were probably Mark Brady's choice, with a glassed-in cabinet containing what he imagined was Evelyn's collection of Herend figurines and an art deco cream vase of yellow roses adorning the fireplace. There was no sign of disorder apart from the body on the twill wool carpet. Poignantly, the dead woman's black patent handbag rested half-open on a glass side table next to the sofa.

'No sign of forced entry, so looks like she let them in, guv,' Burton murmured.

'Who raised the alarm?' Markham wanted to know.

'One of the neighbours was expecting her round for coffee at half eleven . . . got concerned when Evelyn didn't show. She has a set of keys, so was able to let us in.'

'Where's Mrs Brady's son?' he asked.

'There's a message from him on the answerphone . . . He rang just after nine to say his meeting in Liverpool had run over and he was going to book into a hotel for the night.'

'Did he sound concerned?'

'No . . . Just told her not to sit up too late and make sure she locked up . . . said he'd be back early afternoon.'

'Not bothered about leaving his old mum on her own with a psycho on the loose,' Noakes's tone was disapproving.

'She should have been safe enough,' Burton pointed out. 'Fairly spry . . . in her sixties, no disabilities or anything like that . . . There's a security system—'

'Cameras?' Markham cut in.

'No, just the alarm sensors and a spyhole . . . But the neighbour said they were safety conscious and Mark was thinking of installing a video intercom because of recent burglaries in the area.'

'"Would've, Could've, Should've,"' Noakes intoned before adding. 'Up late, wasn't she . . . I mean, you'd expect her to be upstairs watching the telly in bed at that time of night.'

Dimples, being of the same generation as their victim, looked distinctly boot-faced at this.

'Not necessarily,' Burton countered hastily. 'If Evelyn had trouble sleeping, she might've wanted to stay downstairs for a while . . . But it looks like she was expecting a visitor given that she let them in. And I reckon she'd touched up her make-up.'

'How can you tell?' Noakes asked curiously.

The three detectives bent over the body, contemplating Evelyn Brady's features.

The dead woman's face was narrow with a high forehead, thin pointed chin and small mouth. A black slime of mascara trailed incongruously down the pale oval of her right cheek.

'I see what you mean, Kate,' Markham said slowly. 'That looks like a coat of fuchsia on her lips.'

'Yes, and she'd applied some more blusher,' Burton told them. 'There's lipstick and a compact in the handbag, and it'd be instinct for her to smarten up if she was expecting someone.'

'A man?' he asked.

'Not necessarily. Women like to look good when they're meeting other women,' she replied. 'It's a question of self-respect . . . high standards, if you like.'

'Yeah, my missus won't even answer the door to the postie unless she's done her warpaint,' Noakes put in sagely.

'She seems pretty dressed up,' Dimples said suddenly. 'Expensive woollen suit . . . cream blouse . . . silk scarf . . . pearls . . . some kind of perfume.' He eyed the detectives dubiously. 'A bit old-fashioned and formal, though . . . Was that her normal look?'

'Well, she wasn't a trendy sixty-something,' Burton said, 'despite being one of Andrew Coxley's customers.'

The pathologist whistled.

'Was she indeed?'

'His OAP clients favour Maggie Thatcher hair,' Burton explained. 'Kind of high-rise and won't move in a force nine gale, if you get my drift.' Mindful that this was also Muriel Noakes's preferred silhouette, she added tactfully, 'Dignified and age-appropriate rather than mutton dressed as lamb.'

'Looks like she were trying to get away from chummy but didn't make it past the door,' Noakes observed.

'I'd say that's about right,' Dimples confirmed. 'The bruising on her arms is consistent with a struggle.'

'An' no-one heard a thing,' Noakes marvelled.

'I've got someone taking a statement from the neighbour, and Doyle and Carruthers are doing house-to-house,' Burton informed them, 'but this is a quiet little close . . . mostly retired couples who tend to mind their own business.'

'Who owns the house?' Noakes enquired.

'Mrs Brady, she was left very well off . . . Apparently Mark sold his own flat in town when he moved in with her.'

Markham looked round thoughtfully. 'Was there a mobile in her handbag, Kate?'

'No. According to the neighbour, she wasn't interested though Mark kept pestering her to get one.'

Markham looked out of the bay window. Whoever it was had come and gone like a shadow, he reflected, most probably cutting through the woods that backed on to the close, the better to avoid detection. Evelyn Brady was almost certainly already dead when her son left that message on the answerphone.

He turned back to his fellow DI. 'Anything significant in the rest of the house?'

'No sign of her organising a meal or drinks or anything like that, guv . . . If she wasn't rolling out the welcome mat, it could mean she didn't want whoever it was to hang around . . . counted on getting rid of them quickly.'

'Not a close friend then,' he mused.

'We'll check the mainline phone records, but they probably didn't want to risk contacting her that way . . . It's more likely they buttonholed her when she was doing her shift at *Age Concern* or somewhere she went during the day—'

'Like the hairdresser's,' Noakes said dourly. 'Her barnet looks like she's just been under the dryer.'

'*The Mane Event* hasn't reopened yet,' Burton said. 'So Coxley's regulars will still be using *Cutting Edge*.'

Markham's expression was alert. 'In that case, we need to check with Des O'Grady to see if Mrs Brady had an appointment or if someone came out to do her hair.'

'On it, guv.'

Burton moved into the hall to make the call.

'It's gotta to be the same scrote who did for Coxley,' Noakes concluded. 'I mean, what are the odds on one of his old biddies turning up dead a week after he's snuffed it?' He regarded the corpse compassionately, clenching his meaty fists. 'She never saw it coming.'

'If Mrs Brady knew who killed Mr Coxley, she would have come straight to the police,' Markham said decisively. 'So it's more likely she picked up on something but didn't realise the significance.'

'Or she said summat that sounded like she were on to 'em, so then they had to shut her up,' Noakes suggested.

Burton slipped back into the room.

'She got her hair done yesterday morning at *Cutting Edge* according to Des O'Grady's receptionist. Came in at half nine just after Jean Gibley but was finished before her . . . This was about a quarter past eleven, and then she planned to get a taxi into town . . . something about wanting to check out bed linen in John Lewis.'

'Did they notice anything unusual about her?' Markham asked urgently. 'Or did anything out of the ordinary happen during the appointment?'

Burton shook her head. 'The receptionist said she was a bit quiet, but not more than you'd expect in the circumstances.'

'Did she happen to mention Mr Coxley or the murder?'

'It was a temp from Calder Vale who did her hair because Mr O'Grady was fully booked. He's discouraged his staff from talking about the murder, but of course she could've had a word with Jean Gibley . . . they were next to each other under the dryers for a bit.'

'What time did Mrs Gibley leave?'

'They always say two hours for a shampoo and set, so Jean's brother came for her at half past eleven. He had to wait outside because the salon was so busy.'

'Nothing like a big juicy murder to bring in the punters,' Noakes observed sourly.

'We need to plot Mrs Brady's movements after she left the salon,' Markham instructed. 'That means checking with John Lewis and her usual haunts — the charity shop etcetera.'

'Righto, guv,' Burton said smartly.

'Do we know where she caught the taxi into town?'

'The receptionist offered to call a cab for her but she fancied getting some fresh air and said she'd pick one up at Greenbank Avenue.'

'Hmm . . . Check with Gordon Rushworth in case he passed her on his way to pick up Jean . . . maybe he noticed her talking to someone or clocked them following her.'

Noakes snorted. 'He ain't exactly Maigret, that one . . . too busy gripping the steering wheel like grim death.'

'Someone arranged to come here,' Markham said thoughtfully. 'They knew her son was away, so no likelihood of interruption. It wasn't a stranger, because she was security conscious and wouldn't have answered the door to random callers. There's no sign of forced entry and,' he turned to Burton with a query in his voice, 'nothing taken.'

'That's right, guv,' she confirmed. 'Evelyn's purse is in her handbag. There's a fifty-pound note in it and all her credit cards . . . Also, the laptop in Mark's study is still there, so the motive wasn't robbery.'

'Was there a diary in Mrs Brady's handbag, Kate?' Markham asked, wondering if the appointment might have been planned and not necessarily spur of the moment.

'No, nothing like that,' she said. 'Just the usual clutter.'

Suddenly they heard the sound of car tyres crunching on gravel, and the next moment Mark Brady burst into the room trailed by a flustered uniform.

'It's all right, Constable.' Markham waved the officer away. 'This gentleman is family.'

'*What the hell happened?*'

The man appeared poleaxed, looking down at his mother's body and then wildly from one face to another.

Noakes stepped forward. 'You don' want to remember your mum like this,' he said with surprising gentleness. 'A scumbag hurt her, but we're going to get them.'

With a deft combination of arm and elbow, he manoeuvred the other out of the living room, talking easily about sorting him a drink for the shock.

'Well handled,' Dimples muttered, clearly relieved there wasn't going to be a scene.

His sidekick always possessed the common touch, Markham reflected, despite the blustering dishevelment and florid complexion that had led to him being nicknamed 'Big Red Tomato' by the junior ranks. With anyone bereaved, vulnerable or dispossessed, the truculent cynicism that was his trademark fell away to be replaced by a curiously tender sympathy which somehow always touched the right chord.

The pathologist had listened attentively to their deliberations but was growing restless. 'I'd better get her moved now, Markham,' he said, knocking on the window to summon the waiting paramedics. 'There's no doubt about cause of death, but I'll do the PM asap.'

Minutes later, Evelyn Brady left her home for the last time as neighbours watched silently from behind the police cordon.

Burton's mobile broke the silence.

'The DCI wants updating as soon as possible, boss,' she said after taking the call. 'Ebury-Clarke plans to be there too.' So the impending Coronation wasn't proving such a useful distraction after all.

Superintendent Ebury-Clarke was possibly Markham's least favourite colleague after Sidney, but there was no dodging it.

'I'll just express my condolences to Mr Brady,' he said, 'and then we'd better head back to base. Forensics will be wanting to get on, so best if we leave them to it.' Not that he had much hope of the SOCOs finding anything that would lead them to a particular suspect, seeing as trace evidence could have come from just about everyone Evelyn Brady crossed paths with and, furthermore, her killer almost certainly wore gloves. It was the same scenario as for the previous murder, so the value of any discoveries forensics came up with depended on there being someone squarely in the frame.

'I'll check where they're up to with the house-to-house and sort out FLOs first,' Burton said. 'Then I can drop sarge back home.' No need to say that Noakes's involvement would be even less palatable to Ebury-Clarke than Sidney.

'I'll catch up with you tomorrow, Noakesy.' Well away from the station.

'Good luck with Slimy Sid an' Toad Face,' his old ally said cheerfully. 'Reckon it's Bushy Haired Stranger time,' he smirked, thinking of the DCI's notorious preference for seeing local 'mentalists' (or the 'neurodivergent' according to HR rubric) under suspicion as opposed to upstanding citizens.

Burton's voice sank to a whisper. 'Are we looking at a *serial*, boss? I mean, with these two murders and the cold cases . . .'

'If we are, then the key to it all lies somewhere in the past.'

But for the life of him, Markham couldn't see a way to unlock the mystery.

* * *

A short time later, the two inspectors sat in Markham's office steeling themselves for Ordeal By Sidney.

'Our cold cases are a non-starter,' Markham said despondently. 'Even though Sidney initially liked the idea of solving Coxley and those two elderly neighbours at one fell swoop, the Holy Martyrs angle is bound to freak him out. And he definitely won't go a bundle on putting respectable types like Mark Brady under the microscope.'

'If that guy was acting, he deserves an Oscar,' Burton said, recalling Brady's distraught demeanour. 'But you're right, guv . . . Our best bet is to give Sidney the idea we've decided that the whole school thing's a blind alley so we're concentrating on local misfits with hang-ups about hairdressers and their elderly clients.'

He laughed. 'Would I be right in thinking you've got a few names in mind?'

'There's nothing like a trawl through social care data for throwing up any number of nutters who fit the profile,' she said demurely. 'We can suggest gerontophobia crossed with homophobia or some sort of histrionic personality disorder . . . Don't forget, there's Stella Casey and the stalking . . . Sidney's bound to latch on to something like that . . . a screwy teenager with all sorts of issues—'

'As opposed to "respectable citizens,' he finished.

'Well, Stella's definitely an oddball, guv. And we don't really want to get into stuff about Coxley maybe running some kind of extortion racket and fleecing OAPs . . . Plus, at least the stalking's concrete evidence that Stella had a hang-up about Coxley. Her dad was openly hostile about him too, so—'

'We can throw him to the lions as well.' As she flushed, he added quickly, 'Don't worry, Kate, I'm not criticising. As a strategy for getting Sidney off our backs, it's ideal. And you're right, so far arguably only the Caseys have broken cover in terms of threatening behaviour.'

'There was that fight between Coxley and Des O'Grady,' she said. 'The one you said your friend, er Mr Dickerson,' somehow she just couldn't use the moniker, 'mentioned . . . when Coxley got a split lip.'

'I'd forgotten about that, Kate,' he said thoughtfully. 'I imagine O'Grady said something derogatory about his sexuality and Coxley wasn't having it . . . or it could have been territorial . . . after they accused each other of poaching customers, something like that.'

'Or Coxley suspected O'Grady of sabotaging his pitch to *Bromgrove TV*.'

'Hmm. Somehow I think Sidney'll be more inclined to give the Caseys top billing.' His dark eyes regarded her keenly. 'Albeit we don't really see them as being in the frame . . .' His voice held a question.

'Difficult to imagine Evelyn inviting Stella round,' she mused. 'Though Philip Casey might have had better luck.'

Markham got up from the desk and looked out of his window, contemplating the pedestrians below intent about their business.

The busy world which for Andrew Coxley and Evelyn Brady was now forever hushed . . .

He turned round to his fellow DI.

'Feels like we're tilting at windmills, Kate,' he said wearily.

'When we're done with the DCI, I'll get the others on to checking alibis, sir,' she said brightly. 'Come to think of it, it's not just Stella Casey and Des O'Grady who kicked over the traces. We're forgetting, the kerfuffle involving Karen Bickerstaff and those two stylists . . .'

His gaze sharpened. 'Oh yes, Sandra Crowley and Becca Drew wasn't it?'

'That's right, guv . . . It was pretty nasty . . . very nearly got physical.'

'I seem to recall Ms Bickerstaff had the upper hand.'

'And she admitted having a fling with Coxley . . . so there was a relationship history as well as her coming off worse in that court case.' Burton warmed to her theme. 'If Sidney doesn't go for the personality disorder stuff, we can always dangle Stella and Bickerstaff in front of him . . . say we're investigating the possibility that Coxley's murder was *sexually* motivated and then Evelyn was killed to stop her talking.' She pulled a face. 'At least this way we're not pointing the finger at Coxley or any pillars of the community . . . not upsetting the status quo . . . As for the press bulletin, we just say there's no cause for alarm but people should take the usual precautions . . . CID have a number of leads and are confident of a successful outcome blah blah.'

He smiled. 'I've always said, you're a master tactician, Kate.'

Burton shyly returned the smile before turning pensive.

'It feels callous to be talking as if all this is some sort of game,' she said ruefully, 'when two poor souls have been snuffed out in an instant.'

'There's nothing unfeeling about *you*,' Markham reassured her. 'And I like to believe that, whatever the fate of their mortal remains, it's not all over for Mr Coxley and Mrs Brady. *Dust thou art to dust returnest, Was not spoken of the soul*,' he quoted softly.

'I remember learning that one at school,' she whispered tremulously.

'Well then,' he told her bracingly, 'you'll remember it tells us to fight hard in the Present. That's how we make the dead *count*.'

He scooped up a buff-coloured folder from his desk.

'Right,' he said, his eyes gleaming wickedly, 'Let's tackle Sidney and Toad Face.'

A short time later, the DI was back in his office.

All things considered, the interview with Sidney and Ebury-Clarke had gone reasonably well, the DCI and slab-faced Superintendent succumbing to Burton's earnest exposition while Markham admired his colleague's ability to maintain a respectful demeanour which avoided any hint of smarm. The text of a press bulletin was approved and an impression given of purposeful activity with multiples lines of inquiry.

His cold cases were on the back burner for now, but Markham had given Burton a watching brief. Somehow he felt certain their murders and the Holy Martyrs deaths were linked.

But for now, there were alibis and witness statements to check.

His murdered dead belonged to the Past.

It was down to the team to ensure nobody else joined them there.

CHAPTER 9: HIDDEN MALICE

Sunday passed uneventfully, with the DI methodically ploughing through his suspects' alibis and the results of the house-to-house on their latest victim.

Like Andrew Coxley, Evelyn Brady had been killed on a Friday night. And as with the previous murder, people were either at home, flaked out at the end of the working week, or making a start on the weekend with family and friends. In the case of Mrs Brady's elderly friends and neighbours, they were variously ensconced in front of the box with a TV dinner, enjoying a nightcap or deep in a good book. Nothing stood out, though Doyle and Carruthers were diligently revisiting all of Andrew Coxley's contacts in the faint hope that the hairdresser's "little black book" might get them somewhere.

Mark Brady had telephoned his mother at nine o'clock and then booked into the Hope Street Hotel in Liverpool at half past nine, which didn't mean they could rule him out of the reckoning. 'That phone call could have been a blind,' Doyle reasoned. 'Brady's meeting at The Cotton Exchange was over at six. According to *him*, he went for a long walk round the city and along the Pier Head to unwind . . . then it was back to the hotel . . . says he was knackered and went out like a light as soon as his head hit the pillow. But it could all be baloney . . . nothing to say he didn't nip over to his mum's place.' On Carruthers objecting, 'Brady's mileage would show if he made an extra trip,' his colleague pointed out that the businessman could have used an anonymous hire vehicle, leaving his own in the long stay Mount Pleasant car park. Kate Burton listened patiently but didn't really buy it. 'The guy's all over the place,' she insisted. 'Genuinely shattered. The FLOs were worried about him doing something stupid, so they got the family GP to knock him out with a sedative.' Markham was inclined to trust his fellow DI's judgment, even though Evelyn Brady had held the purse strings and her son stood to inherit. While Brady undoubtedly harboured considerable animus towards Andrew Coxley, there was nothing to show any ill feeling between him and his mother, with even the crustiest neighbours praising him as a devoted son.

The Mane Event was due to re-open on Tuesday morning with Ed Collins in the role of manager. 'Only *acting manager*, though,' Burton reported. 'Apparently, Coxley's cousins plan to advertise the position . . . Word on the grapevine is that Sandra Crowley and Becca Drew both want a shot at it.'

In addition to this interesting twist, Natalie Noakes — duly prodded by her bloodhound parent — got in touch to say that her friend Eileen had belonged to Ed Collins's crowd for a time and suggested coyly that she might have something for the inspector if Markham cared to call at her fiancé Rick Jordan's fitness centre *The Harmony Spa*. Suppressing a smile at Natalie's breathily flirtatious manner (like Muriel, the Perma-tanned One made no secret of her partiality), the DI readily agreed to an appointment the following morning at ten o'clock. 'You might as well bring dad,' she said at the conclusion of their conversation, 'seeing as he's on board with CID.' Markham was touched by the hint of pride that lurked behind this sign-off and relieved to learn that neither Rick nor his tough-as-nails mother would be in attendance. He had done his best to warm to the pair but had conceived virtually an instant dislike for Natalie's intended on hearing him dismiss his future father-in-law as 'salt of the earth but', with a significant nod in Markham's direction, '*not exactly one of us*'. Given that the Jordans' own antecedents were decidedly humble and that the DI considered George Noakes worth any number of bumptious entrepreneurs, it was hardly an auspicious start although, for his friend's sake, he swallowed his ire and listened kindly as Noakes lavished praise on the undeserving upstart.

Promptly at the appointed hour, Markham and Noakes met Natalie in the foyer of the fitness centre. The DI was somewhat disconcerted to see that she was wearing a smocked grey dress with enormous Peter Pan collar — distinctly reminiscent of Princess Diana in her virginal phase — with her hair coiled in a neat chignon and make-up also decidedly low-wattage (in contrast to the lurid eye shadow and heavy foundation of yore). The DI guessed she was reinventing herself after the rollercoaster of a rocky engagement and miscarriage, and his heart went out to her. His countenance bland as cream, he endured all the preliminary giggling and arch enquiries without a flicker of impatience, delighting her with his interest in plans for the expansion of 'Ricky's empire'. Eventually, however, in the manner of one engaged in a clandestine assignation (Markham could tell she was enjoying the cloak and dagger hugely), Natalie suggested they adjourn to the centre's Juice Bar — an appropriately trendy space with its spotlights, stripped pine and plush velvet banquettes — where Eileen was waiting.

Noakes's face as he surveyed the blackboard with its choice of 'Pick Me Ups' was something of a picture. It certainly didn't look as though he fancied the 'Sports Refueller' of banana, strawberry and passion fruit; still less was he likely to favour the 'Green Haven' combo of spinach, pineapple and apple. Natalie instructed the muscle-bound hunk behind the bar to bring coffee and biscuits, so at least there was no risk of protests about being force-fed such objectionable concoctions.

Once they were settled, Markham turned to the plump, cheerful looking blonde.

'Natalie thinks your acquaintance with Ed Collins might be useful in relation to an ongoing inquiry,' he began. 'We're collecting background information on everyone connected with Andrew Coxley, so there's no need to worry that it's somehow disloyal to speak to us—'

'Or that you're grassing up a mate,' Noakes interrupted.

'Well, I wouldn't say me and Ed were ever exactly close mates,' she said carefully. 'He was in a relationship with my friend Tricia and they shared a flat for three years before splitting up.'

Markham smiled encouragingly. 'Go on.'

'It was pretty unpleasant when they broke up, and he pestered her for money afterwards — even wrote to her parents claiming she owed him for loans and stuff. They ignored the letter, but it wasn't nice.'

'Prince Charming,' Noakes muttered sarcastically.

'Yeah well, like I say, it ended badly.' She bit her lip. 'Probl'y faults on both sides.'

Markham sensed there was more to come. 'Did Tricia have further issues with Mr Collins?'

'The other week, she noticed a whole bunch of stuff on her credit card that didn't make sense . . . There were all these purchases from Ebay that she knew she hadn't made . . . Came to a couple of hundred pounds in all. So she rang them up and said she hadn't authorised any of it. In the end, it turned out there were *two* accounts in her name on Ebay and one of them was for the old address she'd shared with Ed when they were still together. She'd forgotten all about it and never bothered to close it down . . . didn't even remember her password or anything—'

'But presumably *he* could have remembered it,' Markham prompted, 'along with her payment settings.'

Eileen looked uncomfortable. 'She didn't have any way of proving Ed was the one using her credit card details, but whoever was hacking that Ebay account never got stuff posted to them — they always used click and collect—'

'Which meant the purchases couldn't be traced back to the hacker's address,' Noakes cut in before adding with grudging admiration. '*Crafty.*'

'Did she contact the police?' Markham asked.

'Oh yes, she needed an incident number for Barclaycard. But she didn't point the finger at Ed cos she wasn't sure it was really him . . . It *could* have been a scammer or maybe someone at Ebay . . .'

'But she had misgivings about him?' Markham pressed.

'It was the fact that he'd badgered her about money after they split up and then did that thing with her parents,' Eileen conceded reluctantly. 'Plus the stuff that was ordered from Ebay . . . men's fitness wear and gadgets . . . and his favourite scent *Paco Rabanne*,' Noakes wrinkled his nose at that, 'meant she just had this *feeling* it had to be him . . .'

But *feelings* weren't enough for Ed Collins to get his collar felt, the DI reflected. And Eileen was right, the fraud could well have been an inside job by someone at Ebay. However, the attempted blackmail of his girlfriend's parents showed the personable stylist in a less than savoury light and lent some credence to the notion of him being a hustler. Of course, none of it meant that he was a murderer . . .

'Why did Mister Paco Rabanne an' your friend split up?' Noakes asked.

Eileen was visibly uncomfortable, a dark flush creeping up her neck.

'Whatever you tell us will remain confidential,' Markham assured her, 'unless it becomes relevant to our investigation.'

The woman shifted in her seat before taking the plunge.

'Tricia wondered if Ed might be bi.'

'*Bisexual?*' Whatever Noakes had been expecting, it wasn't this.

'She thought he might be cheating on her with a bloke . . . He spent a lot of time with some guy called Darren who used to come here . . .'

'It could have been wotsit . . . *platonic*.' Noakes had recovered his sang-froid. 'Mebbe they were jus' fitness freaks . . . seeing who had the biggest biceps kind of thing.'

'I guess.' But she didn't look convinced. 'Ed was devastated when Darren moved down to London . . . more than you'd be if it was only a friend. Tricia said he was really down in the dumps and took it out on her.'

'Was he ever violent?' Markham asked.

'Oh no, nothing like that. She just thought he was keeping something from her and then there were the mood swings after Darren left . . . Something didn't add up but there was nothing concrete she could point to.'

'Did she ever think there might have been anything going on between him and his boss?' Markham said quietly.

'*Andy Coxley?*' Her incredulity was unfeigned. 'No way! He thought that seventies get-up was seriously weird. And I remember him saying once that Andy was a real dog in the manger.'

'What do you think he meant by that?'

'Well, that Andy kept all the perks for himself . . . like he got the hump if a customer took a shine to Ed and wanted to give something special as a thank you.'

'Money?' Noakes cut in.

'Yeah, I think so . . . tips and . . . presents . . . that kind of thing,' she said. 'Mind you, I had the impression there was a lot of competition going on . . . not only Andy and Ed . . . it sounded like the girls were just as bad. Hairdressing's pretty cut-throat these days. If anyone wanted to move on, Andy made it tough for them to find somewhere else . . . wouldn't think twice about putting the word out that they weren't top dollar.'

'Is that what he did with Helen Mathews?' Markham slipped in.

Seeing that Eileen appeared worried she might have said too much, the DI added, 'Don't worry, we're not gunning for anyone..'

At least, not just yet, said Noakes's bulldog expression.

'It's a case of trying to get a feel for Mr Coxley's world,' Markham continued. With a self-deprecating laugh, he joked, 'The world of posh crimpers is a bit alien to us . . . Though not, of course, to Natalie,' he qualified charmingly as Noakes's offspring bridled with satisfaction.

Disarmed, Eileen visibly relaxed.

'Helen's all right,' she said. 'But she doesn't put up with anyone's BS and Andy didn't like that.'

'Could she be the one who passed stories about him to the *Gazette*?'

Eileen pursed her lips. 'Not really her style,' she pronounced after due consideration. 'Like I said, she's the type who shoots from the hip.'

'How about Ed then?' Noakes demanded.

'*Maybe*,' she said. 'But if it was, he did a good job covering his tracks. Nobody ever pinned anything on him that I knew about.' A thought occurred to her. 'Some people said he sent those poison pen letters, but I reckon it was one of Des O'Grady's lot trying to make mischief.'

Markham tensed. 'What poison pen letters?'

'Oh, a few of Andy's old ladies got stuff in the post about being saddos cos they fell for his shtick.'

Interesting that no-one from *The Mane Event* had mentioned this episode, Markham reflected bleakly.

'Did *you* ever see any of those letters, Eileen?' he asked.

She shook her head vigorously. '*Nah* . . . But it was just a wind-up. Sandra or Becca — I can't remember which — got a peek at one when this old dear came chuntering to Andy . . . They said it sounded like some catty schoolkid trying to get a rise.'

'Who was the customer who complained to Mr Coxley?' Markham wanted to know.

'I *think* it was a Mrs Gibson or Gibbling . . . some name like that—'

'Might it have been *Gibley*?' Markham asked.

She beamed. 'Yeah, that's right . . . Apparently Andy played it cool . . . just said to chuck it down the loo cos that was the best place for garbage.'

Markham knew that low-level malice was often the precursor to something far more sinister. 'Can you remember anything else about the letter to Mrs Gibley, Eileen, anything at all?'

Catching his seriousness, she screwed up her face in concentration. 'Des O'Grady's receptionist Cath came to one of my spinning classes . . . said *she*'d heard it was some woman hater ranting on about pathetic needy types who've got nothing in their lives so they obsess over their hairdresser . . .' Eileen suddenly shivered. 'Cath said it could've been literally *anyone*,' she exclaimed melodramatically. 'One of the customers or staff . . . ever so nice on the surface, but beneath all the smiles and nods and "how are yous?" they've got this twisted agenda . . . like something out of Agatha Christie or *Midsomer Murders*.'

Only this wasn't some cozy village murder and the stakes were much higher, Markham thought grimly.

Aloud, he said, 'You've been extremely helpful, Eileen.' Slipping his card across the table, he added, 'If there's anything else you remember, please don't hesitate to contact me directly.'

Oh God, Noakes thought grumpily as he observed their interviewee's dazzled expression, *there's another scalp for his collection*. It struck him as eminently unfair that Markham only had to gaze at a woman for her to go weak at the knees while *he* might as well have been invisible. But you had to hand it to the guvnor, he never traded on his looks, not like Chris Carstairs who came over all Bergerac at the merest whiff of an attractive female. It wouldn't surprise him if Carstairs didn't whip out a police badge and cuffs for the odd date . . .

Natalie and Eileen bustled off for their cardio funk class, leaving the two men alone.

'Well, old David Hasselhoff's a dark horse an' no mistake,' Noakes pronounced.

'It certainly sounds as though Mr Collins has another side to his character,' Markham agreed soberly.

'Didn't sound like he fancied *Coxley*, though . . . I mean, like the lass said, he were creeped out by that whole Bee Gees vibe an' got a cob on cos of missing out on perks an' fringe benefits.'

'Who can say *what* went on between them . . . It seems to me that Mr Coxley was a man who kept people in separate compartments. Don't forget, he had an affair with Karen Bickerstaff before things went sour and she sued him. For all we know, there could be a similar backstory with him and Ed Collins.'

'I don' see Collins for the poison pen letters,' Noakes said emphatically. 'It sounded like teenage stuff, remember.'

'Yes, but Des O'Grady's receptionist talked about a *woman hater* . . . From what Eileen said, Collins's behaviour towards his ex-girlfriend was vindictive and he may even have attempted to defraud her.' The DI massaged his temples wearily at the realisation that their case had suddenly developed new complications. 'We need to speak to Sandra Crowley and Becca Drew as well as O'Grady's receptionist—'

'An' Old Mother Giblet.' Thinking about the hate mail, Noakes sniffed as though at something evil-smelling and rancid. 'She must've been too embarrassed to tell us about it.'

'Eileen said "a few" elderly ladies had received abusive correspondence,' Markham pointed out, 'so Evelyn Brady most likely received one too.' His voice vibrated with scorn, a disgusted expression crossing his face. 'I imagine the not knowing must really have got to them . . . the thought that someone hated them enough to plot such a nasty campaign.'

'An' incinerate they had the hots for Coxley,' Noakes added solemnly.

Markham's lips twitched at 'incinerate', but it felt like the *mot juste* seeing that the phantom clearly aimed to destroy his targets' peace of mind and lay waste their tranquillity.

'Right,' he said as two Lycra-clad women came into the bar. 'If we loiter here any longer, we're at risk of being offered a lemongrass smoothie or something equally noxious.'

Noakes needed no second prompting.

'I'm not on at Rosemount till this arvo, guv. Reckon I'll hang around an' see what you turn up 'bout them letters.' It was obvious the ex-DS was intensely interested to know more despite his elaborate show of nonchalance. 'I wonder if the cold case oldies ever got anything like that,' he mused. 'Y'know, what with Coxley doing their hair.'

Markham was startled. 'Well if they *did*, it never featured in the case notes.'

'We're looking at, what, ten years ago, so technically any of our suspects could have done summat like that to them other two women . . . got a taste for it, like.'

The DI considered this hypothesis. 'Not Cassie Johnson and Karen Bickerstaff, because they were based in London,' he said. 'And Stella Casey would only have been seven.'

'Mebbe it's the kind of thing a *writer* would do,' Noakes suggested. 'I could see that romantic novelist or whatever she calls herself having a go.'

'I keep coming back to the fact that Eileen said the content was juvenile . . . suggested a "catty schoolkid",' Markham mused.

'Could be a grownup with a case of whatchamacallit . . . *arrested development* . . . Burton says you get it sometimes where folk went through some trauma or had a bad shock . . . or they lost someone they were close to an' never got over it.' For all the ups and downs of their professional history, Noakes respected his former colleague's insights when it came to psychology.

The DI was thoughtful. 'Or it could be someone trying to frame a youngster . . . someone who wants us to suspect Stella Casey, for instance. After all, she's a teenager, plus she has form when it comes to unbalanced behaviour.'

Markham felt his head beginning to throb with all the ramifications.

'I'll check with the cold case team to see if they came across anything like this with Ethel Taylor and Jeanette O'Donnell,' he went on. 'Even if they *were* subjected to some form of harassment, I'm not sure it moves the current investigation any further along . . . But at least now we've got something new to consider and can factor in any psychological co-efficients for poison pens.'

'Who's doing the profiling?' Noakes asked slyly. 'Shippers or that Irish bird you thought were top banana on the allotments case?'

Markham and Dr Eleanor Shaughnessy had indeed struck sparks off each other, but the DI wasn't sorry that she was unavailable to consult on the salon murders. With things still delicate between himself and Olivia — both of them terribly bruised by the recent hiatus in their relationship — he felt the danger of paying the attractive psychologist too much attention. Not least with his friend monitoring them from the sidelines like an outraged Victorian paterfamilias. Mr Barrett of Wimpole Street had nothing on George Noakes in one of his periodic fits of morality!

The muscles of Markham's cheek contracted as if he was smiling, but it didn't reach his eyes. 'The "Irish bird" is otherwise engaged,' he replied inscrutably, 'so Nathan Finlayson is doing the honours.'

Noakes gave a wolfish leer. 'Think him an' Burton will ever sort thesselves out an' seal the deal?' he asked, watching Markham closely.

'I hope so,' the DI said sincerely. 'The two of them have many interests in common, not least their passion for forensic psychology . . . That's not such a bad beginning.'

Something in Markham's voice warned Noakes this was all he was going to get.

'Their kids'll probably be born spouting that bleeding psychiatry manual she lugs round all over the place,' he groused amiably without noticing Markham's sudden tension.

The reference to children grated harshly on the DI as he recalled Olivia's desperate scheme to adopt Natalie's baby and his own secret relief when that plan came to nothing. His partner had never suggested anything of the sort again and these days she laughed and joked as if the entire episode had never been, but there was something in her smile that had never been there before and he fancied would never be absent from it again.

'Kerr-ist . . . *She's nearly wearing that dress!*'

He was jerked back to the present by Noakes's exclamation at the sight of a *Love Island* lookalike striding towards the bar in an itsy bitsy dress that verged on indecent.

'Sorry, boss.' His friend knew the guvnor's dislike of profanity, but women really shouldn't be allowed out looking like that. He thought complacently of Natalie's demure governess outfit, happily oblivious of the fact that his beloved offspring was even then flashing a black Lycra thong at her mixed cardio workout, ignorance in such instances being bliss.

'Let's get out of here,' Markham muttered as the sultry blonde's smouldering gaze came to rest on him.

With one last appalled-yet-fascinated stare, Noakes followed the DI towards the exit.

CHAPTER 10: THE GAME'S AFOOT!

In the event, however, Markham and Noakes ended up making a detour before ever reaching *Cutting Edge*, being summoned to the aftermath of a fire at 29 Meadow Lane, home of Sarah Moorcroft where Simon McLeish of Bromgrove's FIU was waiting for them, watched by a gaggle of neighbours corralled behind a safety cordon.

'The householder wasn't in,' the wiry, sandy-haired FIO told them in his strong Northern Irish accent. 'There'd been a call-out here a couple of weeks back when she was convinced someone deliberately set fire to her garden shed.' His tone quizzical, McLeish added, 'She was giving out to us like you wouldn't believe — all set to report it to the CFO if there wasn't an immediate arrest.'

'She's a writer,' Noakes sniffed. 'One of them emotional types.' He made it sound like a nasty medical condition.

The DI felt further explanation was required. 'There could be an overlap with one of our current investigations, McLeish.'

'I gathered as much when someone said she was caught up in the business with that dead hairdresser,' the other said laconically. 'That's why I asked my boys to get on to you.'

Markham glanced around at the avid faces of the spectators.

'Are we able to take the party somewhere else?' he asked. 'Somewhere less *exposed*.'

Noakes looked up at the white-rendered Edwardian detached property with a puzzled expression. 'Don' look like there's much damage.'

McLeish smiled enigmatically. 'Round the back,' he said quietly, leading them to a well-maintained mature garden where what appeared to be the remains of a small bonfire lay smoking just inside the door of a cedar-clad annexe.

'Apparently it's an *executive garden room*, not a shed,' he told them with a grin. 'She got quite wound up about that when we were here before .'

'What happened the last time?' Markham asked.

'She'd left the side gate open, so they just sneaked round the back and broke in.' He pulled a comical face, 'The door's *real glass, dontcha know*, so it was child's play really. Then they got a small blaze going . . . chucked some of her notebooks and files on top.'

'It's a nice little hut,' Noakes said approvingly.

'The external walls are fire-resistant, so they were never going to raze it to the ground,' McLeish informed them. 'I think it was more about sending her a message.'

Markham frowned. 'And *this time?*'

'More of the same.' The FIO shrugged. 'She wasn't at home, so never in any danger.'

'Doesn't apply to her neighbours, though,' Markham pointed out. '*They* could've been at risk.'

'Well, here's the strange thing.' McLeish's eyes narrowed. 'Both times there was an anonymous 999 call before the fire had a chance to take hold . . . As you can see, the properties in this road are situated well apart,' another wry smile, 'which is presumably why it's such an "*exclusive* address". That meant there was never any real risk to the neighbours. Like I say, it looks like she must've got on the wrong side of somebody,' his wry expression suggested he could easily imagine such an eventuality, 'and they retaliated by sending her a warning . . .

something designed to put the wind up her . . . nothing murderous, just threatening.'

'And nobody saw anything?' Noakes was incredulous. 'In the middle of the bleeding day!'

McLeish gestured to the shrubbery. 'The houses on this side of the road all back on to Meadow Lane playing fields with a cycle path at the end of their gardens, which makes it easy access if they want to nip out the back and have a wander.' The Irishman turned impish again. 'Ideal for authors wanting to think beautiful thoughts—'

'An' for any toerag who fancies a spot of breaking and entering,' Noakes cut in sarcastically.

'That too,' the FIO replied equably. 'The shrubbery screens her house from the playing fields and there's an iron gate . . . but it's relatively easy to slip the bolt . . . That's probably how they were able to get in without being seen.'

'Didn't she get it changed after the last time?' Noakes asked disapprovingly.

McLeish rolled his eyes. 'Waiting for a bespoke timber side-door or something of the sort. Once she'd calmed down, she took the view it was just kids — "teenage yobs" — and now they'd had their fun, they weren't going to try again.' He stroked his chin thoughtfully. 'The 999 call made it seem like whoever did it was just messing around — pulling her strings — but I still advised her not to wait . . . told her she needed to get her security sorted pronto instead of fannying around with ornamental wotsits.' He sighed. 'There's just no telling some people.'

The DI was troubled. 'And now they've had another try.'

'Yeah, same pack drill . . . in through the back . . . then 999 to get the fire service round here.'

'Where's the householder now?' Markham asked, apprehensive lest their celebrity novelist should ambush them mid-conversation.

'That's her BMW round the front . . . screeched up in a hail of gravel about five minutes after we arrived . . . She was only getting in everyone's way, so I packed her off to the woman at number 27 — nice sensible type all set to sort out tea and biscuits.'

They walked round to the front of the house. 'Hopefully Ms Moorcroft will be over the worst by now, so we can interview her,' Markham said.

McLeish's expression had a flavour of *Rather you than me*, but he signalled to one of his hovering subordinates. 'Go and check out number 27,' he instructed. 'See if our vic's okay to talk with the police.'

The FIO turned back to Markham and Noakes, a questioning eyebrow raised.

'You reckon this has something to do with your hairdresser case then?'

Markham scanned Sarah Moorcroft's well-tended garden. 'Well, the timing's suspicious, McLeish. And the lady has an unparalleled knack for putting noses out of joint . . . Mind you, I can't see how it all fits together.' Including the fact that they couldn't rule out Moorcroft as a suspect for Coxley's murder.

McLeish snapped out a smart salute. 'Best of luck, Inspector,' he said sympathetically. 'My lot won't be long finishing up here.' He spotted the victim barrelling along the pavement towards them, trailed by an older woman wearing a resigned expression. 'I'll leave you to it,' he said with a wink, disappearing round the side of the house.

Before Sarah Moorcroft had the chance to unleash any operatics in front of local onlookers, Markham firmly suggested that they move inside. 'Do you need me to come in with you?' the older woman offered politely before withdrawing with what looked very much like relief when her neighbour rudely announced she could cope perfectly well by herself thanks.

'Interfering old biddy,' the writer muttered ungraciously, ushering the two men into her front room. 'Just wants to poke her nose in.' A pronouncement which merely served to confirm the unfavourable impression Markham had previously formed of her.

The living room ran the full length of the house, with French doors opening onto a patio and the back garden. To the DI's surprise, it was both elegant and comfortably decorated — big, overstuffed sofas inviting visitors to relax while bookcases along two walls overflowed with an eclectic range of volumes. The colour scheme was duck egg blue to match the tiles round the fireplace, with draperies and upholstery in shades of lavender creating a soothing ambience. The peaceful atmosphere was enhanced by the pastoral vista in the front garden where spring flowers and foliage seemed to be all bursting out at once.

Altogether it was not what the DI had expected.

Sarah Moorcroft noticed his frank glance of admiration. It seemed to mollify her. 'This was my parents' house,' she said. 'Old-fashioned but I suppose it grows on you.'

'It's delightful.'

She unbent sufficiently to offer refreshments.

'We're fine thank you, Ms Moorcroft,' Markham said politely. He gestured to the Waterford decanter and glasses on a mahogany console. 'But can I fetch you something for the shock?'

Bloody hell, she's practically purring, Noakes thought venomously as his friend quietly and competently settled their hostess with a stiff whisky. *And now she'll be making cow eyes at him and we won't get any sense out of her.*

The DI, being expert at deftly parrying flirtatious manoeuvres without ever appearing brusque or unchivalrous, moved the conversation on to the subject of potential ill-wishers in a surprisingly short space of time.

'I imagine authors like yourself can attract a certain amount of envy,' he said, choosing his words carefully. He allowed the silence that followed his words to stretch before continuing, 'Maybe even outrage and resentment if you tackle subjects that prove . . . controversial or too close to the knuckle for some people.'

'There's always jealousy,' she replied, not without some complacency in her tone. 'Abuse and people creating fake accounts to set up negative reviews online, that kind of thing.' She took a slug of whisky. 'Anyone with a local profile has to put up with it . . . goes with the territory . . . sad little nobodies wanting to derail your career and drag you off your pedestal.'

'But we're talking *arson* here, luv,' Noakes said bluntly.

She put her glass down carefully on the coffee table Markham had positioned at her elbow.

'The first time round, I assumed it was just hooligans . . . probably kids or someone who'd seen my picture in the paper.' She preened slightly as she said this. 'Pathetic types who fancied having a pop.' Her voice faded slightly. 'But after *this* . . .'

Markham's eyes were intent on her face, flushed now with the alcohol.

'Do you have any projects coming up?' he asked. 'Anything in the pipeline that might pose a risk to someone . . . let's say a book that someone might want you to *drop?*'

At this she stiffened, twitching the thick blonde plait over her shoulder as if the room was suddenly too warm.

'It's important you tell us if you were planning anything along those lines, Ms Moorcroft,' Markham said earnestly. 'Anything that might be perceived as a threat. Anything that might trigger a killer.'

As he paused to let this sink in, the DI saw expressions of confusion, bafflement and fear chase each other in quick succession across her face.

'Are you saying this might have something to do with Andy's murder?' she croaked, her hands shaky as she picked up her drink once more. '*Seriously!*'

'Believe me, I'm only too serious, Ms Moorcroft,' Markham replied with no trace of his earlier social manner.

He waited implacably.

'I was trying out ideas for a new novel,' she said finally. 'Something I had to put on the back burner when I was just starting out because it was too,' she seized on his earlier word, '*controversial* . . . There's been a lot of water under the bridge since I first pitched my proposal, so the time feels right.'

'Would this new book by any chance concern two students at Holy Martyrs School who died in mysterious circumstances?' Markham enquired with an almost imperceptible curl of his lip.

Her pupils dilated in alarm. 'How did you know about that?'

'The police file on those two deaths — together with the murders of Ethel Taylor and Jeanette O'Donnell — isn't closed, Ms Moorcroft,' he went on, aware that he was pushing his luck by implying the pupils' deaths had ever been regarded as anything other than accidental. 'Moreover, we have reason to believe they could be linked with the deaths of Mr Coxley and Mrs Brady.'

'I heard about Evelyn,' she stuttered. 'That poor woman never hurt a soul.'

'No, but she died nonetheless.' The handsome inspector's keen dark eyes, almost the same colour as his hair, weren't warm and solicitous now. In fact they were as cold and unreadable as the depths of her whisky. 'You'll appreciate that I want to prevent a similar fate befalling *you*.'

'But I don't see *how*,' she began inarticulately. 'I mean, we're talking about bygone tragedy . . . ancient history . . . What possible relevance could any of it have to *me*?' It sounded as though she was trying to convince herself.

Noakes leaned forward, beefy arms resting on his thighs. 'Look luv,' his voice was almost fatherly, 'don' play games with the guvnor. He ain't got time to explain the ins and outs, but you c'n take it from me these deaths are all linked. *Linked*,' he repeated with an impressive air of finality. 'So you gotta tell us what you're up to,' he added with wheedling insistence as Markham watched in admiration. When it came to the not-so-gentle art of bluff, George Noakes had few equals.

The writer looked from one to the other and appeared to make a decision.

'After it came out in the *Gazette* that you were connecting what happened to Andy with unsolved murders, I had a word with Gavin Conors who said it might be worth my while taking another look at Holy Martyrs,' she confided looking simultaneously shamefaced and defiant. 'He also mentioned how you had a cold case team checking out Ethel Taylor and this other woman and both of 'em got their hair done by Andy.' She bit her lip. 'To be honest, I didn't really think that stuff from the past had any bearing on what happened to Andy and Evelyn . . . but it had the makings of a good mystery,' she added lamely.

Bloody CID leaking like a sieve, Markham fumed silently. *Carruthers better not be behind it. On the other hand, this arson attack on Sarah Moorcroft seemed to confirm a link to Holy Martyrs and the cold cases, so at least that was some consolation . . .*

The woman shifted uncomfortably. 'I mentioned to a few people at *Gallery* that I was thinking about revisiting Holy Martyrs . . . dropped the odd hint here and there when I did stuff for Waterstone's and local book clubs . . . y'know, to get some advance hype going. But I wanted to tread carefully . . . There are still people around who were involved in what happened . . .'

Markham's lips tightened. 'But it's too attractive a proposition to shelve,' he pointed out acidly. Taking pity on her embarrassment, he continued in a milder tone, 'Did it ever occur to you, Ms Moorcroft, that you might be putting yourself in danger?'

'I can look after myself,' she retorted sulkily with another violent twitch of the blonde braid. 'And anyway, if you're right and this is someone connected to Holy Martyrs, it looks like they didn't mean to kill *me* cos they made sure I was out and rang 999 . . . seems they just wanted to scare me off writing the book.' She laughed scornfully though the hands clutching her glass were shaking slightly. 'Kiddy stuff really . . . nothing to write home about.'

Kiddy stuff, Markham thought uneasily. *A case of arrested development, Burton had called their poison pen.* Deep in his bones, he suddenly felt sure that the firesetter and malicious letter writer were one and the same.

'Here's what's going to happen next, Ms Moorcroft,' he said in a flinty tone that brooked no argument. 'You will let everyone know that you've decided *not* to research Holy Martyrs for your next book.' He held up a peremptory hand to forestall objection. 'Whatever measures you planned to take for your personal protection are likely to prove inadequate should this killer decide to come after you.'

'You don't *honestly* believe that's likely, do you?' she demanded. 'Look, I figured the whole local connection was intriguing enough to be a good hook . . . the idea that someone deliberately murdered those kids and then did for the two women before burying his past — in some nice tidy house behind a privet hedge with nobody any the wiser—'

'Don' forget Coxley an' Brady makes it *six*,' Noakes cut in beadily.

'Yeah, but I mean, that would be pretty incredible, wouldn't it,' she said faintly. 'Besides, what kind of serial killer goes without killing for *decades* and then starts up again?'

'Someone with intermittent explosive disorder,' Noakes advised solemnly, having listened to many a lecture from Burton on the subject.

'Someone very dangerous indeed,' Markham echoed. In reality, of course, Sarah Moorcroft was right to challenge his premise that the deaths of Andrew Coxley and Evelyn Brady had their roots in decades-old enigmas, but if he *was* correct about there being a link, who could say what might press the killer's buttons. While on the one hand the notion of using Sarah Moorcroft to flush the killer out had its attractions, on the other, it would be irresponsible as things stood to take the risk. The best he could hope for now was to keep her safe — in spite of herself.

He eyed the novelist shrewdly. 'Is there anything else you can help us with, Ms Moorcroft?' he asked suavely.

'Like fights between Coxley an' Des O'Grady,' Noakes put in.

'Oh you know,' her laugh tinkled gratingly on Markham's ears, '*Boys Will Be Boys* . . . That was just willy-waving—'

'*You what?*' Clearly this phrase was not in Noakes's lexicon.

'Both of them doing the Alpha Male thing,' she went on with a condescending smile in the neanderthal's direction. 'Trying to be top dog in the local hairdressing stakes . . . Des is a bit . . . *forthright*, so he probably made a few digs about Andy being, well, *gender-fluid* or something.'

Spare me these liberals and their ghastly inability to tell it as it is, Markham thought, amused to note that Noakes was wearing his sturdiest Witchfinder General's expression.

'Right, so you're saying Des O'Grady was most likely homophobic,' the DI commented ruthlessly, as she blinked at his frankness. 'What about Ed Collins . . . would there have been any reason for hostility between him and O'Grady . . . sexual competition or otherwise?'

His tone was needle-sharp sarcastic and Sarah Moorcroft flushed.

'I don't know about that,' she mumbled. 'Most likely it was cos they were competing for the same clients . . . trying to outshine each other . . .'

The DI felt a pang of compunction. He shouldn't regard this vain, silly woman as an equal adversary. Whatever his personal antipathy, he needed to remember that in the current instance she was a victim. And if appearances were anything to go by, a bewildered and nonplussed victim at that.

'Hairdressing's a strange new world for us, Ms Moorcroft,' he said gently.

She looked at his rumpled sidekick as though she could well believe it.

'Dog eat dog,' he elaborated, remembering what Eileen had told them earlier that day.

'Yeah.' She was recovering some of her poise now, keen to be seen as assisting the police. 'Sandra Crowley and Becca Drew look like butter wouldn't melt, but you wouldn't believe what it's like when their claws are out.'

Markham's voice was calm and casual. 'I understand Sandra's mother Margaret was the teacher who had difficulties with Preston Taylor at Holy Martyrs,' i.e. the woman whose problems Moorcroft planned to *monetise*, 'and she might therefore have been reluctant to have you resurrect the past . . . Becca Drew likewise, since she was Margaret's niece.'

Something unhappy and uncertain flickered across the woman's face.

'That's all in the past,' she said. 'These days they're focused on their careers.'

'If you say so,' Markham replied with a noncommittal smile.

Moorcroft bristled at that. 'It's no secret Sandra thinks she can run the salon and make a better fist of it than Ed. If it comes to a run-off, I reckon she stands a good chance of taking the place over.'

'And Becca Drew?'

'If Sandra bags the top spot, most likely she'll make Becca her number two.'

'Leaving old Ed out in the cold?' Noakes suggested.

'That one will always land on his feet,' she laughed.

Markham regarded her steadily.

'Do you know anything about poison pen letters to some of Mr Coxley's elderly clients?' he asked.

She eyed him warily.

'Oh, that was just a load of hooey.'

'Not for the recipients, I imagine,' he said with a hint of steel.

'What I meant to say is, someone was obviously trying to get at Andy through his clients.'

'*You* weren't always his biggest fan,' Noakes interjected slyly. 'An' seems like you'd know how to get your own back, what with being a writer an' all.'

Her plait was swinging like a metronome.

'What are you suggesting?' in a voice from Siberia.

'Jus' that you'd be able to stir things up good an' proper,' he said unrepentantly. 'Make some of the oldies have second thoughts about using his salon.'

'If I wanted to bring down a little spiv like Andy Coxley, then believe me I'd choose a classier method than *that*,' she said heatedly. 'And there's no point badgering people about those letters cos I guarantee everyone'll close ranks and send you away with a flea in your ear. Nice old folk like Jean Gibley and the rest of them don't need upsetting with that kind of garbage.'

For the first time, Sarah Moorcroft sounded genuine and infinitely more likeable.

Standing to signal the end of the interview, she added, 'Look, I think there's some kind of *Scissorhands* show on at Hope Academy this evening—' Markham dimly recalled Olivia having mentioned this to him in passing, but he hadn't really paid much attention at the time.

'*Eh?*' Noakes gawped at her. Where did the Johnny Depp film fit into this?

'Kind of a workshop for sixth former thinking about a career in hairdressing,' she explained with weary tolerance. 'If you *really* want to pick up some more industry vibes, why not give that a go.'

And leave me the hell alone.

'I'd better get off to Rosemount,' Noakes said reluctantly once they were back outside. 'But I'm up for this evening if you an' Liv fancy a look at this workshop hoojah.'

'I don't see why not,' the DI replied. 'Might be worth a whirl.'

If Sarah Moorcroft was right, then there was little to be gained by harassing people about the poison pen campaign. Even if he avoided tackling Jean Gibley directly, he could imagine the likes of Gordon Rushworth shrivelling with embarrassment were he to broach the subject. And in any event, Monday was a day off for both *The Mane Event* and *Cutting Edge*, so the salons would be closed.

He would arrange for discreet patrols around Meadow Lane before checking in with Olivia. It surely couldn't hurt to drop in at this demonstration event or whatever it was. At the very least, Noakes's commentary was bound to be enlivening. And who knew, perhaps seeing the hairdressers busy about their professional tasks would shake something loose.

Something that would help him to catch a killer.

* * *

The *Scissorhands* show was productive of little for Markham other than gnawing jealousy as he observed how Olivia and Hope's deputy head Mathew Sullivan skirted round each other.

Was it his imagination, or was their studied avoidance of eye contact, or any sort of personal interaction, altogether *natural?* Surely a department head and member of the senior management team would normally intersect at some point . . . But no, Olivia and the lanky, bespectacled deputy exchanged barely a look or remark when it would have been almost de rigueur for them to do so.

Was there still something between Olivia and her colleague, he wondered, or was this just the self-consciousness of exes feeling uncomfortable about the past? Markham had himself at one time experienced an attraction to clinical psychologist Dr Eleanor Shaughnessy, but not enough to threaten the deep connection that he felt knotted him inextricably to Olivia. However, he was sometimes tormented by misgivings as to whether her feelings for him ran as deep.

He liked Sullivan whose *dégagé* world-weariness and irony were always entertaining. Under the skin, the man might almost be considered a soulmate of Noakes and Doggie Dickerson, such was his disdain for woke shibboleths and the PC world view. Sullivan came over to exchange a few pleasantries as soon as he spotted Markham, but it seemed to the DI he was under some constraint and the old easy affability was gone. Would this new awkwardness between them ever go away . . . ?

To the amusement of both Markham and Sullivan, Noakes staggered in with a bouquet for Olivia, like a knight of old wearing his lady's favour. Somewhat hilariously, he held the flowers awkwardly down at his side, so the soggy brown paper-wrapped offering bumped along any old how until Olivia swooped down and relieved him of his tribute.

'*George!*' she cooed. 'How incredibly thoughtful. Gil hardly ever brings me flowers, but I might have known I could count on *you!* I'm going to put them in my classroom right away.'

As his friend shuffled after her, Markham reflected that Noakes was nailing his colours firmly to the mast.

In the lists for Olivia Mullen, with the rest of them nowhere!

He was glad Kate Burton and the team — back at base trawling through witness statements and background data — weren't around to observe the spectacle. Somehow he felt he couldn't bear his "eternal triangle" to become the stuff of canteen gossip.

From the point of view of suspects, there was little to be gleaned, though he observed Stella Casey hovering on the periphery of things, huddled at one point in earnest colloquy with Ed Collins. It seemed to him there was a kind of electric tension between Collins, Sandra Crowley and Becca Drew, though this was presumably due to the fact that they each hoped to take over as manager when their salon reopened. Des O'Grady and his employees maintained a deliberate distance from *The Mane Event* team, finally bearing away the palm for 'best local hairdresser'. Not that it mattered all that much in the scheme of things, such events being all about creating a local "buzz". He was amused to observe that charity fundraiser Carol Davidson was doing her best to snaffle freebies from the various stands, though when she approached Cassie Johnson's cosmetics counter the do-gooder got decidedly short shrift.

When Olivia and Noakes rejoined him, Markham was struck by his partner's air of suppressed excitement.

With a sharp pang, noting the many eyes which followed her animated gestures, he thought that he had never seen her look more alluring, her deep-set heavy-lidded eyes sparkling as she impatiently ran a hand through the geometric bob that gave her the air of a handsome troubadour.

'*Gil,*' she hissed out of the corner of her coral-pink mouth. 'I think I've got something for you . . . I think I know who your murderer is!'

As Markham's eyes met Noakes's, his former wingman gave an emphatic nod.

The game's afoot!

CHAPTER 11: HORNETS' NEST

Markham stared at Olivia incredulously as she uttered the last name he had expected to hear.

Mindful of his murmured injunction to be discreet, she had waited until they were safely back at The Sweepstakes before embarking on the subject, while Noakes clattered away in the kitchen banging cupboards and plates as he sorted hot drinks and biscuits — no booze, however, since he decided that uncorking the Chateauneuf-du-Pape should wait until there was a suspect firmly in custody.

Padding through to the living room with the snacks, their friend plonked his booty down on a coffee table and installed himself in the comfortable armchair that he thought of almost as his by right, wondering if he would ever learn to like the array of ballet prints and figurines which adorned his friends' living room. Not all his admiration for Olivia would ever quite reconcile him to Rudolph Neveroff and the rest of them. Muriel had refrained from overt criticism, contenting herself with the reflection that poor dear Gilbert no doubt *pined* for something less *bohemian* and more *conventional*. The likes of Margot Fonteyn were fine — after all, she was an ambassador's wife and friend of Princess Margaret — but luridly made-up males with names like *Vadim* and *Sergei* were quite another matter. Him and the missus were pretty much on the same page when it came to all that malarkey, Noakes reflected.

The guvnor's voice recalled him to the present.

'What's *your* take on all this? Can you really see *Jean Gibley* as a murderess?'

The question arrested Noakes mid-reach into the Pringles can that he had requisitioned for himself. Putting it down with as much dignity as he could muster in the circumstances, he said, 'Mrs Giblet looks a bit unlikely at first glance, granted—'

'*A bit unlikely!*' It was rare that Markham lost his cool, but on this occasion he was clearly floored. 'We couldn't find anyone more respectable if we tried!'

Olivia, cross-legged on the floor at his feet (her favourite position for debate), leaned forward earnestly. 'Jean Gibley wasn't always some sweet little old lady straight out of *Miss Marple*.'

Her partner smiled wryly at this. 'I wouldn't describe her as a "sweet little old lady"—'

'More like a right old battle-axe,' Noakes interjected.

'But she's a pillar of the local community — the personification of rectitude and upright living,' Markham insisted.

'The thing is, Gil, *she wasn't always like that*,' Olivia repeated.

'Who says so?'

'I had it from Helen Mathews . . . y'know, the girl who does my hair,' she fluffed out her bob melodramatically. 'The one who gave me this makeover.'

'The stylist Andrew Coxley sacked,' Markham pointed out.

'Just hear me out.' Tucking her hair behind her ears, Olivia prepared to fight her corner. 'Jean Gibley and Evelyn Brady were boy-mad when they were at Holy Martyrs—'

'Hardly a capital offence,' he countered.

'Yes, but they apparently both had the hots for *Preston Taylor* and *Gerry Beck*,' she went on.

His gaze sharpened.

'That's right,' she said. 'The two boys who both died in accidents . . . or what everyone *presumed* were accidents. You told me Jean and Evelyn were on that trip when Preston died and they gave each other an alibi for Gerry, remember.'

'Go on,' he instructed as Noakes made another surreptitious raid on the Pringles.

'Jean and Evelyn weren't sugar and spice and all things nice . . . There were various teenage spats and some of it got quite nasty.'

'*Okay,*' Markham said slowly, 'but that's not unusual with adolescents . . . it doesn't necessarily point to homicidal tendencies.'

'*Hey, George,*' Olivia declared theatrically, 'think I need something to whet my whistle for the next bit . . . as in a splash of the red stuff.'

Markham was amused by the way disapproval contended with Noakes's usual indulgence towards Olivia, his friend disappearing into the kitchen, since it looked like the Chateauneuf-du-Pape would be making an appearance after all.

'Right,' she announced once fortified by a hefty glug, while Markham put his own glass down after barely tasting it and Noakes snapped open a can of Stella Artois, 'that's better. Feel I can focus now!'

'Stop grandstanding, Liv,' Markham chided her affectionately.

She grinned, pleased at the effect of her revelations.

'Helen said Jean Gibley got a couple of nasty anonymous letters that practically accused her of killing Preston and Gerry.'

'And how exactly did Helen know about that?' Markham demanded, his expression unreadable.

'Mark Brady confided in her one day . . . He was sympathetic over how she'd been treated by Andrew Coxley . . . thought she'd had a raw deal . . .'

'Ah, I see . . . Mr Brady was operating on the principle of "my enemy's enemy is my friend".' Markham's tone was sardonic.

'Something like that,' Olivia admitted. 'But Mark seemed genuinely disturbed and Helen's a good listener . . . His mum and Jean had both got letters and he wondered if Helen knew anything about it.'

'There *was* some sort of poison pen targeting a few of Mr Coxley's elderly female customers,' Markham said slowly.

'So Helen was on the level!' Olivia crowed triumphantly. 'It sounded so far-fetched — so Agatha Christie — I wondered if she might be exaggerating.'

'Unfortunately not,' he said grimly. 'A friend of Natalie's let slip that something of the sort had gone on.'

Olivia normally looked as though she was sucking a lemon whenever the subject of Natalie came up. But on this occasion, her devotion to the doting father won through. She smiled brightly at Noakes. 'How clever of Natalie to put you on to all of this.'

Noakes shuffled his feet and endeavoured to look modest.

'Nat likes helping the police,' he said, tapping his nose in the age-old gesture that signified a freemasonry of professional knowledge. 'Her mate has an "in" with Coxley's crowd.' He sounded absurdly proud, but Olivia's smile never wavered. '*Such* an asset, George,' she murmured, as his ears turned pink.

Markham interrupted this love-fest.

'What else did Helen Mathews tell you?' he asked, finally taking a draught of his red wine.

'That was pretty much it,' Olivia said, clearly wishing she had more nuggets to offer them. 'But it kind of ties Jean and Evelyn into your cold cases, right?' she pressed him eagerly.

'I'm not sure the DCI will see it in quite the same way,' he muttered, envisaging Sidney's likely reaction to the idea of Jean Gibley as prime suspect.

'But you'll still have to bring Jean in, won't you?' Olivia persisted.

'I need to speak to her informally first,' he replied. 'Okay, so maybe there's a connection with what happened to those two boys at Holy Martyrs.' A very big maybe in his opinion. 'But it's tenuous at best . . . and there's no obvious reason for her to go and finish off Ethel Taylor . . . still less the other woman, Jeanette O'Donnell.'

'It could have been some kind of vendetta against them, Gil.' Olivia retorted, clearly unhappy at the way her big reveal was fast receding into the realms of improbability. 'Maybe there was some festering resentment . . . to do with Preston perhaps . . . or Ethel and Jeanette could've cottoned on to her being involved in something iffy . . . So she did for them and then later maybe Evelyn tried to blackmail her, so she had to be got rid of too . . .'

'What about the murder of Andrew Coxley, Liv?' Markham asked gently, reluctant to puncture her enthusiasm but remorselessly logical in his approach. 'Surely it makes no sense for Mrs Gibley to have killed Mr Coxley when by all accounts she was utterly devoted to him.'

His partner was only momentarily disconcerted. 'That could all have been some kind of front,' she insisted. 'Designed to conceal how she really felt.' Flushed and eager, Olivia clutched at an idea. 'She might've come on to him . . . made a total fool of herself . . . he gave her the brush-off, and it was all so humiliating that she was out for revenge.'

'P'raps when Coxley died, *that's* when Evelyn got the wind up an' thought about telling the police her mate was loony tunes,' Noakes put in.

Markham's reproachful look said, *Oh, you're a fat lot of help you are.*

Noakes ploughed on undaunted.

'Mebbe if Evelyn were a loyal friend an' knew Jean had got into some kind of mess when they were at school, she could've decided to keep schtum about what went down . . . Then when the two oldies got bumped off, she wondered whether Jean had anything to do with it but looked the other way . . . kinda closed her mind to her bestie being a crazy woman . . . could've been frightened what Jean might do to *her* if she decided to make waves . . . So she kept her trap shut all those years—'

'Only then Andrew Coxley died,' Olivia burst in eagerly, 'and Evelyn knew she couldn't stay silent any longer.'

'Signed her own death warrant,' Noakes agreed solemnly.

'*Oh for heaven's sake!*' Markham exclaimed in exasperation. 'You've thought of everything . . . but there are too many hypotheticals and somehow it all sounds like a penny dreadful . . . There isn't a cat in hell's chance that Sidney will buy a word of it.' He frowned. 'I mean, the bare *idea* of Jean Gilbey sticking a pair of scissors into Coxley's neck . . . like something out of *Tosca!*'

He might have *known* the guvnor would bring opera into it, Noakes reflected dourly.

'More like *Fatal Attraction*,' Olivia suggested.

'Dimples didn't rule out a woman for Coxley,' Noakes said stubbornly.

'True,' Markham conceded. 'With the element of surprise, it could have been a woman.'

'Think about how Ethel Taylor and Jeanette O'Donnell were killed — smothered with a cushion, right?' Olivia followed up eagerly. 'That's just the sort of *genteel* method you'd expect a woman like Jean Gibley to choose . . . take the victims by surprise, press down and *finito!*'

'Yeah, jus' like Shipman.' Noakes's obsession with Britain's most prolific serial killer still burned brightly.

Markham looked at their eager faces.

'You may be on to something,' he said more mildly. 'But as things stand it's too speculative . . . certainly nowhere near enough to bring Jean Gibley in for questioning . . . And don't forget her brother . . . He's protective enough that he'll have her lawyered up in no time if we even make a move in that direction . . . Plus, there's zero forensics and she's got two solid alibis for Coxley and Mrs Brady.' He intercepted a glance between Olivia and Noakes. 'Okay, okay, *solid-ish*,' he conceded, 'but Gordon Rushworth's word has to count for something, so if he says she was at home with him then I don't see much chance of breaking him down.' He thought hard for a moment. 'Don't forget, she must have had a decent alibi for Ethel Brady and Jeanette O'Donnell too, otherwise they'd have pulled her in.'

Noakes looked dubious. 'Most likely old Gordy again,' he said. 'D'you reckon *he's* got any idea about all of this?'

Markham thought of Gordon Rushworth with his narrow, closed-in face and awful sludgy clothes. The man reminded him of a neighbour of theirs when he was a child. A prissy, prurient old fuss-budget who was a terrible busybody and made himself and Jon crack up but his mother insisted was kindness itself. Markham had reason to be grateful that the neighbour in question always looked out for his mother, hence had a certain feeling of warmth towards Jean Gibley's brother.

'I imagine he'll be shocked and appalled that we'd even *countenance* an investigation into Jean,' he said. Looking sternly at his partner and friend, he added, '*Fools Rush In*, as they say. Which is why I intend to do nothing in haste.' More kindly he continued, 'Plus, don't forget there's a host of other people with motives.'

Noakes grunted. 'Yeah,' he conceded. 'That Ed Collins an' a few others were giving us the evils back there.'

Markham quickly updated Olivia as to what they had learned about Collins's chequered past, as well as the arson attack on Sarah Moorcroft. 'So you see, Liv,' he concluded, 'there's more than just Jean Gibley in the mix . . . besides, I have some difficulty in imagining her as Ms Moorcroft's arsonist.'

'She only had to come in the back way and set a fire going, Gil,' his partner objected. 'And ringing 999's exactly what a respectable type like that would do . . . send a message to the novelist lady to back off without endangering life or limb.'

Noakes's stomach rumbled loudly.

Olivia burst out laughing. 'Feeling a bit peckish, George?'

'Well now you come to mention it . . .' Squitty little snacks were no substitute for solid nourishment.

'Right. I've got *The Lotus Garden* on speed dial,' she said with a roguish glance at her old friend. 'How about some Dim Sum to get your synapses firing.'

'Sounds like a plan.'

Indeed it did, Markham thought resignedly, somewhat grateful to have the entire Jean Gibley imbroglio shelved for the time being.

Later, however, as they munched their way through her favourite restaurant's platter of Hors D'oeuvres, Olivia returned to the attack.

'So what next then, Gil?'

He might have known she wouldn't back off for long.

'I need to speak to Jean Gibley,' he said.

'Big Brother's going to want a piece of the action.'

'You make it sound like *Goodfellas*, Noakesy. We're talking about suburban Bromgrove, remember.'

His friend speared a King Prawn and dipped it in the Kung Po sauce with an air of ineffable satisfaction.

'How 'bout you an' me pay the Giblet a visit tomorrow,' he suggested.

'Can Rosemount dispense with your services for that long, Noakesy?'

'Kev can cope,' was the firm response. 'Besides,' with a shy sidelong glance, 'I'm thinking about branching out on my own . . . mebbe starting up a private agency or summat like that . . . so it's all good experience.'

Olivia broke out delightedly, '*Seriously*, George! But that's *wonderful* . . . Isn't it, Gil?'

God help us, Sidney and the top brass are going to break into a tarantella hearing this, Markham thought.

But he was piercingly aware of his friend's anxious regard.

'Whatever you do, Noakesy, I'm with you through thick and thin.'

If Superintendent Ebury-Clarke had anything to do with it, then "thin" might be the operative word.

'Ta. 'Course it's early days . . . jus' mulling things over at the moment.'

Did he intend to make it a family concern and recruit the fair Natalie as assistant gumshoe, Olivia wondered suddenly. Come to think of it, the Pneumatic One could play a blinder on those honey trap investigations or whatever they were called . . .

Markham locked eyes with his partner, calling her to attention.

'I'm sure I speak for us both when I say we're behind you all the way, Noakesy.'

Olivia's gaze was soft.

'Any room for a Miss Moneypenny in the new enterprise, George? It'd be much more glamorous than toiling away at the chalkface.'

Seeing that his friend didn't know where to put himself, Markham reverted to business.

'Let's pay Mrs Gibley a visit tomorrow morning,' he said. 'Kate'll have to come along,' he added. 'I need an experienced female detective onside in case they start screaming about oppression.'

Noakes didn't miss the unhappy cloud that passed over Olivia's face.

'You know the way things go,' he said awkwardly. 'Any sniff of the police being heavy- handed an' them leftie lawyers'll be all over it . . . some minority focus group or whatnot will get a bandwagon going before you can say OAP.'

'Quite right, George,' she said. Markham wasn't deceived by Olivia's dazzling smile but Noakes fell for it hook, line and sinker.

Later that night, as she lay curled up in the crook of his arm, Olivia's mind was still running on the investigation. 'Is this *really* it, Gil?' she wanted to know. 'Is Jean Gibley the key to all those murders?'

What could he say?

'Somehow it feels like the end of the beginning, Liv.'

As he lay still in the darkness, listening to her soft breathing, Markham's thoughts drifted to his pool of suspects and the hard-eyed stares of Andrew Coxley's staff as they watched him head for the exit earlier that evening.

Could an elderly woman really be behind those long-ago deaths at Holy Martyrs and the murders of Ethel Taylor and Jeanette O'Donnell . . . to say nothing of CID's most recent homicides . . . Despite his initial instinct that answers lay with the cold case enquiry, going after Jean Gibley somehow felt like the wildest of wild goose chases.

And where the hell did the poison pen campaign fit in? Was Jean Gibley behind that as well? Had she sent hate mail to herself so no-one would suspect she was behind it all? And what was her motive in the first place?

They needed to make her or that dry stick of a brother crack asap. Otherwise, they might conceivably end up facing the heftiest lawsuit in the history of Bromgrove CID.

Sarah Moorcroft was safe for now, while tomorrow's priority was a make or break interview with the unlikeliest suspect in his experience as a detective.

Pray God he didn't screw everything up . . .

* * *

Tuesday morning found Markham, Noakes and Kate Burton parked around the corner from 4 Porlock Drive.

Burton listened attentively and without interruption as Markham expounded the latest theory. At the conclusion of his recital, she observed, 'Perhaps best to give the impression we're focused on the cold case enquiry . . . After all, that's perfectly true seeing as we're liaising with DCI Moriarty and DI Hart about Holy Martyrs . . . By the way, do they even know we're looking at Jean as a suspect?'

'I called Moriarty this morning,' Markham told her. 'As you might expect, he was a bit startled.' Understatement of the century. 'They're going to review all the Holy Martyrs background material — see if there are any former pupils knocking around who might be able to shed light on the playground politics . . . Possibly over time they could have wondered whether Jean or Evelyn had anything to do with those deaths, so it's worth trying to jog memories.'

'Most of 'em will have snuffed it,' Noakes said mordantly.

Burton sighed. 'Ever the ray of sunshine, aren't you sarge.'

'*Jus' saying!*' Then, 'Giblet's *bound* to smell a rat, 'specially if you bring Evelyn into it an' she twigs this is really all about Coxley an' the salon.'

'That's a risk we'll have to take, Noakesy.' A risk that he was aware could backfire spectacularly. 'I want to get a feel for her mental state. Things could get extremely dangerous if she's round the bend and we don't get a handle on the situation . . . *fast*.'

'Even if Jean's implicated in what happened to those boys and the two local women, Coxley and Evelyn could be down to someone else.' Burton ruminated.

'*Two* ruddy nutters, thass all we need!' Noakes groaned.

Burton appeared troubled. 'Well, if she's the killer, it's strange to think of Jean's murderous impulses lying dormant for so many years before somehow getting reactivated.'

'It could be intermittent explosive disorder,' came the solemn reply.

She blinked rapidly before breaking into a surprised smile. 'You're right, sarge. I was forgetting about incubation and cooling-off periods . . . Funny that . . . Nathan and I were only talking about it last night. He's writing a paper on biopsychosocial factors including time frames.'

Noakes grunted noncommittally. Poor old Shippers, he thought. Boffin talk was probably Burton's idea of foreplay.

Her thoughts turned from academic theories to more immediate practical difficulties.

'What if her brother tries to close us down?' she asked. 'They're both fairly on the ball and he's bound to see where this is going.'

'Can't we get him out of the way somehow?' Noakes said. 'Get the library to ring up and tell him his books are overdue or summat . . . He'd be round there in a flash, all steamed up in case he gets a fine.' He chuckled evilly. '*Outraged of Bromgrove*.'

Markham was hard-pressed not to laugh as he contemplated this unlikely student of human nature. Then suddenly, he stiffened.

'Looks like we may not have to resort to any ruses after all,' he murmured.

Their eyes followed his gaze.

'So Gordy's off out for a walk,' Noakes observed as they watched the stoop-shouldered elderly man on the opposite side of the road. Instinctively, the trio slouched down in their seats until they were sure he had disappeared from sight.

Then without further ado they headed for the house that he had just left . . .

As Markham had feared, the conversation with Jean Gibley did not go smoothly.

The angular purse-faced woman with her Olive Oyl colouring gave him a distinctly uncomfortable feeling, but he could have sworn she appeared genuinely bewildered by their carefully worded enquiries about Holy Martyrs. Even with Burton exercising utmost tact and circumlocution, Jean Gibley visibly bristled at their 'intrusive questions about sad events that she preferred to forget'. Two spots of red burned on her cheeks like warning beacons as she demanded 'what on earth they supposed she could tell them about tragic accidents that had long since been fully investigated by the *proper authorities*'. Her emphasis on the last two words, accompanied by a basilisk glare at Noakes, was eloquent in its contempt for the current proceedings. She professed indignation at the suggestion that she and Evelyn Brady had any romantic interest in the two boys who had died and poured scorn on the idea that either of them might have 'gone creeping around in the middle of the night' at Colomendy.

When Burton introduced the subject of Ethel Taylor and Jeanette O'Donnell, the woman drew herself up into a long column, positively quivering with rage.

'What may I ask has that got to do with *me*?' she demanded.

'Just one of our cold cases, Mrs Gibley,' Burton said in her most emollient tone. 'We're assisting colleagues by speaking to people who might have crossed paths with those ladies. And since you and Evelyn knew Mrs Taylor's son . . .'

Suddenly Jean's eyes turned bright with suspicion.

'This isn't just about Holy Martyrs, is it?' she accused them. 'You're thinking I might have something to do with what happened to poor Andrew Coxley and *my best friend*.'

It was at that juncture — before they even had a chance to broach the poison pen campaign — that Gordon Rushworth, who had just been out to post a letter, returned.

For all that he looked like an old bird, looking anxiously from his sister to the three visitors, the man had a certain dignity as he asked them stiffly to leave.

'Well that went well,' Noakes declared sarcastically once they were back in Markham's car.

Burton's shoulders were hunched as if she was repressing a shudder. 'What a depressing house,' she commented. 'Doyle was right about it being like a morgue.'

'Wonder if it's hers or she owns it jointly with Gordy,' Noakes speculated idly.

Burton cast her mind back. 'One of the girls at *Cutting Edge* said she bought it after her husband died and then he moved in with her.' Guiltily, she added, 'Everyone seemed quite fond of them . . . It didn't feel right implying that she could be a murderer.'

Markham recalled Des O'Grady's favourable impression of the brother and sister.

'Somehow I don't think Mr Rushworth is going to take this lying down,' he said heavily. 'Let's get back to base and see if Doyle and Carruthers have anything useful for us.'

Before Bromgrove high command went on the warpath and took the case away from them.

* * *

Markham's office felt like a bunker as the team plus Noakes convened hastily for a council of war, Burton carefully closing the blinds that offered a modicum of privacy in the station's open-plan CID offices.

Carruthers was visibly excited, his usual carefully cultivated nonchalance abandoned as he said, 'We may have got something, sir.'

Seeing his intensity, Markham sensed something unusual was in the offing and felt a faint stirring of hope.

'We were going through the Holy Martyrs cold case stuff again,' Carruthers said nodding towards the duplicate files that DCI Moriarty had supplied. 'There was this schoolkid they interviewed and drew a blank . . . name of David Blaketon.'

'David was there with Preston Taylor, Gerry Beck and the rest of them,' Doyle explained. 'But later on after school he sort of dropped out . . . mental breakdowns then in and out of the Newman,' he went on, referring to the large psychiatric hospital situated behind Bromgrove General on the outskirts of town. An architectural mishmash of gothic and modernist design, the facility had played a part in previous investigations, inspiring the two sergeants with a mixture of repulsion and fascination. 'Well anyway,' the DS continued, aware that Noakes was becoming restive, 'he was a pretty unstable character . . . The police had another crack at him when Ethel Taylor and Jeanette O'Donnell were murdered, but it looked like he was alibied . . . family swore blind he was at home both times and nothing would budge 'em . . . And besides, the local GP weighed in and said there was no chance of David doing anything like that.'

'Why're you so worked up about this loser then?' Noakes demanded belligerently.

'He's in assisted accommodation now over at Eldred Court,' Carruthers took over. 'When we checked in with his care worker, she said he'd been really agitated over the salon murder . . . kept hinting that he knew something about a killer . . . talked about "a secret from the past".'

'An' she didn't think to tell the police!' Never a fan of social services, Noakes was unimpressed.

Carruthers rolled his eyes. 'She said if she had a fiver every time one of her service users claimed to know about a murder, then she'd be a millionaire. Besides, when she played along with it and asked what he meant — kind of humouring him — David got all anxious and furtive cos the killer said he'd come after him if he ever blabbed.'

Doyle nodded vigorously. 'She didn't reckon anything to it initially . . . But when we told her we were doing a cold case investigation with possible links to Coxley and Evelyn Brady, she wondered if David might really know something after all.'

'How stable is he these days?' Markham wanted to know. 'Given the medical profile, we can't be sure he's reliable.'

'Doing really well apparently,' Carruthers replied. 'Spells of grandiose delusional disorder, which is why the carer didn't take much notice when he started spouting about knowing a killer. But he's had a range of interventions and is in a stable phase . . . even has a part-time job at Medway food bank.'

The DI was beginning to catch some of their excitement.

It sounded as if this might, *just might*, be the break he was looking for.

Burton's voice cut into his thoughts. 'You said *he*,' she told Carruthers. 'As in the killer said *he'd* come after David if he ever blabbed.'

'Christ,' Noakes groused. 'Here we've been giving old mother Giblet the third degree and now it turns out she's in the clear.' Then catching Markham's eye, 'Sorry guv, but it ain't great timing.'

'All of this might turn out to be a false lead,' the DI said levelly. 'On the other hand, it doesn't look like this David is some kind of attention-seeker or fantasist seeing as the carer reckoned he was genuinely frightened and clammed up when she asked for details.'

'Are we going to bring him in, boss?' Carruthers pressed.

'Once Kate has lined up an appropriate adult and ticked the various safeguarding boxes, then yes,' Markham replied simply.

'What about Sidney?' Doyle wanted to know, anxious that their guns shouldn't be spiked.

'After we've spoken to David, hopefully we should have a prime suspect to serve up,' Markham replied calmly, praying that neither Jean Gibley nor her brother would have been on the blower to his boss.

It was a vain hope.

At that very moment, the telephone on his desk rang.

The DCI practically came down the line in his fury.

'I want you in my office *right now*, Inspector, to discuss a *very serious* complaint of police harassment,' he honked. 'Unless you can provide me with a satisfactory explanation for this morning's antics, then I'm taking you off this case.'

Markham replaced the receiver with a careful deliberation that let Kate Burton know he badly wanted to smash it into his superior officer's smug face.

All he said, however, was, 'Bring David Blaketon in *now* while I go and tell the DCI that we're on the brink of snaring a six-times killer.'

He knew it sounded melodramatic, but if the prospect of forensic glory didn't get Sidney off his back, he didn't know what would!

CHAPTER 12: OVER THE TOP

Markham was breathing heavily as he returned to his office some time later on Tuesday afternoon, collecting Kate Burton (from her neighbouring cubicle) and Noakes (from the canteen) en route.

One look at the DI's face as they drew up chairs told them that he had, as Noakes was wont to put it, gone ten rounds with Sidney.

'Tricky?' Burton ventured.

'That's one word for it,' came the terse reply. Markham's pale, patrician features were taut with the strain of placating his boss, while it seemed to Burton that new lines had sprung up round his mouth and the dark rings under his eyes were more pronounced than usual.

'Well, did he buy it?' Noakes demanded, never one for finesse.

'I've got forty-eight hours to make an arrest, otherwise Superintendent Bretherton will take over.'

Noakes snorted. 'Oh well then, if it's down to the People's Peeler, there's nothing to worry about,' he said, sarcastically referencing a nickname bestowed by Gavin Conors. Normally the ex-DS and *Gazette* hack were daggers drawn, but their estimation of 'Blithering' Bretherton was broadly similar, Conors having incurred the superintendent's lasting enmity with a cutting pen portrait entitled *And Plod Those Feet*.

'The thing about Bretherton is, he won't antagonise anyone,' was Burton's gloomy verdict. She pulled a face. 'A "safe pair of hands" and all that.'

'So what happened . . . old Gordy have a whinge, did he?' Noakes wanted to know. 'Come out swinging to defend baby sis?'

'Something like that,' Markham answered wearily. 'Apparently he and Jean are generous contributors to the North West Police Benevolent Fund . . . their uncle was an inspector down south somewhere, so according to Sidney that means they belong to the "extended police family".'

Noakes mimed throwing up as Burton smiled weakly.

His voice hard, Markham continued, 'Plus, as Ebury-Clarke was swift to point out, they are "people of substance" in Bromgrove.'

'You could've fooled me,' Noakes said, remembering the depressing house in Porlock Drive which looked as though nothing had been spent on it in a very long time.

'What did Sidney think to us bringing in batty Dave?' he went on, ignoring Burton's chastising frown.

A cool smile flickered across Markham's face.

'Obviously I played down the "battiness", Noakes, and focused on our belief that Mr Blaketon has vital information which will help us to identify a murderer . . . *a multiple murderer.*'

'Bigged him up then,' Noakes nodded approvingly.

'Correct.'

Despite his ordeal with the powers that be, the guvnor looked as chilled as if he'd just stepped out of a refrigerator, Noakes thought admiringly. He could only imagine how all that pinstriped elegance went down with Sidney and Toad Face. He'd had it from the desk sergeant (in strictest confidence) that some woman from the *Gazette* had been badgering the press office saying she wanted to do a piece on

Markham and calling him a 'moody heartthrob'. If that ever happened, The Ugly Sisters really *would* go into orbit.

A stern glance from Burton made him realise that he was grinning like an ape.

Hastily, he said, 'Okay, so what's the plan?'

'I've been on to Eldred Court,' Burton told them crisply. 'The care worker Sharon Dench is bringing David in around half four. I've let social services know what's going down. They said best just to have Sharon sit in on the interview as the appropriate adult otherwise he might be overwhelmed . . . He's developed a good rapport with her apparently and she's laid the groundwork . . . told him he's not in any trouble and we'll keep him safe, but laid it on about how he can't keep secrets because it looks like the person he's afraid of has killed several people and there's a chance more might die . . . He seemed to take it all on board.'

'Think he might go wobbly on us?' Noakes didn't appear as if he had much confidence in their key witness coming up to proof.

'The FME's going to check him over before we get started . . . see that he's up to it. With breaks and the rest of it, he should be fine,' Burton assured them before adding firmly, 'We can't go in mob-handed, sarge, so you and the other two will be next door behind the two-way mirror.'

'Fine by me,' Noakes said affably. Then more doubtfully, 'D'you reckon this is *really* it then, guv, even though Mrs Giblet was shaping up nicely as prime suspect?' He sounded almost wistful.

The DI raked a hand through his thick dark hair. 'When we called round at her house, it felt almost as though I was seeing everything through the lens of a telescope held the wrong way . . . like a distorted reality.'

Burton was interested. 'You mean you still think Jean Gibley's the key to it all, guv?'

'I'm not sure, Kate . . . Only that when we were with her, I had the feeling *she* was the one who could lead us to the monster in the maze.'

Noakes wasn't sure he liked the sound of this. Some sort of highbrow reference which, judging from the gloopy look on Burton's face, meant he was in for a whole load of boffin talk.

But Markham caught his expression.

'You're all right, Noakesy,' he said evenly. 'I'm not going to come over all metaphysical.'

His friend didn't care to be thought of as being outside the literary loop. 'You'll make the maze collapse an' the monster die,' he said firmly, just to show that Burton wasn't the only one who grasped metaphors.

As this comical declaration of belief fell on his ears, Markham smiled his first genuine smile of the day. He crossed over to the window, momentarily forgetting where he was. Outside, pedestrians were sauntering in the early afternoon sunshine, the day having turned unexpectedly balmy. CID, by contrast, felt claustrophobic as if a caul stretched across it dividing him from normal humanity, without a chink to admit either light or air. And now he was preparing for an encounter with something deformed and monstrous . . . an abortion of humanity.

He turned back to the others.

'Let's get set up for Mr Blaketon.'

'Do we need a script, sir?' Burton never liked anything too extempore.

'We'll follow Ms Dench's lead,' he said quietly. 'Reinforce the message that he's perfectly safe but we desperately need his help to catch this killer . . . If he suffers from bipolar grandiosity, that's most likely the best way to frame it.'

'A messiah complex,' Burton breathed at the same time as Noakes muttered 'white knight syndrome'.

'Well, some form of narcissistic personality disorder,' Markham agreed.

His fellow DI's mind was racing. 'Psychologists used to think that someone with NPD couldn't identify with other people's emotions or vulnerability even though they might be able to understand it at a rational level. But nowadays things aren't so clear-cut . . . it depends where they are on the spectrum and what kind of treatment they've had . . . Nathan says it's all bound up with shame-avoidance, so if someone feels safe and secure they're more likely to open up.'

To put it in a nut-house, what she meant was the trick cyclists didn't have a clue, Noakes thought sourly. *All the Gear, No Idea*. Next thing they knew, she'd be tracing bleeding NPD back to prehysterical times and boring them all rigid with statistics from that big fat manual she carted everywhere.

'You can take that look off your face, Noakesy,' Markham laughed. 'Mr Blaketon's made significant progress according to Carruthers, so provided we adopt a *non-judgmental* and *sympathetic* approach, he should be able to tell us about Mister X.'

Mister X. He felt a strange insistent singing in his ears as he said the words. It seemed to grow louder and more insistent until the stale fug of his office and even Noakes's mutinous stare were quite blotted out.

With an effort, he recalled himself to the present.

'Mr Blaketon is our best hope of catching this killer,' he said quietly. 'If the man's been fearful all this time, it may come as a tremendous relief to unburden himself to us.'

Typical of the guvnor to pity some screwball who'd kept schtum while people were being bumped off, Noakes reflected crossly, wondering if there was a label for folk who had *too much* empathy. Burton was just as bad if it came to that, but he admitted to himself she was the best choice to interview Blaketon. *He'd* likely have spent the whole time fighting an urge to give the sick twist a thick ear.

After Burton had bustled off to prepare the interview room they reserved for vulnerable adults, Markham and Noakes sat in reflective silence for some time.

Noakes had a weird feeling that his friend already knew the name Blaketon was going to give them. It was there in Markham's pallor and the fixed look on his handsome face.

A premonition or something. The kind of fey oddness that Sidney *hated* but that he had come to accept as part and parcel of what made the guvnor special.

However, he knew better than to ask.

All he said was, 'I'll let your Liv know it'll be an all-nighter.'

Markham nodded. Whatever the outcome of their session with Blaketon, this was the investigation's crisis point. He experienced a spasm of self-contempt that he was leaving it to Noakes to brief Olivia, but he needed all his strength for the final push.

Like a soldier going over the top.

* * *

'Pinch me, I must be dreaming.'

'Bloody hell, did he *really* just say that?'

Markham might have intuited what David Blaketon was going to tell them, but Carruthers and Doyle were thunderstruck.

Doyle shook his head.

'It can't be right,' he muttered, stunned by what he had heard. 'The bloke's gotta be a fantasist or something.' Even Carruthers, previously optimistic about the interview with Blaketon, appeared disconcerted.

The door to the viewing room opened and Kate Burton appeared.

'We're giving him a break,' she said, looking drained. As well she might. 'The boss has gone upstairs to brief Sidney.' And to make sure there was no risk of Bretherton getting dumped on them.

Doyle continued to stare incredulously at David Blaketon through the two-way viewing mirror. 'Mad as a box of frogs, right sarge?' he murmured, appealing to Noakes.

But Markham's former wingman said hollowly, 'I reckon he's on the level.'

Silently, they returned to contemplation of Markham's key witness. With his watery unfocused blue eyes, sallow complexion, dead-looking hair which lay in wisps across his head and diminutive stature, the man could hardly have been more unprepossessing. But, 'I think he's telling the truth,' Noakes said finally.

'So do I.' Burton's voice had a ring of certainty.

'Just let me just get this straight.' Doyle looked around at his colleagues as though to say, *If I believe this, then I'll believe anything*. 'Gordon Rushworth — Mister Prim and Proper, so upright he's probably never even got a parking ticket — was secretly into boys when he was a schoolkid . . . so when Gerry Beck knocked him back on that trip to Colomendy, he pushed the lad down a well.'

Seeing that his colleague appeared lost for words, Carruthers took over the story as recounted by Blaketon. 'Gordon blackmailed David into saying nothing about how he'd snuck out of their room in the middle of the night . . . threatened to tell everyone it was *David* who had a motive for murder because he was infatuated with Gerry . . . plus, Gordon had the love letters or whatever they were to prove it.'

'How the fuck did he get hold of *those*?' Doyle asked, bemused.

'*Language*,' Burton snapped. Then, more mildly, 'Sounds as though Gerry was friendly enough with Gordon to have shared David's, er, billets doux.'

'Passed 'em around for cheap laughs,' Noakes said sagely.

'Gordon was every bit as hung up on Gerry,' Burton suggested. 'But far cleverer about hiding it . . . and much more manipulative.'

'So Gerry shared the juicy details of David's sad little crush,' Carruthers reasoned, 'without any idea that *Gordon* was the dangerous one.'

'Correct,' Burton said.

'Are we saying Gordon's gay then?' Doyle enquired.

'The Gay Gordons,' Noakes retorted. 'You couldn't make it up.'

The two sergeants sniggered at the feeble witticism but Burton, unusually, didn't reprove them, conscious that her colleagues were struggling to make sense of a bizarre scenario.

'I think Gordon Rushworth may have been conflicted about his sexuality and morbidly sensitive to rejections or slights,' she said. 'Once Gerry got a whiff of Gordon's *own* interest and rebuffed him, the torch paper was lit . . . And then history repeated itself, which is how Preston Taylor ended up getting shoved over a cliff . . .'

'Okay, but even if that's true, why would Gordon have killed Ethel Taylor and that other woman . . . Jeanette O'Donnell?' Doyle demanded.

'Continuing rage at Preston perhaps,' Burton said thoughtfully. 'A desire to punish everyone connected with him . . . And maybe the two women had started to wonder about Gordon. Where Jeanette was concerned, perhaps there was jealousy in the mix as well, on account of her being a success in the academic world whereas *he* never achieved his full potential and ended up a mere schoolteacher at a mediocre comprehensive.'

'*Hey,*' Noakes was struck by a thought,' Gordy taught at Medway High—'

'And Andrew Coxley was a pupil there,' Burton finished soberly. 'Quite possibly Coxley being Jean's hairdresser stirred up all kinds of bad memories.'

'How come?' Doyle asked.

'Back in the day, he could've made fun of Gordon and exposed him to ridicule at Medway,' Burton suggested. 'Students can be very cruel that way . . . And when they encountered each other again at the salon, there may have been some latent attraction on Gordon's side, which resurrected sexual impulses he thought were buried forever.'

'So Rushworth was *closeted*?' Carruthers enquired cautiously.

'I think it's very likely,' Burton replied. 'And if he'd constructed an alternative identity — elderly, well-off bachelor who might be considered something of a catch by the women in Jean's circle — then if someone ripped up that image he had of himself, it could well have triggered an aggressive response.'

'You reckon that's what happened with Evelyn Brady, ma'am?' Carruthers asked. He only ever resorted to 'ma'am' when the stakes were high.

'We'll probably never know what happened between them,' Burton said soberly. 'But I think in their final encounter she may have mocked him and held up a mirror to the truth—'

'D'you think Evelyn was somehow on to him?' Carruthers pressed.

'I think when Andrew Coxley was murdered she may have *sensed* something about Gordon, without knowing what it was that made her uneasy . . . If she believed he was the killer, she would have come straight to the police, so it wasn't that . . . But her instincts — maybe her memories of Holy Martyrs where they were both pupils — were letting her know that something wasn't right . . .'

'Only her mind recoiled from the idea that he could be a murderer,' Carruthers said eagerly. 'She just couldn't equate what her instincts were telling her with the notion that he was dangerous.'

'Too much of a coward to face anything unpleasant,' Noakes concluded brutally. 'But she must've said summat that made Gordy panic an' decide she had to go.'

'Let's assume that Gordon's feelings for Coxley were intensely conflicted,' Burton said. 'There may have been a latent homosexual attraction, but it was all bound up with resentment of Coxley's freewheeling bachelor lifestyle and charisma, to say nothing of the way he had all those women — including his own sister — eating out of his hand. With all of that in the mix, if Evelyn said something that was psychologically threatening to him, it wouldn't take much for him to lose control.'

'Yeah,' Carruthers visualised the scenario, 'if Evelyn started drivelling on about Coxley being the best thing since sliced bread and making tactless comparisons, that could've set him off . . . especially if he'd flattered himself that she might be interested in him . . . hell, he may even have come on to her and then she laughed in his face.'

Despite himself, Doyle warmed to this narrative.

'Gordon could have issues round strong women,' he suggested. 'After all, it's his sister who owns their house . . .

and Evelyn Brady was another moneybags . . . it might've ended up making him feel inadequate . . . *emasculated.*'

'I remember Des O'Grady's receptionist telling me that Andrew Coxley did wickedly funny impersonations,' Burton told them. 'It wouldn't surprise me if his repertoire included Gordon . . .'

'If he got to hear about it, he would have resented Coxley even more,' Carruthers suggested.

Burton's eyes wandered to the listless figure of David Blaketon sitting in the adjacent room sipping his cup of tea and making desultory conversation with the care worker who struggled to maintain her expression of bright professional interest.

'Obviously David can only speak to what happened when they were students at Holy Martyrs,' she said thoughtfully, 'but at least he's positive that he saw Gordon push Preston Taylor—'

'An' he's smashed Gordy's alibi for Gerry Beck,' Noakes finished.

'So he's given us enough of a foundation to argue that he killed both boys,' Burton continued. 'Then there's his claim that Gordon tracked him down years later and threatened to silence him forever if he breathed a word to anyone.'

'Plus Gordy boasted about finishing off a couple of uppity old crones who were too clever for their own good,' Noakes pointed out. 'He must've meant Ethel Taylor an' Jeanette O'Donnell . . . an' it scared poor Dave shitless.' The ex-DS was slowly coming round to Markham's compassionate assessment of their key witness who cut a pathetic figure, almost swallowed up by the oversized cream armchair reserved for vulnerable interviewees.

'Why the heck didn't David tell one of the teachers about what happened at Colomendy?' Doyle asked wonderingly. 'If he'd done that, then maybe Preston and the rest would still be alive.'

'He was this geeky little misfit who thought Gordon would fit him up for Gerry Beck,' Carruthers said. 'And let's face it, who was going to believe what would have sounded like some cock and bull story made up by an attention-seeker.

In those days they weren't up to speed on special needs and all that.'

'As for what happened to Preston . . . like David said back there,' Burton jerked her head towards the viewing window, 'it was just him, Preston and Gordon on that ledge together . . . They were out of sight of the rest and it happened so fast that afterwards he couldn't even be sure what he'd seen . . . It was only because of Colomendy that he was certain Gordon pushed Preston to his death.'

'God, what a bloody mess,' Doyle sighed. 'And David's not exactly impressive . . . I don't see the CPS getting excited about him.'

'Poor sod,' Carruthers said unexpectedly. 'He's wearing a hearing aid, so must be deaf as well.'

They contemplated their star witness through the viewing panel in profound gloom until Noakes attempted to lighten the mood.

'There's these two blokes and one goes, "Fred, do you want to go shares in me new invention?" "What is it?" "A new type of hearing aid." "Hearing aid?" "Yeah, it's this little piece of wire — you put it in your ear an' everybody shouts."'

The two sergeants grinned, and even Burton had to smile.

'What's the position with David's NPD meds?' Carruthers asked, mindful that physical disability was one thing but a personality disorder quite another.

'He's taking Prozac but that's it,' Burton replied. 'No antipsychotics or anything like that. He has a CBT session every other week plus psychotherapy top-ups. Okay, he's got flat affect but that's part of his condition . . . As far as it goes, he's pretty coherent.'

'But his story's so freaking *incredible*,' Doyle demurred. 'I mean, can you just imagine Sidney's reaction. If he blew a gasket over the idea of it being Jean, what's he going to say about *Gordon*?' The ginger ninja was troubled. 'The bloke comes across like Foggy in *Last of the Summer Wine* — and before you say anything, my nan likes it — kind of dead upright and leader-of-men . . .'

Noakes spluttered. 'Leader of men my backside,' he guffawed. 'That one was army catering corps . . . The only action *he* ever saw was handing out tins of spam.'

Doyle grinned. 'You know what I mean, sarge. David looks like this total deadbeat while Gordon's ultra-respectable . . . totally pukka.'

Carruthers looked sardonic. 'And don't forget the police connection . . . his uncle being an inspector and the rest of it.'

'David's story about Holy Martyrs hangs together,' Burton insisted. 'Okay, so the man's got a mental health condition, but he's coping with it. He doesn't have a police record or anything like that, which helps.'

'Wasn't he in the frame for Ethel Taylor and Jeanette O'Donnell, though?' Doyle asked. 'I mean, didn't our lot get the wind up about him?'

'They couldn't break his alibi,' Carruthers reminded him. 'And the GP was positive David couldn't have done it.'

'He's credible on Holy Martyrs and the cold cases,' Burton reiterated. 'And if he's telling the truth about *that*, then Gordon Rushworth has to be our prime suspect for Andrew Coxley and Evelyn Brady.' She fixed her colleagues with a determined stare. 'He may look too womanish and prissy to have done it, but in each case there was the element of surprise and the posing of Coxley definitely points to some kind of psychosexual hang-up . . . If Gordon's a repressed homosexual with a secret fear of strong women, it's not such a stretch to imagine him as the killer.'

'It's hunch territory,' Doyle mumbled.

'It's a lead,' Burton amended firmly.

As she said this, Markham joined them. He looked absolutely wrung out, Burton thought, but she could see from the set of his jaw and something unwavering in the dark eyes that he had won the battle with Sidney. Being no stranger to dirty fighting where necessary, the DI wouldn't have pulled his punches in making the case for an operation to trap Gordon Rushworth . . . the elusive salon killer. She felt a warm sense of triumph wash over her along with a profound relief that they were at last on the home straight.

Markham watched the trio with an idle smile playing about his lips, but his gaze was razor sharp.

'I take it you've been weighing all the variables,' he said.

'Yes, boss. But is Sidney really onside with it?' Doyle blurted.

The DI gave a brief, bitter bark of laughter.

'After a fashion,' he rasped. 'Though if Mr Blaketon isn't the genuine article, I may well end my days directing traffic.'

Noakes smirked. *As if!*

'What's the plan, guv?' he demanded.

'David's going to get in touch with Gordon and invite him over to Eldred Court,' Markham announced as coolly as if they were discussing the weather.

With a thin-lipped smile as he looked through the two-way mirror, he continued, 'You heard him say Gordon's kept track of his whereabouts down the years and always made sure they had each other's contact details—'

'In case Dave got any funny ideas about splitting on Gordy,' Noakes growled.

'Exactly,' Markham nodded. 'Well, now he gives Gordon the idea it's crunch time and he's gearing up to do just that.'

'So we stake out David's accommodation in advance,' Carruthers said eagerly. 'Wire him for sound and listen in.'

'Exactly.'

'What's David going to say to Gordon?' Doyle asked.

'That his nerves are in bits and he just *knows* Gordon killed Andrew Coxley and Evelyn Brady . . . he can't stand the strain of keeping the past bottled up and it's driving him mad . . . wants Gordon to confess to the police blah blah.' Burton had it off pat.

Doyle's brow was furrowed. 'Won't Gordon be suspicious?'

'He has no reason to think we're interested in David and the cold cases,' Markham pointed out. 'I'm guessing he'll show his true colours when David starts ranting and raving about Holy Martyrs and the past.' He locked eyes with each of them in term. 'As in he'll threaten to expose David as an accessory to Gerry Beck's murder — possibly Preston Taylor's as well.'

'We need to get him on tape acknowledging that he killed those boys along with Ethel and Jeanette . . . in addition to implicating himself for Coxley and Evelyn.' Burton frowned. 'It's asking a lot of David.'

'That's where the grandiosity helps us,' Markham said quietly. 'We encourage him to see himself as literally our only hope of calling a halt to Gordon's murderous career. His narcissism will do the rest, because it's likely he wants to pay Gordon back for the way his life has turned out and all the mental difficulties.'

'You don't think Gordon will try to kill David?' Doyle wondered.

'He'll know that's a non-starter because Eldred Court's covered by CCTV,' Carruthers answered. 'His best option is to try the same bully-boy tactics as before.'

'Only this time *we'll* be listening,' Noakes said complacently.

'There's an outside chance Gordon might hold back and decide to attack David somewhere away from his sheltered accommodation,' Markham said. 'But I think with his long-standing psychological dominance, he'll be confident of talking him out of any plans to go to the police. Of course, if he doesn't play ball, David might eventually be lined up for an "accident" . . . just like Gerry and Preston.' It was a chilling thought.

Markham turned to his fellow DI. 'Right, let's get in there and talk them through it,' he said. 'If all goes well, the techies will set up at Eldred later tonight and then David makes his call to Gordon tomorrow morning asking him to come round in the afternoon.'

'I'll ask Nathan to help with prompts for David,' Burton said evenly.

'Excellent. I also want round-the-clock surveillance on 4 Porlock Drive. Not only do I believe Gordon Rushworth is a dangerous killer, I think he was behind the poison pen campaign — a covert way of tormenting Jean and other women he resented for their fawning devotion to Andrew Coxley.'

'And the arson attack on Sarah Moorcroft?' Burton asked.

'That too,' Markham replied grimly. 'Her interest in Holy Martyrs had rattled him — too close to home — so he tried to warn her off.'

Markham smiled at his colleague, trying to raise her energy level. 'Once more unto the breach,' he exhorted.

After they had left, Doyle turned to Carruthers.

'Reckon the boss can pull it off?'

'He'd better. If he screws up, it won't just be a case of getting busted down to Traffic.'

It was a sobering thought for the two young men who had hitched their star to Markham's.

To their credit, however, potential career suicide wasn't at the forefront of their minds.

Nailing the salon killer was all that counted.

CHAPTER 13: ENDPIECE

Markham had a restless night and ended up pacing his study in the small hours of Wednesday morning.

In his dreams, while Olivia slept oblivious beside him, he found himself lying at the bottom of a dank well. After repeated attempts, he somehow dragged himself out of its slime-covered depths to the surface. But then, as he lay gasping half-out and half-in, a dark figure with a vice-like grip clamped his shoulders and thrust him back down.

He never saw his attacker's face.

Rationally, he knew his thoughts had been running on Gerry Beck, the teenager thrust into an abandoned well in Colomendy and callously left to drown, hence the nightmare. There was a perfectly logical explanation, but he still felt odd: light-headed and weightless as though trapped in a floatation tank.

Olivia crept down around 5 am, bringing a cup of strong black coffee.

He slumped into the chair behind his desk as she perched on the edge.

'Sorry I didn't ring last night,' he murmured.

Her hand reached for his. 'No worries. George said there'd been a breakthrough and filled me in.' Softly, she asked, 'Was it a surprise?'

'Somehow, deep down, I must've known it was Gordon Rushworth when I went to his sister's house that second time,' Markham told her. 'There was something in the atmosphere . . . something foul and rotten that felt like a flood of poison swamping everything. I think even *she* sensed it—'

'Sensed her brother was a killer?'

'Had the feeling something wasn't right . . . but she was afraid to face it . . . I think her instincts were telling her loud as a ringing bell that something was badly wrong with Gordon, but her mind slid away from the truth because it was just too awful to take in.'

'I suppose she knew him better than anyone else,' Olivia said, wondering what secrets the siblings might have shared.

'They went to the same school and she could have guessed his latent attraction to boys like Gerry Beck and Preston Taylor . . . confident, virile, popular lads who were all that he could never hope to be.'

'D'you reckon she realised that he had killed them?'

If she did, thought Markham grimly, then Jean Gibley had the blood of four other victims on her conscience.

'I think she scented danger but just wasn't strong enough to grasp the thread and let it lead her to the truth.'

The monster in the maze.

Quietly they looked out onto the neighbouring municipal graveyard as long grey streaks of daylight illumined the Victorian obelisks and monuments. Olivia smiled as she recalled her childhood obsession with claiming tombstones and monuments as *hers*. Her parents had been concerned about this trait being 'unwholesome' until the local vicar put their minds at rest and told them she was welcome to come and contemplate the local resting places whenever she liked.

'It's kind of weird. Rushworth sounds like Doc Abernathy,' she said, referring to her eccentric former head of department who went on to become a deputy head. 'Another Mister Chips . . . a harmless schoolteacher, almost a stereotype.'

'His record is impeccable . . . twenty-seven years without so much as a blemish.'

'So how did he manage to batten down the hatches for so long?'

Markham knocked back a draught of coffee before answering.

'I think he compartmentalised for dear life, Liv . . . It was the only way he knew how to survive . . . And reputation was everything, so he reinvented himself as a local model of propriety . . . it was crucial to maintaining his self-image intact. I imagine that over the course of time, he was almost able to convince himself that everything to do with Holy Martyrs belonged to another existence.'

'Like a bad dream.' Olivia was intrigued by the feats of dissociation Gordon Rushworth must have performed. 'Talk about a double life . . . Walter Mitty eat your heart out!'

'A double life . . . yes, I think that's exactly what it was,' Markham told her. 'But then Andrew Coxley came along to threaten his peace. Not only had Coxley made fun of Gordon when he was a pupil at Medway High, but the hairdresser became a fixture in his sister's life and virtually an idol to women like Evelyn Brady whom Gordon secretly wanted to impress . . . Worse than all, however, were his feelings of attraction towards Coxley, a dreadful reminder of his tormented schoolboy obsession with Gerry Beck and Preston Taylor.'

'It sounds like you pity him, sweetheart,' Olivia observed shrewdly.

Markham's gaze rested on a lavishly ornamented gravestone featuring an archangel crushing the devil beneath his heel. There was no compassion in the seraph's countenance, only a stern determination to subdue the Enemy.

'I think I *do* pity him,' Markham replied slowly. 'Gordon Rushworth had these gaping rents in his personality — tears that he was trying to hold together.' Like a ragged garment that could never be made whole.

'You really think he'll spill his guts to this David bloke . . . enough for you to pin the murders on him?'

Markham's fingers sought hers, moving caressingly, erotically, across the back of her hand, around her wrist.

He felt a sudden wild urge to take his partner back to bed, before telling himself this was merely a physical reflex . . . energy coursing through him before the final push to snare a murderer.

'After the latest murders, I think he won't be able to help himself.' Suddenly, he knew with the certainty of absolute conviction that Gordon Rushworth would need to remain in control and prevent his carefully constructed existence from falling apart. There would also be relief in talking to the only other person who knew his secrets. 'I imagine the ghosts of Gerry Beck and Preston Taylor have haunted him down the years, so David represents some sort of safety-valve.'

'What about Ethel Taylor and Jeanette O'Donnell?' she asked with a hint of indignation in her voice.

'Collateral damage, my love,' was the sad reply. 'Whatever made him lash out at the two women, with Gordon it was only ever about those lost schoolboy loves.' He thought for a moment. 'Whether they were uneasy about him or were somehow an affront to his self-image, I doubt we'll ever know.'

'What about Andrew Coxley . . . was that a sex attack?' she asked. 'Did Gordon make a pass or what?'

'We know he went to the salon late at night and Coxley let him in . . . Either they arranged to meet or Gordon knew Coxley would be there—'

'And then Gordon staged some kind of romantic stunt,' she interrupted eagerly, 'but Coxley laughed himself silly . . . and that was all it took . . .'

Markham had to smile at her enthusiasm.

'It's difficult to know what happened between them,' he said. 'I'm not sure Gordon went there with any intention of declaring himself or anything like that . . . I think it's more likely he intended to confront Coxley about rumours that he was mocking Gordon and disrespecting his sister.'

Olivia frowned. 'Was Coxley *really* making fun of Jean?'

'I think he probably sent her up, along with the other elderly ladies who constituted his "harem" . . . not with any malicious intent, more because he was conceited and couldn't help himself . . . Gordon was thin-skinned with a keen sense of what was due to himself and Jean. The mockery stung — not just because it was an echo of Coxley's behaviour as a pupil at Medway High, but because Jean and other customers like Evelyn Brady *had* made themselves a bit ridiculous with their slavish adoration, even to the extent of Evelyn giving Coxley presents . . . Gordon's resentment turned him into a poison pen. And bear in mind, he wasn't the only one to worry about undue influence. Mark Brady also had misgivings.'

'But rather than confronting Coxley, *he* preferred to let his mum's infatuation die a death.' She bit her lip. 'Sorry, Gil, unfortunate turn of phrase.'

'You're absolutely right,' he said, giving her a reassuring squeeze of the hand. 'Mark Brady was a businessman . . . a man of the world without Gordon's demons. Preserving the family honour wasn't a matter of life and death to *him*. But where Gordon was concerned, image was everything.' Markham's expression was taut as he added, 'Coxley would have had no idea of the danger. As far as he was concerned, Gordon was this fusty character whose sister was a useful source of income. He could never have dreamed the old fusspot was a killer.'

'So, d'you reckon Mister Chips gave him the glad eye but Coxley was so revolted he came out with something offensive and Gordon lost it?'

'Darling Liv, you're starting to sound more and more like Noakesy with every passing day.' As in his friend's remorselessly cynical prurience and penchant for calling a spade a blunt instrument.

She beamed, taking his words as a compliment.

'*Well?*'

'I doubt we'll ever know what triggered Gordon,' he said quietly. 'In many ways he's an enigma . . . looks like some hero out of *Bridge on the River* Kwai,' definitely preferable to Doyle's comparison with *Last of the Summer Wine*, 'but, if David Blaketon is to be believed, the man is a lethally dangerous sociopath.' He drained the mug of coffee. 'Gordon's very good at melting into the shadows . . . I think he must have worried about Evelyn Brady being some kind of weak link and got to her ahead of us.'

Olivia knew from something in his tone that her partner blamed himself for the killer stealing a march on the police.

'But now it's his endpiece,' she said gravely. 'A choice between finding a way to muzzle David — stop him going to the police — or silencing him permanently.'

Endpiece. The word hung in the air between them. It had a satisfyingly final ring to it, but Markham knew real life was rarely neat.

The morning light over the cemetery was turning pale-pink, its gentle radiance gilding and softening the lichen-covered monuments with their sober inscriptions. Many of his murdered dead slumbered there, and now it seemed that dim forms moved and whispered to him in the dawn, beseeching him to bring this sad chapter in Bromgrove's annals to a successful conclusion. As if for all of them.

Markham had a dull pain under his ribs that felt as though it had been there for ever and was now a part of him. But he knew it was merely the corporeal manifestation of an endless longing to bring his shadowy victims closure. *Endpeace*, he thought wistfully.

Again, Olivia reached for him.

'Steady as a rock,' she said comfortingly, patting his hand. 'You can do this, Gil, I know you can.' Then, timidly, 'When d'you reckon it'll all be over?'

'Blaketon's putting in a call around eleven. Assuming that Gordon takes the bait, our stakeout's on for later this afternoon.'

'David's vulnerable, right?' she asked. 'George said there's any number of "isms". Apparently, Freud and Jung would have a field day.'

'Well, let's just say there's a big fat medical file on him.'

'And you really think he can hold it together long enough to trap Gordon?' she asked anxiously.

'I'll let you into a secret, Liv,' Markham said wryly. 'I don't have a clue which way this will go. But it's bunker mentality right now, and all I know is it's my last throw of the dice before Blithering Bretherton takes over.'

She grimaced sympathetically.

'I remember *him*,' she said. 'Real MCP. Kept calling me "little lady" at that bloody awful Rotarian bun fight last year.'

Markham grinned. 'That's him. So dull and cautious, that even the toadies are hard put to find a good word . . . gilding the lily-livered, Noakes calls it.'

She giggled. 'Well, best of luck with *Operation Stop Bretherton*.'

The silly inconsequential banter had the effect of lifting Markham's spirits. Olivia was relieved to see that he now looked marginally less haggard and washed out than before.

'What are *you* up to, Liv?' he asked, forcing himself to behave as though this was just like any other day.

'Another "enrichment" session on sex education . . . Difficult to top yesterday's postbag,' she laughed. 'Some kid — strictly anonymous obvs — wanted to know where a girl's *volvo* was . . . could've had a bit of fun with that, Gil, but thought I'd better play it straight.'

He was still chuckling as he headed out to his car.

It was shaping up to be a lovely day, he thought wistfully, looking at the bank of Japanese azaleas which stood like a proud regiment to the rear of the landscaped gardens where they bordered the municipal cemetery.

Thinking of what Doyle had said about Gordon Rushworth reminding him of 'Foggy' Dewhurst , that quintessential retired military type from *Last of the Summer Wine*, he found it almost impossible to imagine such a man could be a deadly serial killer weaving a contagion of evil and deceit around unsuspecting innocents.

If they were right about Rushworth, this was his last day as a free man.

Time to lance the boil.

* * *

Eldred Court was a modest sheltered housing complex not far out of town. Gabled but modern, the sturdy redbrick lowrise was set in delightfully landscaped gardens, with tulips and rhododendrons well to the fore.

Sharon Dench was calm as she showed Markham, Doyle and Carruthers to a suite adjoining David Blaketon's bedsit, the DI warming to the diminutive brunette who seemed to be coping admirably at finding herself smack bang in the middle of a murder investigation.

Kate Burton was already there, supervising the technical support crew as they made last minute adjustments to the audio surveillance.

'Gordon's coming in at half three,' she told Markham.

'Any problems with the 'phone call?' The DI still dreaded that something might occur to derail the longed for denouement.

'All went like clockwork, boss,' Burton reassured him. 'Actually, David really rose to the challenge. 'Totally convincing.'

'Happen he should think about auditioning for RADA,' Noakes muttered disdainfully.

'Nathan's written him up some prompts,' Burton continued, ignoring the Greek chorus, 'but I reckon he'll be fine.' She met Markham's eyes. 'He's lived in a mental straitjacket for so long, I reckon he can't wait to break free.'

And so it proved . . .

Initially, after David produced tea and biscuits, the two men circled each other warily, with Gordon Rushworth giving nothing away.

It was a shock to Markham to hear the former schoolmaster's dry, precise tones over the intercom as he made carefully polite small talk on a range of subjects. For a while, it looked as though the conversation was going nowhere.

But then David moved up a gear.

'Look, enough of the chit-chat,' he said. 'You gotta understand, knowing about Gerry and Preston is *killing* me,' he whined in a convincing display of childish, maudlin self-pity. 'I can't *stand* it anymore.'

'You don't have any choice.' Gordon's answer was like a shard of ice, and it seemed to the listeners in the next room that the temperature of the warm day had suddenly dropped several notches.

'Why should I have to live with a secret like that on my conscience when *you're* the one who killed them?'

The detectives and Noakes held their breath.

'Yes, I killed them . . . but who's going to believe a word you say? And don't forget, you spied on the meet with Gerry — gave me an alibi — so that makes you guilty as sin.'

'*You threatened me.*'

'Sez who?' came the mocking reply. 'You had the hots for Gerry and Preston *and I can prove it.*'

'I know you killed those women too.' It came out as an abject whimper, and for a moment Markham understood how Gordon Rushworth must despise this millstone with the puling, beggar-like voice to whom he was irrevocably yoked. 'Mrs Taylor and that friend of hers were asking questions, right?' David persisted. 'I guessed it was *you* who did for them the minute I heard it on TV.'

'*Stupid bitches.*' The vulgarity, from Rushworth's lips, was shocking in its unexpectedness. 'Killing them was a walk in the park . . . O'Donnell thought she was one up on me with all those books, but I shut her big mouth in the end.'

'And the hairdresser, was that you as well?' There was naked horror in David's tone. 'You taught at his school, right? And your sister went to his salon?'

'My goodness, what a busy little bee you've been, keeping tabs on us all.' Rushworth had recovered himself after the momentary loss of composure, affecting a jocularity that made Markham's skin crawl. 'Yes, that was me. Not that it's any of your business, but Andrew Coxley was *vermin*,' he continued in a peculiar seer-like voice, 'not fit to breathe the same air as Jean . . . a posturing upstart with ideas above his station.'

Ideas above his station. Noakes rolled his eyes in silent ridicule. Burton was very pale, but her gaze met Markham's with fierce sharpness. *We've got him.*

Not yet, Kate, he telegraphed. *One more to go.*

David knew it too, but in line with Nathan Finlayson's coaching, he didn't move straight to the most recent victim. Instead he proceeded to give a convincing impression of an unstable individual consumed by self-pity and the certitude that Gordon Rushworth had ruined his life. He even managed to inject a note of masochistic slavishness that hinted at something darker and more complex than simple fear of his old schoolfellow, causing Markham to wonder if there had ever been something sexual between the two men. Judging from the looks Doyle and Carruthers exchanged, the same thought had occurred to his subordinates. As advised by the psychologist, David also left the door open to blackmail, concluding on a note of vague menace. 'You've ended up with *everything*,' he whinged, 'while I've got *nothing*. It don't seem fair somehow.'

By carefully calibrated degrees, David came round to the subject of Evelyn Brady. 'Can't get my head round killing old women,' he mumbled. 'That customer of Coxley's was a step too far in anyone's book.'

The prissy, slightly high-pitched, niminy-piminy voice sounded as detached as if this was a completely normal conversation to be having over the teacups.

'Such a *foolish* person,' Gordon said with gentle regret. 'Ran her mouth off so *thoughtlessly* . . . told me she thought *I* was the one sending anonymous hate mail and planned to report me if it didn't stop . . . She said some very *hurtful* things,' he continued in the soft even tone that was somehow infinitely more terrifying than a raised voice. 'Even hinted that she wasn't interested in marrying again, without my having asked her . . . and then rabbited on about Coxley as if she was totally *besotted* . . . so *undignified* in a woman of her age.'

So that was it, Markham thought grimly. Evelyn Brady had been openly contemptuous of the retired schoolteacher . . . shattering his make-believe that she had any ambitions to become Mrs Gordon Rushworth and killing his tentative courtship stone-dead . . . then she compounded her sin by praising Andrew Coxley to the skies. But the woman had never believed her friend's brother capable of murder, which is how he had been able to secure access to her house on some pretext or other.

'Now, what to do about you, David,' the killer mused, in the manner of one faced with a backward student.

Markham's colleagues stiffened as he held up a warning hand.

Wait!

'I told the warden you were coming round today . . . and my care worker Sharon knows too . . . plus there's the CCTV. If anything happens to me, they'll know it was you.'

'But nothing's *going* to happen to you, David . . . *unless* you start making foolish allegations.' The visitor was all sweet reason. 'Obviously you're safe enough in here with your *babysitters*,' the last word was uttered in a sibilant hiss, 'but you can't stay cooped up indoors forever, and when you decide to emerge, who can say what might happen.' Now his voice vibrated with malice. 'You're a bit of a sad case, aren't you . . . and people with a history of mental instability so often come to a sticky end—' There was a sudden choking sound followed by a faint bubbling moan.

Markham's hand came down.

Go!

When they burst into the room, David Blaketon stood over the crumpled body of his tormentor, a bloodstained knife in his hand.

He made no resistance as Doyle and Carruthers wrestled the weapon from him and cuffed his hands behind his back, an obscene high-pitched giggle the only reaction to what he had done.

'He shouldn't have called me a sad case,' David Blaketon called over his shoulder to Markham as they bundled him out of the room.

* * *

Some weeks later, after the Coronation of King Charles — with Bromgrove Police Station to the forefront of civic celebrations (cue more photobombing by Sidney and assorted higher-ups) — Markham's Gang and Olivia met in The Grapes for their usual post-investigation catch up.

The afternoon being mild, they repaired to the little beer garden behind the hostelry, Denise the landlady (a dead ringer for Corrie's Bet Lynch and an ardent fan of Markham's) waiting on them personally and flirting outrageously with Noakes whose extravagant compliments on the pub's toad-in-the-hole went down a treat.

'Bloody hell, sarge,' Doyle said after she sashayed away down the crazy paving, 'carry on like that and your missus'll have grounds for divorce.'

'You've either got it or you ain't,' Noakes retorted. ''Sides, Denise knows a connoisseur when she sees one,' he added, clearly not at all averse to being thought of as Bromgrove's answer to Michel Roux and oblivious of the amusement provoked by 'conny-sewer'.

After a time, the lasagne, toad-in-the-hole, spaghetti carbonara, organic vegan special (Burton) and Caesar salad (Olivia) being disposed of, their talk turned to the salon murders.

'That poor lass Sharon were beside herself,' Noakes recalled. 'But the sheltered wotsit ain't a hospital an' she couldn't have known he'd go for Gordy . . . 'Sides, the medicos cleared him beforehand . . . said Dave were doing okay . . . not seeing things or hearing voices or owt like that.'

'Well, it looks very much as if he'll be spending the rest of his days in the Newman,' Markham said grimly. 'A section 41 order for sure.'

'At first he carried on like he was *looking forward* to lording it over the other freaks in there,' Doyle commented with a shudder. 'Like he's some sort of mastermind . . . the hero of the hour who finished off the salon killer, leaving the cops with egg all over their faces. Seriously, Carstairs said back at the station they couldn't get him to shut up, he was that excited by it all . . . And then suddenly he switched . . . came over all bulging-eyed and paranoid . . . took four of 'em to hold him down.'

'Jean Gibley'll most likely be joining Blaketon in there,' Carruthers opined. 'Keeps insisting Gordon was framed and it's some kind of stitch-up by the police cos we couldn't solve the murders.'

'She's headed for a breakdown when everything comes out,' Burton agreed. 'I think she had the key to some of it at the back of her mind, but the poor woman slid away from the truth into a weird kind of fantasy life—'

'Starring Coxley?' Doyle asked, interested in his colleague's theory.

Burton nodded. 'Yes, I reckon that was a distraction—'

'God knows she needed it, living with Mister Crippen,' Carruthers interjected.

'Not just that,' Burton said slowly. 'Somehow I think she *knew* that Gordon was attracted to Coxley, and this was her way of placing him off limits' . . . kind of keeping him safe . . .'

'Only in the end she didn't. Keep him safe,' Noakes intoned lugubriously.

'No,' Markham said sadly. 'Her and Evelyn's passionate devotion to Mr Coxley essentially sealed his fate.'

'Well, Mrs Giblet won't get anywhere with the *Gordy Wuz Framed* malarkey,' Noakes said happily. 'Sidney's so cock-a-hoop at solving this an' the cold cases that his "extended police family" crip crap's gone out of the window an' she can whistle for all the sympathy she's gonna get from *him*.' Slyly he added, 'Typical, the way he never gave you, Moriarty an' Hart a shout-out in the press conference, guv.'

'Stop stirring, Noakesy. As far as I'm concerned, it's a team effort.'

'Bretherton an' Toad Face were dead sickly,' his friend scowled. 'Talking like *they* were your biggest fans when everyone knows they'd knife you in the back soon as look at you.'

'You're forgetting what Oscar Wilde says, George,' Olivia laughed. 'A true friend stabs you in the *front*, not the back.'

Noakes was divided between pleasure that he was assumed to be on nodding terms with the renowned aesthete's canon and outrage that Olivia was giving his two least favourite policemen a free pass.

Markham chuckled. 'I'm happy to be a backroom boy on this one. What matters is that we finally solved the salon case and achieved *justice* for so many victims.'

'It feels like Gordon somehow cheated justice,' Doyle said tentatively. 'Causing all that pain and then with one slash of Blaketon's knife, he's out of it.'

Markham's mind travelled back to the murderer's dead face as the paramedics worked on him . . . lips drawn back in a ghastly sneer and the eyes those of a predator baulked of his prey.

'Somehow I don't think he's "out of it", Sergeant,' the DI said quietly. If Gordon Rushworth's dying expression was to be believed, an unfathomable chasm had opened up before him in those final seconds. An abyss that told him precisely where he was headed.

There was an awkward silence, Doyle and Carruthers never entirely comfortable with the guvnor's 'RC weirdness' but anxious nonetheless to signal their respect.

Markham watched them with an ironical smile splaying about his lips.

'You and Noakesy should drink up and get off,' he said lightly. 'I've no doubt *Match of the Day* trumps my metaphysical speculations.'

After they had gone, he turned to Burton.

'Should I be worried about Carruthers, Kate?' he asked almost idly. 'Not succumbed to the lure of filthy lucre from the *Gazette*, has he?'

'I don't know what may have gone down with Gavin Conors, guv,' she said. 'But I let it drop casually that you'd wondered about leaks during the allotment case . . . said this would be a case of "two strikes and you're out" if anyone was nabbed for it further down the line.'

'Good,' he replied quietly. 'Even if Carruthers has blabbed to the press and somehow lost his way — maybe through Conors having got to him- I think he's a decent detective and still want to keep him. But he can't serve two masters.'

Olivia chuckled, puncturing the tension. 'That sounds positively *biblical*, Gil!'

Her partner laughed too, but his eyes met Burton's in a long hard look.

Message received and understood. Somehow, she would ensure the young sergeant kept to the straight and narrow.

A short time afterwards, his fellow DI took her leave.

Olivia wasn't sorry to see Kate go. Her private jealous fear of Markham's colleague had never entirely subsided. There was just something about the way the woman looked at him . . . like a sodding *mooncalf*, she thought savagely, before smoothing out her expression as she became aware of Markham looking at her.

'So that's the salon investigation done and dusted,' she said lightly.

'Well, no doubt there'll be an enquiry into how David Blaketon managed to secrete a weapon and attack Gordon Rushworth,' Markham replied. His lips curled slightly. 'But Sidney and Ebury-Clarke will make any unpleasantness go away . . . CID hasn't had a result like this in years and there's no chance anything will be allowed to tarnish their lustre.'

'Have you broken the news of George's career plans to them?' she enquired roguishly. 'Guaranteed to give the top brass a collective coronary.'

'I thought I'd let them enjoy the moment,' he grinned. 'What with them basking in post-Coronation glory, it seems unfair to take the gloss off it all.'

'Might you think of going in with George?' she asked tentatively. 'Tell Sidney and the rest of them where to shove it.'

Markham reached for her hand.

'I reckon it's a new chapter for Noakesy,' he said gently. 'And who knows, maybe for me too . . . But right now, I'm happy just to be here with you . . . not worrying about what's around the corner.'

Olivia smiled back.

The pages of the next instalment in their story lay before them.

She was content to wait for what the future would bring.

THE END

THE JOFFE BOOKS STORY

We began in 2014 when Jasper agreed to publish his mum's much-rejected romance novel and it became a bestseller.

Since then we've grown into the largest independent publisher in the UK. We're extremely proud to publish some of the very best writers in the world, including Joy Ellis, Faith Martin, Caro Ramsay, Helen Forrester, Simon Brett and Robert Goddard. Everyone at Joffe Books loves reading and we never forget that it all begins with the magic of an author telling a story.

We are proud to publish talented first-time authors, as well as established writers whose books we love introducing to a new generation of readers.

We won Trade Publisher of the Year at the Independent Publishing Awards in 2023. We have been shortlisted for Independent Publisher of the Year at the British Book Awards for the last four years, and were shortlisted for the Diversity and Inclusivity Award at the 2022 Independent Publishing Awards. In 2023 we were shortlisted for Publisher of the Year at the RNA Industry Awards.

We built this company with your help, and we love to hear from you, so please email us about absolutely anything bookish at feedback@joffebooks.com

If you want to receive free books every Friday and hear about all our new releases, join our mailing list: www.joffebooks.com/contact

And when you tell your friends about us, just remember: it's pronounced Joffe as in coffee or toffee!

ALSO BY CATHERINE MOLONEY

DETECTIVE MARKHAM SERIES
Book 1: CRIME IN THE CHOIR
Book 2: CRIME IN THE SCHOOL
Book 3: CRIME IN THE CONVENT
Book 4: CRIME IN THE HOSPITAL
Book 5: CRIME IN THE BALLET
Book 6: CRIME IN THE GALLERY
Book 7: CRIME IN THE HEAT
Book 8: CRIME AT HOME
Book 9: CRIME IN THE BALLROOM
Book 10: CRIME IN THE BOOK CLUB
Book 11: CRIME IN THE COLLEGE
Book 12: CRIME IN THE KITCHEN
Book 13: CRIME IN THE SPA
Book 14: CRIME IN THE CRYPT
Book 15: CRIME IN OXFORD
Book 16: CRIME IN CARTON HALL
Book 17: CRIME IN RETIREMENT
Book 18: CRIME IN THE BOUTIQUE
Book 19: CRIME IN THE HIGH STREET
Book 20: CRIME IN THE ALLOTMENT
Book 21: CRIME IN THE SALON